China couldn't bring herself to look back at Ben for fear the look of hunger she'd seen on his face would still be there.

Long after the house was quiet and everyone had gone to bed, China sat in a chair by the window, staring out into the night. Her thoughts were on replay, from the time Ben had tied the hood beneath her chin to the moment he'd told her good-night. She kept remembering the feel of the horse's nose on the palm of her hand and Ben English's mouth upon her lips. One had tickled, the other had made her knees go weak. She couldn't be falling in love. She was in enough danger already without giving another man entry into her heart.

But then she reminded herself that Ben wouldn't hurt her. He wasn't that kind. He was a man who kept the promises he made.

Now all she had to do was learn to believe in herself as much as she believed in him.

Award–winning author, **Sharon Sala**, has been writing since 1985 when family tragedy brought her to the conclusion that life was too fleeting not to pursue wholeheartedly her dream of becoming a writer. She is recognised for her skill and sensitivity in exploring a variety of controversial topics in her books. Sharon Sala is also published by Silhouette books® as well as writing under the name of Dinah McCall.

Available in
MIRA® Books

SWEET BABY
REUNION
REMEMBER ME

SHARON Sala

Butterfly

MIRA® BOOKS

*All the characters in this book have no existence outside the
imagination of the author, and have no relation whatsoever to
anyone bearing the same name or names. They are not even
distantly inspired by any individual known or unknown to the
author, and all the incidents are pure invention.*

*All Rights Reserved including the right of reproduction in whole or
in part in any form. This edition is published by arrangement with
Harlequin Enterprises II B.V. The text of this publication or any part
thereof may not be reproduced or transmitted in any form or by any
means, electronic or mechanical, including photocopying,
recording, storage in an information retrieval system, or
otherwise, without the written permission of the publisher.*

*This book is sold subject to the condition that it shall not, by way of
trade or otherwise, be lent, resold, hired out or otherwise circulated
without the prior consent of the publisher in any form of binding or
cover other than that in which it is published and without a similar
condition including this condition being imposed on the subsequent
purchaser.*

*MIRA is a registered trademark of Harlequin Enterprises Limited,
used under licence.*

*First published in Great Britain 2001
MIRA Books, Eton House, 18-24 Paradise Road,
Richmond, Surrey, TW9 1SR*

© Sharon Sala 2000

ISBN 1 55166 616 2

58-0701

*Printed and bound in Spain
by Litografia Rosés S.A., Barcelona*

I dedicate this book to the butterflies in all of us,
and to my Bobby,
who made me believe I could fly.

A great big THANK YOU must go to Pistol Pete Cormican, premiere DJ of Dallas, Texas, and one of the most open and generous men with whom it was ever my pleasure to speak.

By telephone, he helped me through the geography of his fine city, leading me through the maze of streets and suburbs with patience and ease.

Any physical discrepancies you might find in various locations are nothing more than creative license, and any mistakes are mine, not his.

Prologue

Detroit, Michigan
July 13, 1980

Sweat ran down the middle of six-year-old China Brown's forehead as she crouched in the cool, dry dirt beneath the porch of her mother's house. Inside, she could hear the murmur of voices and the occasional thud of footsteps as her mother and her stepfather, Clyde, moved from room to room. Every time she heard Clyde's voice she shuddered. It was only a matter of time before he realized his favorite coffee cup was broken. She hadn't mean to do it, but Clyde wouldn't care that it was an accident. He didn't like her any more than she liked him and seemed to look for reasons to reprimand her.

Time passed, and she had almost drifted off to sleep when she heard a loud, angry shout, then the sound of running footsteps coming toward the door.

"China Mae, you get in here right now!" Clyde yelled.

China flinched. He must have found the cup. She'd

wanted to hide the pieces, but she'd heard her mother coming and had tossed them into the wastebasket before bolting out the door. Now it was too late. They'd been found.

"China…so help me God, I'm gonna whip your ass if you don't answer me!"

China held her breath. Answer Clyde? No way. He was gonna whip her ass no matter what. Why hurry up the inevitable?

She heard another pair of footsteps—lighter, quicker—then the anxious tone of her mother's voice.

"Clyde? What's wrong?"

Clyde Shubert pivoted angrily, jamming a knobby finger into the woman's face.

"I'll tell you what's wrong. That stupid kid of yours broke my favorite coffee cup."

China heard her mother's swift intake of breath and just for a moment thought about revealing herself. Sometimes Clyde took his anger out on her mother, too. But her fear was greater than her guilt, and she stayed immobile, closing her eyes and praying as she'd never prayed before.

"I'm sure it was an accident," Mae offered, and tried to placate Clyde with a pat on his arm.

But Clyde would have none of it. He shrugged off Mae's touch and cursed aloud before striding to the edge of the porch. China followed his path with a horrified gaze, watching the dirt sift down through loose wooden planks above her head, then blinking furiously when some of the dirt drifted into her eyes. Suddenly her nose began to tickle, and she pinched it between her thumb and forefinger, willing herself not to sneeze.

"China! You get yourself into the house this instant!" Clyde yelled.

China pinched her nose tighter as the urge to sneeze persisted.

"Please…Clyde…it's just a cup."

The sound of flesh hitting flesh was as abrupt as China's exit from the house had been, and she knew without doubt that her mother had just been slapped. The need to sneeze disappeared, replaced by an overwhelming urge to cry. She did neither, instead curling tighter into a ball and wishing she could disappear.

"Today a cup. Tomorrow something else. You're always excusing the little bitch. That's what's wrong with her!" he yelled.

Mae flinched, but held her head high. It wasn't the first time he'd hit her. Doubtless it wouldn't be the last. There were days when it shamed her that she'd let herself come to this, but she didn't have the guts to leave.

"Don't call my daughter names. There's nothing wrong with her! She's just a little girl."

Clyde snorted beneath his breath. "Yeah, and one of the skinniest, ugliest kids I've ever seen. You just keep her out of my face, you hear me?"

China bit her lip as she heard Clyde stomp back into the house. Ugly? She was ugly? Tears welled. She didn't want to be ugly. Her thoughts began to race. Was that why she didn't have any friends? Did the kids down the street think she was too ugly to play with?

"China...where are you?"

Mae's voice startled her, and she almost answered. But a sense of self-preservation kept her quiet, and moments later she heard her mother go back inside.

As soon as she knew she was alone, she rolled over onto her stomach and buried her face in her arms. Ugly. She hadn't known she was ugly. Now it made sense why Clyde didn't like her.

Hot tears welled beneath her eyelids as she lay belly down in the dirt and buried her face in the curve of her arm, her thin little shoulders shaking with suppressed sobs.

The neighbor's yellow cat sauntered into their yard and started beneath the porch, then stopped short, hissing with displeasure as it saw China. Ordinarily she would have jumped and run away, but today she didn't care. Nothing mattered anymore, not even the chance that old Scruffy might scratch her.

The cat sniffed her bare feet, then the backs of her knees, then worked its way up to her face, sniffing and licking at the wash of wet, salty tears streaming down the side of China's cheek.

She gasped and jerked, raising her head too fast and bumping it on the underside of the porch. Scruffy hissed at the unexpected movement and scampered out the other side of the porch to disappear beneath a volunteer stand of Castor beans her mother let grow to keep the moles and gophers out of the yard.

China held her breath, certain that the thump of her head against the underside of the porch had given her away, but when no one came running, she began to relax.

Scruffy seemed to have forgiven her for frightening him and was already in the act of stalking a grasshopper that had landed on a nearby blade of grass. The big cat pounced, and she absently watched the demise of the grasshopper as it disappeared down Scruffy's throat. The cat soon moved on in search of bigger game, leaving China alone with a sense of growing dread. Sooner or later it was bound to get dark, and when it did, she would have to come out. It was a sad but true fact that she was more afraid of the dark than she was of Clyde.

She shuddered on a sob, then wiped her nose on the back of her hand and started inching her way through the dust toward the yard beyond. Just as she reached the edge of the porch, a small brown caterpillar dropped from a blade of grass and began inching its way toward the shade beneath the porch. China hesitated, then rested her chin on her hands, watching in fascination at the undulant movement of the tiny body—at the way it seemed to thread itself between the twigs and pebbles without disturbing a single grain of dust. It was so small. If she hadn't been eye to eye with the little creature, she would never have known it was there.

As she watched, a thought began to occur. If only she could become as small and insignificant as the lowly little worm, then maybe Clyde would never bother her again. And if she was as ugly as Clyde said she was, being invisible would protect her from offending people with her presence. It seemed like a good idea, and she even closed her eyes and tried to think herself small. But when she finally looked up, she was still China and the caterpillar was gone. She crawled out from under the porch and began dusting off the front of her clothes. Some things just weren't meant to be.

She made herself scarce for the rest of the afternoon until the sun began to set. Then, when the shadows in the yard began to lengthen and turn a dark, somber blue, she dawdled through the grass to the front steps and sat, waiting until the last possible minute before going inside to face Clyde's wrath. The hinges suddenly squeaked on the screen door behind her, and she jumped and stood, wild-eyed and poised to run. It was her mother.

''China Mae, where on earth have you been?'' Mae asked.

She shrugged and looked down at her bare toes, unable to come up with a suitable answer.

Mae pushed the door open wide. ''Well, come on in then,'' she said softly. ''And go wash,'' she added. ''Your clothes are filthy. What have you been doing?''

''Nothing,'' China mumbled and slipped past her mother on near silent bare feet.

Mae reached for her child, trying to brush the wayward hair from her little girl's face, but China was too fast. She was gone before she could catch her.

As Mae eased the door shut, she cast a nervous glance toward the living room on her way to the kitchen. Clyde was intent on the evening news and unaware that China was back. All she could do was hope that the meat loaf and mashed potatoes she'd fixed would sidetrack him from going on again about a broken cup.

Staying with Clyde bothered Mae's conscience on a daily basis. It was one thing for her to tolerate Clyde's abuse, but it shamed her that, by staying, she put China in danger, too. Yet leaving was even more frightening. She had no skills and a tenth-grade education, so her choice of jobs was never great. They needed Clyde's paycheck to put a decent roof over their heads.

Inside the bathroom, China pulled the little step stool out from under the sink and stepped up on it so she could reach the faucets. The old pipes groaned as she opened the taps, and she flinched, certain that Clyde would come bursting through the door at any moment and give her a thrashing. In her haste to finish, a goodly portion of the water dribbled down the front of her dress, mingling with the dust to make thin streaks of mud. She swiped at the streaks with the palms of her hands, which only made things worse, and then she had to wash her hands again to get them clean. By the time she got to the kitchen, her legs were shaking and her stomach was in knots. She slipped into her chair without looking up, but she knew Clyde was there—watching her, waiting for her to make another mistake.

"I thought you told her to wash up," Clyde growled.

China ducked her head as Mae turned, nervously clanking a spoon against the inside of the bowl in which she was dishing up the potatoes.

Mae saw the smudges on her little girl's face and dress, then looked past them to the stiff set of China's shoulders and sighed.

"She's fine. As soon as she's had her supper, I'll give her a bath."

Clyde muttered beneath his breath, satisfied he'd made his point.

Mae set the last bowl of food on the table, then slid into her chair with a heartfelt sigh and gave Clyde a tentative smile.

"I made meat loaf."

Clyde rolled his eyes as he stabbed at a roll. "Hell, woman, I can see that."

Mae frowned, then shrugged. The way she looked at it, she'd made an overture of peace. If he didn't want to accept it, then that was his problem, not hers. She reached for China's plate.

"Here, sweetie, Mama will fix your plate. Are you hungry?"

China dared to look up. The scents surrounding her were varied and enticing, and had she not been so certain that Clyde wasn't through with her, she might have done justice to the meal.

She sighed and then fixed a dark, anxious gaze on her mother's face.

"Not really," she whispered.

"Speak up, damn it," Clyde yelled, and thumped the handle of his knife on the table, making the dishes and cutlery rattle.

China flinched and moaned and gave her mother a frantic look.

Mae's frown deepened. "I heard her just fine," she told Clyde. "Help yourself to the meat loaf and please pass it on."

Clyde grabbed the platter and defiantly slid over half the slices onto his plate before setting it back on the table with a thump. Then he reached across China's plate for the bowl of mashed potatoes without caring that his elbow just missed hitting her in the nose. She started to slide out of the chair for a hasty exit when Clyde grabbed her by the arm and gave it a yank.

"You sit," he ordered, and then proceeded to spoon a huge portion of mashed potatoes onto her plate. "You ain't gettin' up until you eat every bite."

Mae reached for her daughter's plate. "Clyde, you've given her too much. That's even more than I could eat."

Clyde backhanded Mae, catching the edge of her chin with his ring and leaving an angry gash that quickly started to seep a thin ribbon of blood.

China gasped as her mother cried out, then held her breath, afraid that Clyde would take umbrage with her response. Again she thought of the little brown caterpillar and wished she could just disappear.

Clyde muttered an oath beneath his breath and grabbed a bowl of spinach.

"You got anything to say to me, whelp?"

China shook her head vehemently, her eyes wide with fear.

"That's what I thought," he muttered, then slid a helping of the dark, juicy greens onto her plate as Mae turned away to staunch the increasing flow of blood. Clyde picked up China's fork and slapped it into the palm of her hand.

"Eat!"

China looked up to her mother for help, which angered Clyde even more.

"Your mama ain't gonna help you this time," he warned. "You eat or so help me God, I'll whip your ass until you can't sit down."

Mae pivoted angrily. "You won't touch my daughter."

Convinced that if Clyde hit her mother again, he would kill her, China gave her stepfather a nervous glance.

"It's all right, Mama," she said quickly. "I can eat it."

Across the room, Mae watched her baby girl and knew that, at that moment, China had more guts than she did, and it shamed her.

China looked down at her plate, then up at Clyde as she stuck her fork in the top of the potatoes. An uneasy silence filled the room as she lifted a bite to her lips and then closed her eyes.

Suddenly the back of her head exploded in pain as Clyde hit her with a doubled fist, driving her face into the plate of potatoes and spinach. She came up gasping for air as her fork clattered to the floor. In a panic, she began digging potatoes from her eyes and nose, knowing that to sit blind with the enemy was to taunt death.

"Now look what you did, you ugly little bitch," Clyde snarled, and yanked her up from the chair.

"No!" Mae screamed, and dashed toward the table. But she wasn't in time to prevent Clyde from dragging China from her seat and out of the room.

China was sobbing now, certain she was going to die.

"I didn't mean to break your cup. I didn't mean to break your cup."

But Clyde was beyond reason. He hit the bathroom door with the flat of his hand and shoved China into the shower stall.

Mae was pounding on Clyde's back with both hands, begging him to leave her baby alone, but he was mute to her pleas. He turned on the cold water faucet. Immediately water came spewing from the shower head and down onto his arms.

In desperation, China kicked and screamed, begging for Clyde to stop, and in doing so, she accidentally kicked him in the eye. With a mighty roar, he grabbed her by the throat and turned her head up to the jets of chill water.

"I'll teach you to mess with what's mine," he yelled. "I'm gonna wash that filth off your face if it's the last thing I do."

Clyde's fingers tightened around China's neck as her view of the world began to spin and then narrow dangerously. Water peppered into her eyes and up her nose, mingling with the tears and mashed potatoes. Choked sobs alternated with frantic gasps for air, and in her peripheral vision, she could just see an outline of her mother's face and the footstool she was holding above her head.

Then everything went black.

One

The baby kicked in China's belly as she bent down to pick up her bag, a frightening reminder that she wasn't the only person about to become homeless. George Wayne, her landlord, shifted nervously behind her as he stood in the doorway to the apartment, watching her gather her assortment of meager belongings.

"It ain't my fault, you know. Rules is rules, and you're more than three months behind on rent."

China turned, the bag in her hand, her head held high. "If you'd told me sooner that Tommy wasn't giving you the rent money, I wouldn't have kept giving it to him. I would have given it to you myself."

George Wayne frowned. "That's what you say, but you ain't got no way of provin' that to me. For all I know, you both partied up the money, and when it was all gone, he split on you."

China's heart sank. The fact that Tommy Fairheart,

the father of her unborn child, had disappeared from her life eight days earlier was secondary to the fact that he'd stolen every penny she had to her name when he left. That he had also kept the last three months' rent money instead of paying George Wayne, as China had believed, was, as the old saying went, the last straw.

She gave George a scathing look, pulled the front of her coat as far as it would go across her tummy and shouldered her bag. With her head held high, she moved past George in long, stilted strides, hoping she could get out of his sight before she started to cry.

It was a long walk from the third floor of her apartment down to street level. She made it in record time. But her defiance died when she stepped out the door and turned to face the bitter bite of Texas winter.

Again the baby kicked, then rolled. China placed her hand across the swell of her stomach and shifted the strap of her bag to a more comfortable position on her shoulder. Her mouth was twisted into a bitter grimace, her eyes flooded with tears, but there was determination in her voice.

"Don't worry, baby. Mama will take care of you."

Uncertain as to how that would yet come to be, she started walking. Her plan was to find a church. She'd seen several on the bus route that she rode every day to work. Maybe there would be someone there who could give her some temporary shelter. She had a job waiting tables in a barbeque joint. The pay wasn't much, but the tips were good. All she needed was a place to stay until she could save up enough money for another apartment.

For thirty minutes her hopes were high, but after more than a mile of walking and still no sign of any church, she began to get nervous. Her feet were so cold she could no longer feel her toes, and though she'd dressed as warmly as possible in sweatpants and a sweatshirt and two pairs of socks, her lack of gloves and the bite of the wind against her flesh was taking its toll. And, as if that wasn't enough, to add insult to injury, it started to snow.

Minuscule bits of something that felt more like sleet than snow stung her eyes. She squinted and ducked her head against a cruel winter gust that parted her coat. With shaking hands, she yanked it back over her belly, as if trying to shelter the child she was carrying.

A garbage truck rumbled past her as she paused at a street corner to get her bearings. She told herself that the pain in her lower back didn't matter. The buildings looked festive in their Christmas decorations, but she didn't see anything that resembled a church. As she waited for the light to change, she couldn't help but wish she'd paid more attention to the route the bus had taken instead of putting on her makeup and adding the finishing touches to her hair as she'd ridden to work each day.

"There's got to be one around here somewhere," she said, and headed for a florist on the opposite side of the street to ask for directions.

As she stepped inside Red River Floral and closed

the door behind her, the strains of "White Christmas" filled the air. She leaned against the door to rest, letting the warmth envelope her.

"Hi, honey, can I help you?"

China's focus shifted at the woman's approach. She was broad and tall, and had the reddest hair she'd ever seen. It took China a bit to realize that a goodly portion of her height came from the highly teased hairstyle.

"Um…yes, I hope so," China said. "I'm looking for a church."

The redhead grinned. "You lookin' to join it or…"

"No," China said. "I'm sort of lost, and I thought someone there could help me. I saw plenty of them when I rode the bus to work, but now I can't seem to find a single one."

"You ride the bus?" the redhead asked.

China nodded.

"Then why didn't you just get back on that bus and ride it to the church?"

China shrank within herself. Admitting she didn't have a dime to her name wasn't something she was comfortable with, especially to a stranger.

"I missed it, that's all," she said shortly. "Can you help me?"

The redhead's smile shifted slightly as compassion filled her eyes. "Well, sure. We'll get the phone book and take us a look. How's that?"

China smiled. "I would appreciate it," she said softly, and unconsciously patted the swell of her belly as she followed the woman to the back of the store.

While they were in the midst of searching the yellow pages, a bell jingled, signaling the appearance of another customer, and this time a paying one.

"Excuse me just a minute," the florist said, and moved toward the customer, leaving China alone at the counter.

She scanned the listings, one by one, trying to figure out where she was in accordance with the nearest churches. At this point she wasn't in a position to be picky about denomination; all she wanted from them was charity. She was still looking at addresses when the florist and the customer came to the counter.

"Find what you're looking for?" the florist asked.

China shrugged. "I'm not sure. Are any of these churches nearby?"

The customer, a tall, well-dressed woman in her midthirties, gave China an impatient stare.

"I'm in a hurry," she said, eyeing the florist.

"Yes, I'm sorry," the florist said, and began writing the work order.

"Do you mind?" the woman drawled, elbowing China out of the way in order to set her purse on the counter, then staring pointedly at China's bag on the floor between them.

The woman's attitude was nothing more than another slap in China's face, and for a woman who'd already had one too many blows to her self-esteem that day, it was one too many.

China picked up her bag and headed for the door without getting the address she'd come for.

''Wait, honey!'' the florist called. ''I'll be with you in a minute.''

China paused, then turned, the length of the store carrying the clear, quiet tone of her message.

''Thank you for being so kind.''

A frigid blast of wind and its accompanying sleet hit her squarely in the face, reminding her of why she'd sought shelter there. She'd wasted precious time and still didn't know any more now than she had when she went in. She hesitated, considering going back inside, when she caught a glimpse of herself in the store window. Her hair was wild and windblown, her cheeks reddened from exposure. Her all-around appearance was bedraggled. With the bag hanging over her shoulder, she looked like the homeless people she often saw walking the streets. And in that moment, the bitter truth of her situation hit.

She didn't just look like one. She had become one.

Two

As the sun began to set, China was forced to accept the truth that pride did go before a fall. If only she hadn't stormed out of the florist's before getting the information she needed, she might not be in this fix. From that realization, self-pity moved her thoughts in another direction.

If only her mother were still alive, she would never have gotten mixed up with a man like Tommy Fairheart. Her mother had always had a way of seeing through pretty words to the heart of a person. She'd left Clyde Shubert the day after he had nearly drowned China in the shower. She could still remember her mother apologizing to China over and over as they made their way to the bus station. The determination on her mother's face had been fierce and her faith in men definitely over. Mae wouldn't have been fooled by Tommy's pretty words as China had been.

China sighed as she stopped at a street corner, waiting for the light to change. She stomped her feet and stuffed her hands into the sleeves of her coat. Never would she take being warm for granted again.

As she stood, her thoughts drifted back to Tommy.

When they'd first met, he'd been so sweet. In the beginning there wasn't anything he wouldn't do for her.
She wasn't so sure she would have listened to her
mother—not then. She had been ready for love—for
her own life to begin. She was so willing to believe
his good looks were a reflection of his soul. Obviously
she'd been wrong.

The light changed. Just as she stepped off the curb
into the street, a car came around a corner at a high
rate of speed, skidding dangerously toward her on the
snow-packed street. She jumped back to the curb just
in time to keep from being hit as the tires sent a nasty
mix of sand, salt and slushy snow onto the legs of her
sweatpants.

"You jerk!" she shouted.

The girth of her belly was restricting, and she
grunted as she bent down to brush off the mess. This
time, when she stepped off the curb to cross, she made
a hasty sprint to the other side, breathing a sigh of
relief when her feet touched the sidewalk. She started
walking. A few blocks back, someone had told her
about an all-night mission in the area, and she needed
to find it quick. Her lower back was throbbing, her
belly was in knots and now her fingers were as numb
as her feet.

The streets were well lit, and the bars she was passing seemed to be doing a healthy business. The sounds
of holiday music seemed to be everywhere—spilling
out of passing cars and from inside different establish-
ments as the patrons came and went. More than once

she had to sidestep rowdy crowds standing in front of the doors to continue down the street. The smell of food was making her nauseous, yet she knew she needed to eat.

A few blocks down, the patrons thinned out, as did the quality of the businesses. Her steps quickened as she moved past the varying signs over these darkened doors. She'd ventured into the Oakcliff area—a place that people in the know called the Sunny South Side. Only it wasn't sunny, and it wasn't a place she wanted to be.

Topless dancers inside.

Lap dances.

Nude Strippers.

The Flip Side.

When a pair of men came out of the last bar arm in arm, she knew she was out of her element. She'd seen plenty of these places before, but always from within the confines of a car or a bus. Never had her vulnerability been more evident. And just when she thought it couldn't get much worse, three young men stepped out of the shadows of a nearby alley. One grabbed her by the arm and began pulling her toward the darkness.

"Baby, baby, come 'ere to me…I'll show you how to stay warm."

"Let me go!" China cried, then kicked at his shins as she yanked her arm free and began to run.

He cursed in pain and bolted after her, catching her before she'd gone more than a few steps.

China screamed.

Anger slashed across his face, and he drew back his hand to silence her when one of the other men suddenly spoke.

"Let her go, Ruiz, she's got a baby in her belly."

The man called Ruiz snarled, "So much the better for me," and curled his hand in China's hair.

Then the man who'd spoken on China's behalf stepped into the light and curled his fingers around Ruiz's wrist. As the pair glared at each other, it became obvious to China that there was more than a physical struggle going on. The look that passed between the two was more of a challenge for dominance than for doing what was right.

Suddenly the pressure on her scalp ceased. Ruiz had turned her loose. She was free. Hastily, she reached down to pick up the bag that she'd dropped, but the man who'd spoken up on her behalf beat her to it. The look on his face made her take a hesitant step back.

Miguel Hernandez stared long and hard into the young woman's face, looking past the cold that had long ago pinched her features into frozen caricatures, then to the coat that was two sizes too small for her belly.

China held her breath, waiting to see if this savior was going to turn on her, too.

"Where is your man?" he asked.

The question was unexpected, and it cut to the pain China was carrying in her heart.

"I don't have one," she muttered.

The man pointed at her stomach. "Where is the man who put the baby in your belly?"

Her chin began to quiver. "I don't know. He stole my money and left a few days ago."

The man's dark eyes glittered. "Why are you here? It's not safe for a *chica* like you."

"A mission...someone told me there was an all-night mission."

"You have no home."

It wasn't a question. It was a statement. And it cut to China's heart like a knife. She tried to speak, but the words wouldn't come. She found herself staring at him through a thick wall of tears.

"Ahhh, don't cry," he said softly. "Come..." He led her out of the alley and back to the street, then pointed. "See? Just a few blocks away. You are almost there, little mama."

China looked in the direction he was pointing and saw the outline of a lit cross, bright against the skyline of Dallas like a beacon in the dark. It stood silhouetted against the neon debauchery like a lifeline for the lost. She started to shake. It was a normal reaction to the adrenaline rush, but it left her feeling breathless and weak.

"I see it," she said, and eyed her dark-eyed savior nervously.

He almost smiled. "When you get there, tell Father Doyle that Miguel said to treat you right."

"You are Miguel?"

He shrugged, as if remembering that, on the streets, identity was not something one easily gave away.

But China wasn't insulted by his lack of response. She glanced over his shoulder to the pair of men who'd slunk back into the shadows, then back at him. There was something in his eyes that told her he wasn't as far gone as the others. Caution told her to start walking, but she felt guilty at just walking away. Tentatively she touched his arm, feeling the strength of him through the layers of his coat.

"Thank you, Miguel, more than I can say."

A muscle jerked in his jaw, and his eyes suddenly glittered dangerously.

"Just get off the streets," he said, thrusting her bag into her hands, then disappearing into the alley.

China heard an angry exchange of voices and then receding footsteps. With a last nervous glance over her shoulder, she started walking, ever mindful of the snow-packed sidewalks and the baby she carried.

Two blocks came and went, and China's gaze stayed firmly fixed on the cross above the mission. The humble landmark promised warmth and safety and, if she was lucky, maybe some food. Because she was so focused on where she was going, she forgot to pay attention to where she was at.

One moment she was in midstride, and the next thing she knew she'd collided with a tall, elegant blonde in a full-length fur coat. Her bag slid off her shoulder onto the sidewalk as she scrambled to stay on her feet. Certain she was going to fall, she was surprised by the sudden impact of strong, gripping hands on her shoulders, steadying her stance.

"Careful there, honey," the blond woman drawled. "You don't want to hurt yourself or that little baby in there."

"I'm so sorry. I didn't see you," China said.

The woman's smile was wry, but her drawl held a hint of laughter as she brushed the slight dusting of snow from her fur. Then she patted her hair, as if checking for disarray.

"Obviously."

China straightened her coat and bent to pick up her bag. As she did, she heard someone shouting and then the woman beside her starting to curse. Startled by the sound of someone running through the muck, she spun in fear. A series of lights began flashing, and she screamed. It took a few seconds for her to realize someone was only taking pictures.

To her horror, the blonde suddenly pulled a gun from her purse and fired three shots in rapid succession. The man with the camera staggered, then turned, trying to run. The last shot hit him square in the back. He dropped facedown in the street, sending a small shower of slush into the air as he hit. A pool of red began spilling out from beneath him, discoloring the snow.

China stared in disbelief, first at the blonde with the gun, then at the man in the street. Her mind kept telling her to run, but her feet wouldn't move. Instead, she pressed both hands over her mouth, willing herself not to scream. There had to be a logical explanation for what she'd just witnessed. The man must have been going to attack them. That was it. The blonde had been defending herself.

But when the woman leaned over the dead man and yanked the camera from around his neck, China knew that claiming self-defense would never fly. Pictures might be incriminating, but they were hardly lethal. She took a tentative step backward, and as she did, the blonde looked up, an expression of pure rage on her face, and China knew then that the danger she'd faced earlier with the three men was nothing to what she faced now.

''Please,'' China whispered, and unconsciously spread her hands across her stomach.

''Well, shit,'' the blonde drawled, and gave China's belly one last glance before taking aim.

''No!'' China begged, and began moving backward. ''I won't tell. I don't know you. I don't know him. I won't tell.''

''Can't take the chance, darlin','' the blonde woman drawled. ''But it's nothing personal.''

China didn't feel the first shot, although it knocked her off her feet. The second shot hit high in her shoulder as she fell, ripping her flesh and ricocheting off the pavement beyond as it passed through her body. Pain was muted by the quickening onset of impending unconsciousness. She had a few fleeting moments of awareness, of staring up into the night sky and seeing thousands upon thousands of snowflakes coming toward her, just like the water from the shower all those years ago when Clyde had tried to drown her. Her head lolled to the right as a wave of weakness came over her. From the corner of her eye she could see the outline of the cross, and in that moment she knew she was going to die. Within seconds, the cross began to fade. A single tear slid from the corner of her right eye, and then everything got quiet—so quiet that China imagined she could hear the impact of each single snowflake as it fell against her face. In the distance came the sounds of running feet, but they would come too late.

The darkness was here, waiting for her to catch up.

She was tired—so tired—and so very, very cold.

Her eyelids fluttered once, twice, then closed.

A quiet sigh escaped from between her lips, and then it was over.

The air was warm—without gravity. China was moving without walking—floating toward a distant humming sound—when she heard a child call out for Mommy, shouting for her to wait.

She stopped and turned. A little dark-headed girl, who looked to be no more than three or four, was running toward her and laughing aloud. China smiled. Her daughter. Of course. What had she been thinking? She couldn't go without her. They clasped hands as if they'd done it countless times before and resumed their journey toward the distant rhythmic sound. It didn't seem strange that the child beside her was older than the child she'd been carrying. It was her baby, just the same.

They walked and talked, pointing at a bird sitting on a nearby tree, stopping to smell a patch of wild-flowers nestled by the path. The longer they walked, the louder the sound became. Before long, China could just make out the sound of voices, and within a short time, she could hear what they were saying.

"Welcome…welcome. We've come to walk you home."

Joy flooded her as she bent down and picked her daughter up, suddenly anxious to reach them. The child's hair was thick and soft, and it blew against her cheek like so many strands of black silk, and then they were there in the midst of the murmuring crowd.

"China Mae, I'm so happy to see you, child."

China started to laugh. Mother. It was Mother.

"We're home, Mother, we're home," China said.

The murmuring began again, only louder, encompassed by an ever-growing light. China stood in awe of the illumination and knew a quiet recognition. Love filled her as she lifted her face to the light, then everything began to change. Her daughter was in her arms and then she was not. In fear, she saw her mother carrying her away.

"Wait," China cried. "Wait for me."

But the light blocked her path, and she couldn't move through it.

"No!" China begged. "Don't leave me here."

Mae stopped and turned, her granddaughter perfectly balanced on her hip.

"It's not your time, China Mae. You have to go back."

China had no time to protest. One moment she was standing before the presence of God, and then she felt herself falling…falling…back to the pain and the cold.

And she was going alone. -

Detective Bennett English pushed his way through the gathering crowd and then slipped beneath a strip of yellow crime scene tape, flashing his badge as he went.

"English. Homicide."

The patrolman on duty nodded to let him pass and then turned his attention to some overzealous onlookers, forcing them back behind the barrier.

Ben shivered as he slogged his way through the muck on the street, thankful he was wearing his boots instead of street shoes. He approached a pair of officers standing near a parked ambulance. One of them was sipping coffee, while the other was using his baton to knock ice from the bottom of one shoe.

"I see you got the luck of the draw tonight, huh, English? Where's your buddy Fisher?"

"Home with the flu," Ben said, then pointed to the bodies. "What have we got?"

One of the officers shrugged. "Dead people," he said, then took another sip of his coffee. "No witnesses. No nothing, which is no surprise around here."

Ben gave the area a quick glance. It was true. This part of the city was not a hangout for Dallas's more law-abiding citizens.

"Hell of a night to die," the other officer said.

Ben frowned. "Is there ever a good time?" he asked, then turned, looking toward the blanket-covered body in the street.

"Do we know who they are?"

"That one's a male. The Medical Examiner is almost through with him. As soon as he is, we'll check for ID."

Ben nodded, pointing toward the other body on the sidewalk and the paramedics hovering around it.

"What about that one?"

"Woman—mid to late twenties—pregnant."

As cold as he was, Ben felt a deeper sort of chill invade his body.

"Damn," he muttered, as he gave the paramedics a closer look. "So we're looking at three deaths and not two."

Suddenly there was a flurry of activity around the woman. Ben moved closer to the scene.

"What's going on?" he asked.

"We've got a live one," one of the paramedics said, as they began moving her toward a gurney.

Ben's focus shifted. If she lived, it would make getting answers to this mess a whole lot easier. As they pushed her past him on the way to the ambulance, he glanced at her face.

Even with the snow melting on her cheeks and plastering her hair to her head, she was beautiful. She had a small straight nose above lips softly parted, and eyelashes so black and thick they looked like shadows. Her cheeks were pale and pinched from the cold, but the delicate cut of her features was impossible to miss, as was the small, perfect dimple in the middle of her chin.

Ben's gaze moved from her face to the wound near her shoulder. His gaze dropped from that to her abdomen and the wide slash of red staining her coat.

"What about the baby?" he asked.

The medic shook his head as they moved past.

Sadness quickened. He could only imagine her despair if she lived—waking up in a hospital and learning that she had survived while her baby had not. He shifted his stance and looked away, unwilling to pursue his thoughts. He was letting his emotions interfere with his objectivity, and that was something he couldn't afford.

As he watched, the last paramedic climbed inside and reached out to close the ambulance doors.

"Where are you taking her?" Ben yelled.

"Parkland," he said.

Within seconds they were gone, speeding away into the night with a woman in need of a miracle.

Ben took out his notebook and moved back toward the body in the street. The ME was leaving. He caught him at the door of his car.

"Hey, Gregson, got a minute?"

Bob Gregson looked up. "Evening, English. I see

you got the luck of the draw tonight. Where's your shadow?''

"Red's down with the flu. What can you tell me about the victim?''

"He died of multiple gunshot wounds. Won't know which one did him in until we do an autopsy, but I doubt it matters. Someone wanted him dead real bad and kept shooting until the job was done.''

"Send a copy of the autopsy to my office, okay?''

"Don't hold your breath,'' Gregson muttered, as he slid behind the wheel of his car. "We're backed up as it is.''

Ben empathized with the frustration in the ME's voice, but knowing as much as possible within the first twenty-four hours of a homicide was crucial to solving the case. The coroner drove away as Ben moved back to the body.

"Find any ID on him?'' Ben asked.

One of the officers handed him a plastic bag with a wallet and a couple of business cards inside.

"Some guy named Finelli...Charles Finelli.''

Ben's pulse surged.

"Wait,'' he said, and reached down, unzipping the body bag just enough to view the victim's face. He grunted in disbelief.

"You know him?'' one of the officers asked.

"By reputation,'' Ben said. "He's a bartender by trade and a psycho with a camera by night. He's been booked a half-dozen times for trespassing. Thinks he's some sort of Hollywood paparazzi type. Was there a camera on him?''

They all shook their heads in denial.

"Did you search the area?"

"We looked all over," an officer said. "When we first arrived on the scene, we figured this for a domestic situation. You know…a man, a pregnant woman, probably an argument gone wrong. But neither one of them had a gun. We canvassed the area for everything from witnesses to gum wrappers, and if there'd been a camera to be found, we would have it." He motioned toward the sky and the snow still falling. "Even the hookers took the night off, and according to the bunch inside the bar, no one heard a thing."

Ben nodded. "Figures. No one ever wants to get involved. What about ID on the woman?"

"No purse, but she had this bag. We found it on the sidewalk near her body. Haven't had time to go through it."

They handed Ben the duffel bag and moved toward their patrol cars. They'd secured the scene, passed along all they knew to the detective division. It was Homicide's problem now.

Ben tossed the bag into the trunk of his car, along with the plastic bag containing Charles Finelli's personal effects. He would take it all to headquarters as soon as he made a few inquires of his own inside the bar.

A few officers were still on-site as he stepped inside. It was a sleazy, inconsequential establishment, unremarkable in any respect except for the sign over the door—a bright-blue parrot in flight and the words The Blue Parrot glowing a bright neon-orange beneath.

He paused inside, ignoring the smoke and welcoming the enveloping warmth. The underlying murmur of voices silenced almost immediately as several patrons at the bar turned to stare. Their judgment was silent and brief. Moments later they turned back to their drinks, but the silence continued.

Ben stifled a sigh. Obviously he'd already been made, which did not bode well for getting any questions answered. He moved toward the bar.

"What'll it be?" the bartender asked.

"Got any coffee?" Ben asked.

"No."

"Then I pass," Ben said.

The bartender shrugged and started to move away when Ben laid his badge on the counter. The bartender looked at the badge then up at Ben, obviously unimpressed.

"Two people were gunned down in front of your place about twenty minutes ago," Ben said.

The bartender's stare never wavered. "Yeah, so I heard."

"Don't suppose you heard the shots?"

"I don't suppose I did," the bartender drawled.

"Then who called the cops?" Ben asked.

The bartender shrugged. "Some guy came in off the street, said there were two bodies in the snow. I showed him where the phone was. He used it. That's all I know."

"Is he still here?" Ben asked.

"Nope."

"Can you tell me what he looked like?"

"Nope."

Ben had to resist the urge to grab the bartender's shirt and shake that insolent tone out of his voice.

He turned around and raised his voice so that it could be heard throughout the small room.

"Anybody in here see what happened outside?"

Nobody answered.

"Anybody hear anything…like gunshots…or a car speeding away?"

Total silence.

"Well now," Ben drawled. "I want to thank you for your assistance. I know the young woman they just took to the hospital will appreciate knowing how much cooperation you gave toward finding the person who just shot her unborn baby to death inside her belly."

Ben laid his card down on the corner of the bar and walked out, disgusted with them and with the human race in general. He was halfway to his car before he realized it had stopped snowing. The streets were eerily silent, making the sound of his own footsteps seem ominous as he stomped through three inches of snow. As he unlocked his car, a cat squalled from a nearby alley. Instinctively, he spun, reaching toward the semi-automatic he wore in a shoulder holster under his coat, but there was no one there. Silently cursing Red for succumbing to the flu, he slid behind the wheel and drove away.

Three

Ben hit the period key on his computer keyboard, then leaned back in his chair, eyeing the report he'd just finished. The shooting down in Oakcliff wasn't the worst case he'd ever worked, but there was something about it that bothered him more than usual. His gaze moved from the typewriter to the wallets next to his phone. Notifying next of kin sucked.

Charles Finelli's father lived in Krebs, Oklahoma, a small, predominately Italian community known for thriving vineyards and fabulous food. Anthony Finelli had cried when Ben informed him of his only son's demise. After several phone calls he'd learned that there was no one left to cry for China Brown.

He picked up the old red wallet he'd found in her bag and opened it again, as he had off and on for the past hour and a half. It was thin and cracked and held together with a large rubber band. No money inside, and the picture on her driver's license was typical of most—a self-conscious smile in the process of being born—but the tumble of thick, dark hair framing a delicate face was not. Even there, her beauty was evident.

He laid it aside and then leaned forward, resting his

elbows on the desk and closed his eyes, and still he couldn't rid himself of China Brown.

Last known address—no longer valid.

He thought of the landlord he'd spoken to earlier. What a jerk, evicting a pregnant woman into the snow. According to the landlord, the boyfriend was a guy named Tommy Fairheart, who'd gotten her pregnant and skipped out on her days earlier, taking all her money with him.

Ben stood abruptly, grabbed his coffee cup off the desk and headed toward the break room. He hoped they both burned in hell.

The coffee was bitter, but it was hot, and for now it was enough. He sipped it slowly, expecting the warmth to envelope him. Instead, the image of China Brown's snow-covered face slipped into his mind. He shuddered instead. God, would he ever be warm again?

He glanced at his watch. It was already morning. He needed to go home, get some food and a shower, at least pretend to sleep. But he knew sleep would be long in coming, if at all. So much about this shooting didn't ring true, and the detective in him couldn't turn loose of the puzzle, not even for the night.

Suddenly he set his cup down on the cabinet and strode to his desk, yanked his coat from the back of the chair and headed for the door. There was something he needed to do before he could sleep.

The nurse on desk duty in the ICU unit of Parkland Hospital was monitoring a patient's erratic heart rate when the doors to the unit swung open. She stood abruptly, eyeing the tall, tousled-haired man with dismay.

"I'm sorry, sir, but you can't just come in here like this. Visiting hours aren't for another hour and..."

He flashed his badge.

"I don't care who you are," she said. "I don't have any patients healthy enough for interrogation."

"I didn't come to talk," he said softly. "I just need to see her."

The nurse frowned. "See who?"

"China Brown...the pregnant woman who was shot."

The nurse's expression shifted, alarming Ben.

"She's still alive...isn't she?"

The nurse nodded. "But her baby didn't make it."

"Yeah, I know," Ben said. "What's her condition?"

The nurse checked the chart. "Critical." Then she gave Ben a pleading look. "Please, Detective English, you have to leave."

He turned, searching the beds for a glimpse of her face.

"Where is she?" he asked.

"Fourth one from the end."

He took an impulsive step forward, then stopped when the nurse touched his coat sleeve, giving his arm a gentle squeeze.

"Come back tomorrow."

He hesitated before nodding, his shoulders drooping with fatigue.

"Yeah, maybe I'd better. Sorry for the interruption. It's just that she's been on my mind ever since the—" He stopped, unwilling to bare his soul to a stranger.

"It's a tragedy about the baby," she said softly. "It was a little girl."

Ben nodded. Halfway out the door he stopped and turned. He knew the routine. The baby would have been taken by Caesarian and sent to the morgue for an autopsy, even though it would have been assumed that the shooting was the cause of death. But then afterward…?

"About the baby…"

"Yes?"

"She doesn't have any next of kin—Miss Brown, I mean."

The nurse stood her ground. "I don't know about that, sir. You'll need to check with the doctor who handled the surgery."

"What's his name?" Ben asked.

"Dr. Ross Pope."

"I'll talk to him in the morning," Ben said. "In the meantime, if it matters, I'll take responsibility for claiming the body until Miss Brown is able."

"Yes, sir, I'll make a note of your name for the records."

Ben glanced back at the bed where China Brown was lying, then handed the nurse his card.

"If there's any change—any change at all—I want

to be notified. My home and office number are there. Call either, any time.''

She clipped the card to China's chart.

Ben stood for a moment, staring down the length of the room to the woman on the fourth bed from the end, then stalked out as abruptly as he'd come in.

Bobby Lee Wakefield looked good and he knew it. The Armani suit he was wearing fit perfectly, accentuating his slim, wiry build and making his legs look even longer. The thousand-dollar Justin boots he was wearing were an affectation with the suit, but, here in Texas, quite appropriate.

He gave himself one last look in the mirror, smoothed his hands on both sides of his hair to pat down any loose ends and then headed for his desk. Ainsley Been, his campaign manager, would be here any moment to escort him to the Wyndham Anatole, where the press would be waiting. It was an elegant hotel, worthy of the announcement he was going to make. He glanced at his speech, then tossed it aside. He knew the damned thing by heart. He'd been planning it for years.

Bobby Lee Wakefield had come a long way from being a wildcatter's son from Amarillo, Texas. Wearing clothes all through his school years that had been bought from the Goodwill store had not endeared him to any of his classmates, and he'd been deep in the jungles of Vietnam when his daddy finally struck it rich. Coming home to luxury had been as foreign as the jungle he'd nearly died in. He had taken one look at the elegance of their new home and known instinctively that it would take more than an endless supply of money for his family to match their surroundings. Within six months of coming home, he'd enrolled at Southern Methodist University and never looked back. Interning for every politician who would have him on staff had occupied his summers, and by the time he was ready to graduate, he had more than a foot in the door of state government. By the time he was thirty-five, he was serving his second term in the House of Representatives, and by his forty-second birthday he had been elected to a seat in the Senate. Here in Dallas, the city was his. He'd been divorced for years, was wealthy and handsome, popular as hell on Capitol Hill—and he was about to announce his plans to run for president of the United States of America.

His daddy would have been proud.

Just as he checked the time, the door to his office flew back, hitting the wall with a reverberating thud. He didn't have to look up to know who'd just entered, although he turned to face her.

The tall, elegant blonde in white silk sauntered into the room in a cloud of expensive perfume. His eyes narrowed, and he stifled a curse. Daddy had never known what to do with the woman, and God help him, neither did he.

''Mother, did it ever occur to you to knock?''

Mona Wakefield blew him a kiss and sidled up to

where he was standing, pulled her long blond hair over her shoulder and offered him her back.

"Bobby Lee, honey, I do not knock on doors in my own house. Now zip this up for me like a good boy. I want to be ready when Ainsley comes."

Bobby Lee gawked. There wasn't enough back to the dress she was wearing to warrant a zipper, much less anything else.

"Hell's fire, Mother, you are not wearing this to my press conference. You look like a hooker."

Mona shrugged, glancing over her shoulder and batting her eyes.

"Maybe a call girl—an expensive call girl—but not a hooker. Besides, how many sixty-eight-year-old women do you know who look as good as me? I'll tell you how many. None. Now zip me up and stop telling me what to do."

Bobby Lee grabbed her by the shoulders and spun her around.

"You get that goddamned thing off now and put something else on, or so help me, I'll have Waymon lock you in your room. You want to stand by my side and bask in the so-called 'glory' of being Senator Wakefield's mother, then you'd better be wearing something more suited to the occasion."

A dark angry flush stained her cheeks as she stared him in the face. To an observer, they would have appeared quite similar. Their tall, slender bodies were firm, their facial silhouettes surprising alike. High foreheads, straight noses, stubborn chins.

Their staring match was a draw until suddenly Mona shrugged.

"You don't like it? Fine. I'll find something else."

She tilted first one shoulder down and then the other, defiantly letting her dress fall down around her ankles in a puddle of white silk. Only after she saw shock replace Bobby Lee's anger did she turn and saunter out of his office as calmly as she'd come in. The fact that she was wearing nothing but high-heeled sling-back shoes, see-through underwear and the white lace garter belt holding up her hose didn't seem to faze her.

Just as she disappeared from sight, the doorbell rang, echoing throughout the downstairs portion of the mansion.

"Jesus Christ," Bobby Lee muttered and grabbed her dress off the floor. Ainsley was here.

He dashed into the hall, grabbed the maid on her way to the door and stuffed the dress in her arms.

"Delia, you make damn sure my mother gets something decent on, you hear? Don't let her downstairs until she does!"

Delia nodded and took the dress on the run. Working in this household was crazy, but the pay was good, and she never got bored.

Bobby Lee hesitated, waiting until he was sure that his mother's bare backside was no longer visible, then he pasted on a smile and strode toward the door.

"Ainsley, you look ready for war, boy," he drawled, affecting his best Texas good-old-boy routine. "Cook has a fine bunch of snacks in the library.

Why don't you go on in and make yourself at home? I'll just tell Mother you're here.''

Ainsley Been smiled and smoothed a hand down the front of his vest as he aimed for the library. Being hired as Wakefield's campaign manager had been a coup. It would be his first presidential campaign, but if he did this right, hopefully not his last.

''Thank you, Bobby Lee, I believe I will have myself a little snack. I missed my lunch today.'' He moved on as he'd been directed, unaware of the undercurrents in the senator's household.

Within the hour, the trio was in a white stretch limousine and headed toward the hotel, where the press were awaiting their arrival. Mona was sitting opposite the men, her long legs crossed, her anger still high. She stared out the window, refusing to meet her son's gaze. She'd come downstairs in a two-piece suit, as her son had requested, sauntering across the floor in her black stiletto heels to meet the men. The fact that the skirt was three inches above her knees and the jacket's top button was just below the beginning of her cleavage was bad enough. But it was the fabric about which Bobby Lee was most pissed. Black leather. He was announcing his candidacy for president, and his mother was going to be standing at his side in black leather. All she needed was a whip and a Harley to complete the image.

''Well, now,'' Ainsley said as the driver pulled up to the front of the hotel. ''We're here. Ya'll put on a smilin' face and let's knock 'em dead.''

Bobby Lee took a deep breath and gave his mother a warning glance. She arched an eyebrow, then smiled.

"Now, Ainsley, I'm here merely to lend support. After all, this is my son's night."

Ainsley smiled broadly. "Yes, it is, and you must be very proud."

Mona looked at her son then, at the glitter in his eyes and the muscle jerking at the side of his jaw. She gave him a wink. To her delight, she could see him struggling to stay angry.

"Of course I'm proud of him. What mother wouldn't be?" she said.

Bobby Lee shook his head, then grinned wryly. When all was said and done, whatever Mona did, it was going to be done her way or else.

"Thank you, Mother."

"You're quite welcome, Bobby Lee. Now let's go give those reporters something to talk about. Put a smile on that handsome face and strut your stuff."

"Yes, ma'am."

The door to the limousine opened.

Ainsley looked at Bobby Lee and then gave him a thumbs-up.

"After you," he said.

Bobby Lee took a deep breath. By the time he was out of the car, his smile was as wide as his steps were long. He entered the hotel with flashbulbs going off in his face and never looked back to see if they were following. He was on a mission that would not be deterred.

* * *

It was ten minutes past seven in the morning when Ben once again approached the ICU. The nurse who'd been on duty last night was gone and another was in her place. Ben flashed his badge and was asking about China's condition as a doctor came in on his morning rounds. Ben took one look at the name tag on the slim, sandy-haired man's lab coat and gave him his full attention. It was Ross Pope, the man who'd operated on China.

"Dr. Pope?"

"Yes?"

Ben extended his hand. "Detective Bennett English, Homicide Division. I'm handling the case involving China Brown, the woman you operated on last night."

Dr. Pope frowned. "I hope you're here to tell me you have the bastard who shot her in custody."

"No, not yet, but we will."

Ross Pope sighed. "What can I do for you?"

"Grant me permission to see her."

The doctor's frown deepened. "Absolutely not. She's in a drug-induced coma. There's no way she can assist you in your investigation and no guarantee that she will remember what happened when she does wake up."

Ben shook his head. "You misunderstand me," he said. "I don't want to talk to her."

"Are you family?" Pope asked.

"As far as we can ascertain, she doesn't have any," Ben said.

Pope frowned. "Then if she can't talk, why the need to visit?"

Ben hesitated, then glanced toward the ward. He could barely see the outline of her body beneath the sheets.

"Will she live?" he asked.

"Barring any unforseen complications, I would say yes."

"When will she wake up?"

"When her body has had more time to heal, we will decrease the medications. After that, it will be up to her. She'll come back when she's ready."

Ben thrust his hand through his hair, disheveling the style into spiky disarray. A look of confusion came and went on his face, but he didn't know it. All he knew was that seeing her—touching her—was necessary.

"Look, I can't explain it," he said. "But I keep feeling like I need to be there—maybe it's more for me than for her, but she doesn't have anyone else. From what we've gathered, the father of her baby abandoned her. Her landlord evicted her yesterday morning, and by nightfall she was near death. Her baby is dead, and she doesn't even know it yet. When she wakes up, well…it just doesn't seem right that she suffer that alone."

Pope's gaze narrowed as he gave Ben a studied stare. He hesitated briefly, then turned to the nurse on duty.

"Make a note on China Brown's chart that Detective English be allowed to see Miss Brown at his discretion.'' He tapped a finger against Ben's chest. ''I'm trusting that you will have sense enough not to abuse the privilege you've been given.''

Ben resisted an overwhelming urge to grin. ''Yes, sir, that you can.''

''Fine, then. Follow me. I'll check on her condition, and then you may have exactly five minutes at her bedside. I'd advise you to be careful of what you say, if anything. We know now that comatose patients often hear what is going on around them without being able to communicate. Keep that in mind. I don't want anything making matters worse for her.''

''You can trust me,'' Ben said.

Pope almost smiled. ''Yes…well…it seems I've already done that. Don't disappoint me.''

Ben nodded, then followed Dr. Pope to China's bedside. She was a far cry from the bloody, snow-covered woman he'd seen being taken away in the ambulance last night, and yet not so different after all. She was still so very small. So very silent. So very hurt.

He watched the doctor's every move with interest, noting his thorough study of her chart and then the tender manner in which he checked her wounds.

Ben caught a glimpse of pewter-colored staples and winced. He didn't give a damn what modern medicine had to say about the benefits of using metal as opposed to the old-fashioned sutures. They looked grotesque, and he imagined they would hurt like hell. For the first time since this whole thing began, he was glad China

Brown didn't know what was happening. At least for now, she couldn't feel the pain of the trauma her body had endured.

With one last warning look, Dr. Pope moved away to check his other patients, leaving Ben alone by China's bed.

Ben took a deep breath and then let himself look, marking every feature of her face for future reference, noting the delicate shape and the dark, winged eyebrows slightly knitted over the bridge of her nose.

He brushed his thumb along the length of one of her fingers. When it twitched, his pulse jumped. Although it was nothing more than an unconscious reaction to stimulus, it startled him just the same. He leaned over and very carefully lifted a strand of her hair from the corner of her mouth, smoothing it back against her head, then whispered very quietly near her ear.

"I'm here, China Brown. You're safe…and you aren't alone."

Rationally, he had not expected anything, but when she gave no reaction to the sound of his voice, his spirits fell. He straightened up, but he didn't move back. Instead, he laid his hand upon hers and took solace in the warmth of her flesh.

The drug-induced coma she was in was allowing her badly battered body to heal. But it was her sanity that Bennett English was most concerned with. When she woke, and Dr. Pope had assured him that this would take place, would she remember what had happened to her? Would she be able to identify the man who'd shot her and killed Charles, aka Chaz, Finelli, or would the trauma and shock of losing her baby and very nearly her life block everything else from her mind? Only time would tell. Unfortunately, time was not on Ben's side. With every passing hour, the chance of finding the person who'd committed the crime grew slimmer.

It wasn't until someone touched his sleeve that he realized his time was up.

"Sorry," he said softly. "I was lost in thought."

"It happens a lot in here," the nurse said. "You can come back later, but for now, you need to leave."

"I'll be back," he said softly, and gave China's hand a soft squeeze.

It didn't make sense, but his heart was lighter as he pulled out of the parking lot on his way to headquarters. Nothing had changed. The woman was still their only witness and, for now, she wasn't talking. But there at her bedside this morning, he'd made a connection with her that he didn't want to lose.

A half hour later he turned down Commerce Street, then pulled into the parking lot of the Dallas P.D., avoiding a melting snowdrift as he parked. He was halfway to the door when his partner, Red Fisher, came striding out and waved him down.

"Saw you pulling in from the window," Red said. "Thought I'd save us both some time and come to meet you."

Ben grinned. "Glad to see you back, but what's the rush?"

Red waved a piece of paper in Ben's face. "I was halfway through reading the report on the Oakcliff shooting when this call came in. You can fill me in on the rest as we drive."

"Where are we going?" Ben asked.

"To see Finelli's girlfriend. She called this morning to report him missing. When they broke the news to her, she got hysterical."

Ben slid behind the wheel and closed the door as Red got in on the passenger side, still talking.

"Anyway, from some of the stuff she was screaming about, the captain thought we might get a lead on the shooter from her."

"Didn't know he had a girlfriend," Ben said.

Red nodded. "According to her, they've been living together for about a year or so. Maybe she'll know why Finelli was down in that part of town last night."

"Maybe," Ben said, and then turned all his attention to maneuvering through the slushy streets.

A short while later, he pulled to the curb in front of an apartment complex and parked. Gang graffiti was everywhere. On walls, on the sidewalks, even on a couple of parked cars near the back of the lot.

"Jeez," Red muttered. "Rita and I lived in this complex the first two years of our marriage, but it didn't look like this."

"How many years ago was that?" Ben asked.

"Nearly fifteen," Red said. "Garland has changed a lot in the last fifteen years."

Ben thought of China Brown, who became a victim her first night on the streets.

"Fifteen years, hell," he muttered. "A lot can happen between one breath and the next."

Red gave his partner an odd, studied glance. It was unlike Bennett English to be so emotional.

"You all right?" he asked.

Ben shook off his anger and gave Red a grin. "You're the one who's been sick," he said. "Better be worrying about yourself. Now let's go see the lady. What's her name again?"

Red consulted his notes. "Jackie Porter—apartment 610."

Ben rolled his eyes. "Five bucks says the place doesn't have a working elevator."

Red grinned. "I'll give you ten to ride it if it does."

Ben laughed. It was good to have his partner back on the job.

Jackie Porter was still bawling and about ten minutes from a nervous breakdown when her doorbell rang. She jumped reflexively at the sound, then started howling even louder. By the time she got to the door, she was as close to hysterics as a woman could get and not be locked up.

"Who is it?" she yelled, then blew her nose so loud she didn't hear the answer. "Who?" she repeated, then stood on her tiptoes to look through the peephole in the door.

"Dallas P.D., Miss Porter. May we come in?"

She could see their shields and their faces, although it was like looking at them through a fishbowl. Hiccuping on a sob, she undid the locks and the security chain, opened the door, then stepped back to let them in.

"Is it true? Is Chaz really dead?"

Ben steeled himself and nodded.

She let out a wail and covered her face with her hands as Red closed the door behind them. Ben took her by the elbow and led her toward the sofa.

"Please, let's sit down," Ben said.

Jackie Porter fell backward with a plop and reached for a fresh handful of tissues. The men waited while she blew and wiped and managed to compose herself.

"Miss Porter, can I get you some water?" Red asked.

She shook her head. "No, I'll be fine, but thank you," she muttered, then gave her nose a last dainty blow.

"Your name is Jackie, right?" he asked.

She set up a little straighter and wadded the tissues in her hand into a ball.

"It's Jackwilyn Kate Porter, spelled J-A-C-K-W-I-L-Y-N, but everyone calls me Jackie. My mama was a huge fan of *Charlie's Angels* back in the old days. She named me for that Jaclyn Smith woman, and for

Kate Jackson, only she spelled it different. Those were her two favorite angels. Mama didn't go for blondes.''

Ben wouldn't look at Red. He knew if he did, he might grin, and this visit was no laughing matter.

''Anyway, Chaz and I were supposed to go get some barbecue and then go see a movie last night. At the last minute, he called to tell me he had a hot lead.''

Ben looked up. ''Hot lead?''

Jackie nodded. ''Yeah, you know…if someone famous was out and about in the city, Chaz wanted to be on hand to take photos. He got paid good money for them. I know, because sometimes he had me deposit the cash.'' She sniffed a bit, then continued. ''He was going to be famous like those photographers who work for the tabloids.'' Her chin quivered as a fresh set of tears began to roll. ''I knew something was wrong when he didn't come home last night. He always called if he was going to be late.''

Ben had his notebook out and his pen in hand when he spoke. ''So you were living together?''

She nodded. ''For almost a year.''

Ben glanced at his notes. ''But this isn't the address that was in his wallet.''

''Yeah, I know. He kept his old apartment, but he used it as sort of an office. It was where he developed all his pictures. He kept his cameras and files there, too, I think.''

''What kind of files?'' Red asked.

''I don't know. About his work, I guess.''

"So you know for sure he had his camera with him last night?"

"He must have. The only time he ever stood me up was when he was going to take pictures...and I understood, you know. It was his calling. Chaz was real good at what he did."

A few minutes later, after they'd gotten all the information they could from Jackie Porter, including the key to Finelli's apartment and the make of camera he would probably have been carrying, Red arose from his seat and handed her his card.

"If there's anything else you can think of that might help us find the person who shot Mr. Finelli, please give us a call," Red said. "My office number and pager number are both on the card. Call anytime."

"Thanks," Jackie said, and followed the detectives to the door.

They had started down the hall toward the stairs when she called out to them. They stopped and turned.

"Yes, ma'am?" Ben asked.

"When you arrest the man who did this...will you let me know?"

"You'll know," Ben said.

She managed a smile and then nodded before shutting the door. They heard the sound of four locks being turned. Red glanced at the graffiti on the walls and rolled his eyes.

Ben grinned. "What? You some kind of art critic now? At least it matches the exterior of the place just fine."

Red chuckled and shook his head.

When they reached the elevator, they hesitated, gave each other a questioning look, then headed for the stairs. The idea of two cops being stranded in an elevator in a building like this was something like offering to be targets for some gun-happy gang-banger. Neither man breathed easy until they were in the car and driving away.

"So, what do you think?" Red asked, as Ben braked for a red light.

"I don't know," Ben said. "Finelli didn't have a camera on him when the EMTs got to him. Maybe he was shot for the camera and China Brown just happened to be in the wrong place at the wrong time."

"Yeah…maybe." Red leaned over and turned up the heat. "Or maybe he was playing fast and loose with Ms. Brown. Maybe the kid she was carrying was Finelli's. Maybe Brown's boyfriend found out, they had a fight and he split. Maybe Brown was meeting Finelli to get help."

Ben snorted beneath his breath. "Damn, Red, what the hell kind of flu medicine are you taking? I've never heard so much baloney come out of your mouth at one time since you badmouthed the Slickers in their last Super Bowl."

Red frowned. "Just because I'm not a Dallas Slickers fan does not make me stupid. So I was reaching a little with my last theory. So what. It's possible."

But Ben wouldn't budge. "Not her," he said. "She wouldn't cheat."

"Who? Jackie Porter?"

"No. China Brown."

Red turned in the seat and stared at his partner as if he'd never seen him before.

"Now how the hell do you know something like that?"

Ben shifted restlessly, then shrugged. "Call it a hunch, okay?"

"Did you hear what you just said?"

Ben turned onto the freeway and then glanced at his watch.

"Are you hungry?" he asked.

"I'm always hungry," Red said. "And you didn't answer my question."

"While you're deciding where we're going to eat, I'm going to make a quick stop."

"Where at?" Red asked.

"Parkland Hospital. I want to check on China's condition."

"China? We're calling her China now?"

"Red, we've been partners for the better part of twelve years now, right?"

"Yeah, but what's that got to do with—"

"And have I ever asked you to trust me on something that wasn't right?"

Red sighed. "No."

"Then let this go." Ben took the exit to the hospital and headed down the street with single-minded intent.

Red threw up his hands and leaned back in the seat. "Fine," he muttered, then added, "are you buying?"

Ben grinned. "Maybe."

"Then I'm having steak. Chicken-fried steak."

"I thought Rita had you on a low-fat diet?" Ben said.

"You have your secrets, I have mine," Red muttered.

Ben parked and got out of the car. "I won't be long."

"Oh, no, you don't," Red said. "I'm coming with you. I want to see this woman for myself."

Four

Red watched his partner's face as they rode the elevator up to ICU. There was a muscle jerking at the side of Ben's jaw, and his gaze was fixed. The car jolted slightly as it came to a halt, and when the doors opened, Ben English strode through them in haste. Red shook his head as he followed. Ben's behavior was bordering on obsessive, and that made Red nervous.

But Ben didn't care what his partner thought. What mattered most to him was catching the person responsible for the murders and making sure China Brown came to no more harm. As they neared the nurses' station, he lengthened his stride. By the time they arrived, Red was all but running to keep up.

"It's a good thing we didn't have to go any farther," Red muttered, as they waited for the nurse on duty to finish her phone call. "I'm all out of breath."

Ben glanced over at Red and grinned. "Too many chicken-fried steaks."

Red glared. "No, I'm just too damned short. You're what…at least a couple of inches over six feet. I'm five-seven. My legs are half as long as yours, and I have to take two steps to your one. Chicken-fried steak, my ass.''

Ben glanced down at his partner. "Not so much your ass as your belly."

Red shook his head and then chuckled. It was impossible to get ahead of this man. Before he could think of a good come-back, the nurse on duty hung up the phone.

"May I help you?" she asked.

Ben flashed his badge. "Detectives English and Fisher to see China Brown," he said.

"I'm sorry, but only two visitors at a time in ICU, and there's someone with her now."

Ben spun, staring intently through the glass to the ward beyond. He could just make out the figure of a man leaning over her bed.

"Who is he?"

The nurse shook her head. "He didn't say."

Ben's belly knotted. "That woman is the only witness to a murder. Do you let in anybody who presents themselves?"

The nurse looked nervous. "I don't have any orders to the contrary," she said.

Ben leaned over the desk, his voice hoarse with worry. "Either you go get him out of there now, or I'll do it for you."

She jumped up from her chair and bolted through the doors. Seconds later, she was at China's bedside. Ben had his cell phone in hand and was making a call as the nurse began escorting the man toward the door.

By the time they reached the exit, he'd already requested a guard for China.

"Easy, partner," Red said. "It's probably the boyfriend. Remember…the one who skipped out on her. Now and then the jerks do get a guilty conscience."

But the young, thin Latino coming through the doors didn't look like a man filled with remorse. He looked nervous.

Ben stepped in front of him, blocking his way. "Detective Bennett English, Homicide. This is my partner, Detective Fisher. If you'd step this way, we'd like to ask you some questions."

The color faded from beneath the young man's skin, leaving it a pale, ashy gray.

"I don't know nothin'," he said shortly.

"Let us be the judge of that," Ben said, and lightly clasped his arm as they led him toward a nearby waiting room.

As soon as they were inside, they sat him down, then pulled up their chairs so they were both facing him. The implication was plain. He wasn't going anywhere until the officers were through.

"What's your name?" Ben asked. "And how do you know China Brown?"

The young Latino glared, but this time it was anger that fed his emotions.

"*¿Hablo Englese?*" Red asked.

The man's gaze shifted from Ben to Red, and as it did, a look of disdain replaced his fear.

"Yes, I speak English," he said. "*¿Habla usted español?*"

Red looked a bit taken aback and then shrugged.

"Well, then," the man said, "looks like I'm one up on you."

Ben slid his foot between the young man's outstretched legs and leaned forward. The motion of dominance was impossible to mistake.

"If you two are through with your pissing contest, then I want some answers. What's your name, and how do you know China Brown?"

At that point, all the fight seemed to go out of the young man. His shoulders slumped, and he leaned forward, resting his elbows on his knees as he looked down at the floor. When he looked up, Ben was surprised to see tears in his eyes.

"Miguel. My name is Miguel Hernandez. I didn't know her. Not really."

"Do you always visit people in the hospital who you don't know?" Ben asked.

"Look, man, it's like this. Me and my home boys were down cruising Oakcliff the other night and this *chica* comes out of nowhere. Ruiz, he starts hitting on her, but I saw her belly." He looked away, then back at Ben, almost defiant. "My sister, she's going to have a baby. I guess I felt sorry for the woman, okay?"

Oddly enough, Ben was starting to believe the man's story. "So you played Galahad, then what?" he asked.

Miguel frowned. "I don't know this Galahad, and I

haven't *played* since I was *cinco*…five. I told Ruiz to get lost and then told the little mama to go home.''

Ben thought of the woman in ICU. Poor China Brown. She would never be a little mama now.

''Then what?'' he asked.

Miguel shrugged. ''She said she had no home. I asked her where was the man who put the baby in her belly. She said he stole her money and ran away.''

Now Ben was beginning to believe him. This co-incided with the little bit they'd learned from China's ex-landlord.

''What was she doing down in that part of town?'' Ben asked.

''Looking for an all-night mission. She was cold. She was hungry. She was looking to God to protect her.'' Miguel stood abruptly. His voice was hard, his expression bitter. ''God. There is no God. Where was God when the little mama was in danger?''

Ben stood and followed Miguel to a window over-looking the parking lot.

''I don't have any answers for you,'' Ben said. ''But I want some answers from you. Why are you here?''

Miguel spun angrily. ''Because I should have walked with her. I thought about it. It wasn't far to the mission from where we stood. I showed her the cross on the building, then I walked away from her. If I'd gone with her, none of this would have happened and her baby would not be dead.''

Ben sighed. Guilt. The kid had come out of guilt. He ran a hand through his hair and then glanced at

Red. Red just shrugged, as if to say he was on his own. Ben turned back to Miguel.

"Yeah, I suppose that could be true," Ben said. "Or Red and I might be investigating three homicides instead of two if you'd gone."

Miguel shook his head. "Why?" he asked. "Why was she shot?"

"We don't know," Ben said. "Maybe something as simple as being in the wrong place at the wrong time."

Miguel slumped.

"Do you know a man by the name of Charles Finelli?" Red asked.

Miguel looked up. "No, I don't know nobody by that name. Was that the name of the man who was killed?"

Red nodded. "He also went by the name of Chaz."

"Means nothing to me," Miguel said, then gave both men a weary look. "Can I go now? I got places to go, man."

"Got an address?" Ben asked.

Miguel shrugged. "Sometimes I stay with my sister." He gave the men her name and address. "Now can I go?"

"Yeah, sure," Ben said, and handed him his card. "In case you hear anything on the streets."

Miguel frowned. "I don't do business with the 'man'," he muttered, then took it and stuffed it in his coat. "Only for the little mama, you know."

"Yeah, for the little mama," Ben said.

Miguel got all the way to the doorway then stopped and turned. The look he gave Ben was dark and fierce.

"You catch him, Detective. You catch the man who did this to her."

"We're doing our best," Ben said.

Miguel just shook his head and then made a hasty exit.

Red looked at Ben and shook his head. "Why do I have the feeling that our best isn't good enough for him?"

"Sometimes our best isn't even good enough for me," Ben said. "Now come on. There's a woman I want you to meet."

China was in limbo. Mercifully, her brain registered nothing of what was happening to her, and only now and then did a glimmer of cognizance surface. When it did, it came in the form of flesh-piercing pain and an inability to scream. Her body was healing, but if they'd asked her, she would have said, "Let me die."

Unaware of the countless hours of care she was receiving from the doctors and nurses, or of the persistence of one homicide detective from the Dallas P.D., she lay motionless beneath the covers, tied to machines.

In a way, China Brown was in a chrysalis. All her life, she'd been a victim. First at the hands of her stepfather, Clyde Shubert. Then, throughout her school years, as the kid who was too quiet to speak up for herself. After that, she'd been easy pickings for a man like Tommy Fairheart. He'd told her pretty lies for a place to live and food to eat. The fact that he'd left a part of himself behind hadn't mattered to a man like Tommy, because he had no concept of who he was— only what it took to survive. China had been fair game for the predator that he was.

Before, all the people who'd victimized her had been people she knew—men who were supposed to be taking care of her, men who were supposed to love her. Being the victim of an act of random violence became the next logical step. It remained to be seen what kind of woman would emerge.

The moment Ben stepped into the ICU ward, he forgot Red was behind him. He moved toward China with fixed intent, playing a game with himself that by the time he got to her bed, she would awaken. He needed to look into her eyes. She needed to know that he was there.

When he reached her bedside, he stopped, took a slow shaky breath, then leaned down until his mouth was near her ear.

"I came back, just like I promised," he said softly. "I brought a friend. His name is Red." He straightened up and gave Red a hard stare, as if daring him to argue. "Red, say hello to Miss Brown."

Red shifted nervously. This was weird, talking to someone who didn't even know he was there.

"Hello, Miss Brown. I'm real sorry you got hurt."

Ben nodded, as if satisfied with the way Red had

played his role; he touched China's arm, then her forehead. It was cooler than it had been before. A nurse came by on her way back to the desk.

"What's the status on China Brown?" he asked.

The nurse paused. By now, all the staff knew they were cops.

"She's stable, sir."

"Her condition…has it been upgraded?" Ben asked.

She shook her head. "Not yet. She's still listed as critical, but she is holding her own, and that's something to be thankful for." Then she added, "Is there anything else?"

"We're posting a guard outside ICU. No one gets in to see her unless they're okayed by me."

"Yes, sir," she said. "I'll make a note of that on her chart right now."

"Thanks," Ben said, and then glanced at Red. "Well?"

Red looked down at the woman, then back up at Ben. "She's sure small, isn't she?"

Ben laid his hand over her fingers. "Yeah, she's small."

"Looks pretty young, too," he added.

"According to her driver's license, she's twenty-six."

"No next of kin, you say?" Red asked.

"None that we know of."

An awkward silence enveloped the men as they

stood on either side of her bed. Finally, Red had to ask.

"Why, Ben? Why this fascination?"

Ben looked up. He started to unload a big set of excuses that had to do with it being part of the job, and then something stopped him. He glanced back at China—at her pale, colorless skin—and remembered the wounds on her body and the loss she had suffered. He started to speak, but the words wouldn't come. Then he cleared his throat and shook his head.

"I don't know," he said softly. "I honest to God don't know."

"Fair enough," Red said.

They stood in silence, each lost in his own set of thoughts. And then something happened.

China drew a deep breath and then moaned. Ben jumped and reached for her face, gently cupping her cheek with the palm of his hand as he spoke.

"Don't be afraid. I'm here."

As they watched, a single tear slipped out from beneath her eyelid and slid down the side of her face. The sight of it hit Ben like a blow to the gut. He leaned down again, his voice harsh and urgent, his own eyes blurring with empathy.

"You cry, girl. You cry all you want, and when you're through and all this pain is nothing but a memory, I will find a way to make you smile. Do you hear me, China Brown? That's a promise from me to you."

Red looked away. This was starting to get to him, as well.

He cleared his throat and muttered, "It's time to go. We've got a killer to catch."

Ben straightened, his expression cold and angry. "And the first place we're going is to Chaz Finelli's apartment. Maybe there's something there that will give us a place to start."

Bobby Lee strode into the dining room and smiled at the maid who was pouring coffee into his cup.

"Morning, Delia. Tell cook I'd like my eggs scrambled this morning, and bring me some biscuits and sausage gravy, too. I'm a hungry man."

"Yes, sir, Senator. Will your mother be joining you this morning?"

Before Bobby Lee could answer, Mona strolled into the room and answered for herself.

"I'm already here," she drawled. "I'll have fresh strawberries and toast, and bring me some of that herbal tea I like."

"Yes, ma'am," Delia said, and hurried out of the room before the fireworks started. And they would start, of that she was certain, because, although Mona Wakefield was wearing a long, silk robe, it was obvious as all get-out that she didn't have a stitch on under it.

Bobby Lee's eyes narrowed angrily as he watched his mother take her seat. As she leaned forward to adjust the hem of her robe, the top gaped open, revealing a goodly portion of voluptuous breast. Bobby rolled his eyes heavenward.

"For the Lord's sake, Mother, tie that robe a little better or put something on under it first. Have you no shame?"

Mona glanced down at herself and shrugged as she readjusted the robe.

"You are such a prude, Bobby Lee. If I didn't remember the pain of birthing you, I would swear you are not my son."

"If only that were so," he muttered beneath his breath and resumed reading the front page section of the *Dallas Morning News*.

"I heard that," Mona said. "And may I please have some of the paper?"

Bobby Lee took a couple of sections from the back and handed them to her.

"The classifieds?" she drawled.

He cursed beneath his breath and handed her another section.

Their banter was so commonplace that neither one of them took much of it to heart. Silence reigned in the dining room for all of five minutes until Delia returned with their food. A few more insults were traded between passing the butter and sugar. After that, they continued to eat while reading between bites. Mona was taking her last swallow of tea when her gaze fell on a small column of news.

"Well, now, just listen to this, Bobby Lee."

He dropped his paper in his lap and looked up with a sigh. "Mother, you know I don't like to be read to."

She wasn't paying him any mind, which didn't surprise him. When had she ever?

Mona cleared her throat and dabbed at her mouth with her napkin, then began to read aloud, hitting only the highlights of the story.

"'Shooting down in Oakcliff…two killed…no witnesses…police at a loss…'"

Bobby Lee interrupted. "The police are always at a loss," he muttered.

"That's not so," Mona said. "You're just mad because you got pulled over last month and ticketed for speeding."

Bobby Lee's eyes narrowed angrily. "The boy didn't know his place."

Mona grinned. "Why, I believe he did. Just because you're a senator, that doesn't make you God." Her grin widened. "That comes afterward…when you're elected president of these United States. Then you can be God."

A grudging smile centered on Bobby Lee's handsome face. "You are a witch," he said. "You know that, don't you?"

Mona arched an eyebrow. "I know nothing of the sort. Now, let me finish," she said, and ran her finger down the page until she found her place. "Oh yes, here's what I was trying to tell you. The man who was killed. It was Chaz Finelli." She made a face. "I never did like that man."

Bobby Lee's mouth dropped. The man's sleazeball reputation for taking scandalous photos of Dallas's rich and famous was well-known. The fact that his mother spoke personally of him made him nervous.

"You *know* Finelli?"

She glanced over her shoulder. "I'm all out of tea. Where's Delia gone off to, anyway?"

Bobby Lee grabbed his mother by the wrist. "Mother, I asked you a question."

"And I heard you," she snapped.

His grip tightened. "Then answer me," he growled. "Goddamn it, I just announced my candidacy for president. I don't need any surprises coming out of the woodwork. Exactly *how* do you know Chaz Finelli?"

"Why would it matter now? He's dead, isn't he?"

Bobby Lee stood, and in that moment Mona was almost afraid of her son. His voice was shaking with fury as he loomed over her chair.

"You talk to me...now!"

Mona shrugged. "It didn't amount to a hill of beans," she said. "I just got a little drunk at the mayor's birthday party last year."

Bobby Lee's mind was racing. He remembered the incident well. He'd pulled in a lot of favors to keep it out of the press.

"And..."

"Oh, hell, Bobby Lee. A woman has needs, too, you know. John Woodley and I were out in the greenhouse when a bunch of flashes went off. We thought they were part of the fireworks for the party until about a week later. John said he got some pictures in the mail."

She gave Bobby Lee a nervous glance. She'd never seen him so quiet—or so angry.

"What were you and John doing in those pictures?"

She grinned. "Well, we weren't counting daisies, Bobby Lee. What the hell do you think we were doing?"

"Jesus Christ," he muttered. "You will be the death of me yet."

"Oh, calm down. John paid him off and got the negatives, too."

"No blackmailer worth his salt *ever* gets rid of all the evidence. Somewhere, I can guarantee, there's a copy of those pictures, and they will show up just when it matters most."

Mona hated being wrong, and like her son, when faced with a problem, dealt with it in anger. She shoved her chair back with a thump and threw her napkin in his face.

"How? By ghost express? He's dead, Bobby Lee. Dead men tell no tales."

Bobby Lee paled. "I've got to call Ainsley." Resisting the urge to put his fist in her face, he pointed at her instead. "You don't leave this house today, do you hear me? If you're ever connected to his murder, then all of this is over…for both of us!"

Bobby Lee stormed out of the dining room. Mona strode to the window overlooking the snow-covered gardens. Icicles hung from the edges of the roof like long crystal spears. A pair of cardinals darted from bush to bush in search of food—as obvious to the human eye as blood on snow. Mona watched their futile search for food without any emotion. When they finally gave up and flew away, she abandoned the view. It was a hard world out there, and in her opinion, it didn't matter how beautiful the birds were. If they didn't have what it took to survive, then they didn't deserve to live.

A thin layer of dust covered the furnishings in Finelli's apartment, as well as three empty pizza boxes stacked on the table with a mummified piece of pepperoni pizza lying on top. There was a small plastic bowl on the kitchen floor with a handful of dried cat food, and another bowl beside it, obviously a water dish that had long ago evaporated. One could only hope that the cat it had been meant for was long gone from the premises. Either that or the stench that they were smelling was the cat. Ben and Red were hesitant to find out.

"Shoot a mile," Red muttered. "Something sure stinks. I hope it's not that cat. Where do you want to start?"

Ben pulled a pair of rubber gloves from his coat pocket and put them on.

"I'll go in the bedroom and work my way forward. You start in the kitchen, okay?"

"What are we looking for?" Red asked.

"Anything that might get a man killed."

"Okay," Red said, and then hesitated. "You got another pair of gloves? I left mine in the car."

"Yeah, I think so," Ben said, and dug through the inside pocket of his coat. "Here you go. Knock yourself out."

With that, both men went their separate ways, looking for answers to a crime that, so far, made no sense.

Time passed as the men moved from room to room. Red refused to set foot in the bathroom, so it was Ben who got left with the job. As he walked through the doorway, the stench they'd been smelling hit him full force. After a quick search of the cabinets and drawers, he decided that it was the sink that was harboring the smell.

It was streaked with grime and hair, and something that looked suspiciously like chemicals. He supposed they were the kind used in developing, but to be on the safe side, he scraped a sample off the sink. Maybe it was residue from a drug lab. If it was, manufacturing amphetamines would go a long way toward explaining why someone had wanted Finelli dead.

There was an assortment of bottles, mostly chemicals, in the cabinet beside the sink, and Ben was beginning to believe this had been Finelli's darkroom. He moved them around, reading each one label by label, but could find nothing that looked out of place. Yet when he set one of them down, the sound seemed hollow. He shoved several bottles aside and tapped on the bottom of the shelf once more. Again the thumps seemed to echo.

"Hey, Red!" he yelled. "Got a minute?"

Red appeared at the door.

"Yeah, what's up?"

"You got your flashlight on you?"

Red pulled a small flashlight out of his pocket. "Like the Boy Scouts, I'm always prepared."

Grinning, Ben took it from his partner and flipped the switch. He leaned closer to the cabinet, aiming the beam of light at the cabinet floor. Almost immediately, he could tell that it had been altered from its original design. Quickly he took all the bottles out of the cabinet and set them in the sink, then took out his pocket knife and stuck the point at one end of a crack.

"Whatcha got there?" Red asked.

"Don't know," Ben said. "Maybe nothing." But he continued to dig. Within seconds, something popped, and all of a sudden the floor of the cabinet was in his hands.

"Would you look at that?" Red said, and leaned closer, peering over Ben's shoulder. "Is something in it?"

Ben aimed the flashlight into the opening. "Son of a..."

"What?" Red asked. "What's in there?"

Ben began pulling out photos, along with a couple of manila envelopes, and he'd only skimmed the surface of the stash.

Red's eyes widened. "Oh, man. Would you look at these? Hey, isn't that Sonny Harold of the Dallas LoneStars with the needle in his hand? I thought he was on probation."

"He is," Ben said.

Red held up another. "And this one…the naked woman riding that mechanical bull. She looks familiar, but I just can't…"

"The mayor's wife," Ben muttered. "And I must say, I've seen her looking better."

"Jesus!" Red said. "Where do you suppose he got these?"

"With that famous little camera he was never without. You know…the one that's missing. Without doubt, I'd say we've got, at the least, a good hundred or so reasons for murdering Finelli. The question remains, which one of these creeps did the deed?"

Five

Aaron Floyd slapped his desk with the flat of his hand and tossed the list he'd been handed back to Ben and Red.

"Jesus Christ! Do you two have any idea what a mess this is going to make?"

Anger was thick in Ben's voice as he answered his captain.

"Yes, and ask me if I care. Those people in the photographs caused their own set of problems. Finelli exacerbated them and it got him killed. We're just trying to find some justice for the stupid bastard, not that I'm sure he deserves it, but China Brown damn sure does."

Aaron Floyd wiped a hand across his face, then ran it through his hair, giving himself time to calm down. He took a deep breath, and when he spoke again, his demeanor was apologetic.

"I didn't mean that the way it came out," he muttered. "Hell, yes, I want the shooter caught, and if he's on this list, then we'll find out." He glanced back at the list and then shook his head. "The mayor's wife? Larry Dee Jackson? Ariel Simmons?" He rolled his eyes as he repeated her name. ''Ariel Simmons is one of those TV preachers, for Pete's sake. For now, keep your questioning discreet until we find out who's got an alibi and who doesn't. If this gets out, we'll have the Dallas city government, the Country Music Association and even God on our ass if this gets mishandled. I don't want to set the police department up for a lawsuit, do you hear me?''

''Fine. We'll make sure we don't step on too many toes or ruffle any more feathers than we have to,'' Ben snapped. ''But I think it needs to be remembered that we've got a victim who's hanging on to her life by a thread, a woman who has yet to hear the words, *your baby is dead.* When she wakes up—and she *will* wake up—do you want to be the one to tell her that we still don't know who killed her child because we were afraid to make somebody mad?''

Before Aaron Floyd could answer, Ben picked up the list of suspects and strode out of the office. Red shrugged apologetically.

''This one just got to him, Captain. He'll be all right.''

''See that he is, or I'll put someone else on the case.''

''That won't be necessary,'' Red said, and left quickly before he unloaded what was on his mind, too. He was as ticked off as Ben. The way he looked at it, if the stupid fools hadn't gotten themselves into these messes, then there wouldn't be any incriminating pictures to worry about. His mama always said if you lay down with dogs, you were bound to get fleas, and after looking at the pictures they'd pulled out of Finelli's stash, it would take more than flea baths to solve their itches.

"Ben, wait up," Red said, as he grabbed his coat and followed his partner out the door.

Ben spun, his face tight with anger. "Politics suck. If you know the right people, or have enough money, you can buy your way out of just about anything."

"The captain said if you don't pull it together, he's going to put someone else on the case."

"He'll play hell trying," Ben said. "You driving, or am I?"

"Me."

Ben tossed him the car keys and strode out the door. Red shook his head and followed.

Twenty-four hours later, they'd eliminated fifteen of the forty-five names on the list. Some of the people had been out of town when the incident occurred, others had unshakeable alibis. But they had all been appalled to learn that there were still existing pictures of their indiscretions.

At the moment, the man they were interrogating was less than happy to see the picture of himself and the teenage hitchhiker he'd picked up, having sex in the back seat of his car, as naked as they day they were born.

"Sombitch!" Jody Franklin had roared. "I paid that

little weasel good money to get these back. He assured me I had them all, including the negatives.''

"Obviously, he lied," Red said. "When was the last time you saw Mr. Finelli?''

Jody grabbed a cigar from a box on his desk, bit the end of it off with his teeth and spat, sending the bit of tobacco flying.

Ben watched without speaking. Jody was so furious, he half expected the man's cigar to light on its own. That kind of anger could easily escalate into something more—something deadly.

"Mr. Franklin?''

Jody Franklin glared at Red. "I heard you the first time," he snapped. "I'm thinkin'.'' He lit his cigar, taking several long puffs until the end of the cigar was glowing; then he circled his desk and sat down with a grunt and buzzed his secretary to come in. "Eileen, bring me last year's calendar.''

A few moments later, a short, well-dressed woman entered the room, eyeing the detectives with curiosity.

"Any particular date you want me to look up for you, sir?''

"Yeah. When did I go to the Fort Worth livestock show? It was sometime last spring, but I don't remember the exact date.''

Eileen ruffled through the months, running her finger down the dates on individual pages until she found what she was looking for.

"Here it is. May 12 through 15. You stayed at the Hilton.''

"Thank you, Eileen. That will be all."

The secretary exited. As soon as the door had closed behind her, Franklin strode to the window, a wreath of smoke following him as he walked.

"It was May 15, my last night in Fort Worth. The little bastard showed up at my hotel, handed me a copy of that picture you have there and said if I didn't give him ten thousand dollars, he was going to mail copies to my wife, my daughters and my mother." He spun, his face dark with anger. "My mother, for God's sake! She's eighty-four years old. The shock alone would have killed her."

"Did you pay?"

Franklin shrugged. "Hell, yes, of course I did. Money wasn't the issue. I would have given him double without thinking twice. I got the negatives and all the prints." His eyes narrowed as he glanced back at the picture lying on his desk. "At least I thought I did."

"And you haven't seen him since?" Ben asked.

Franklin took a long puff of his cigar, then blew a couple of smoke rings before answering.

"We don't run in the same social circles, Detective."

"Where were you last Friday?"

Franklin took another long, thoughtful puff. "Oh, yeah," he muttered. "Squiring my wife and youngest daughter to see *The Nutcracker* ballet." He grimaced. "Damn boring, dancing around on your toes and all, but you know how it is…sometimes you do what you have to do.''

"We'll have to verify that,'' Ben said.

For the first time since they had walked into his office, Jody Franklin looked scared.

"Check with the box office, they can verify we were there. Call Mayor Devlin. We sat next to him and his wife. Just don't call Mary Sue. I don't want to hurt her.''

"Should have thought of that before you screwed a kid young enough to be your daughter,'' Ben snapped.

"Hell,'' Franklin muttered. "Give me a break, Detective. I'm not gonna lie and say I didn't wish the little bastard dead a hundred times, but I swear to God I didn't have anything to do with his death.''

"We'll be in touch,'' Ben said. "Oh…and don't leave town.''

Franklin was pale and sweating as they left his office.

Red grinned as they reached the elevator. "It just goes to prove that being rich doesn't necessarily mean you've got brains to go with it.'' Then he glanced at Ben. "What do you think? Was he telling the truth?''

Ben shrugged. "Probably. It will be easy enough to find out. As for the brains part, it's for damn sure Jody Franklin could have used some more and a measure of good sense to go with them.''

"Now what?'' Red asked.

Ben glanced at the list. "We've got time for a couple more before—'' His cell phone rang. "Just a minute," he said.

"Ben English."

"Detective English, this is Dr. Pope. You asked to be notified if there was any change in China Brown's condition?"

Ben's heart skipped a beat. "Yes?"

"As you know, we've been decreasing the sedatives for some time now. And, as you also know, her wounds are healing nicely."

Ben interrupted. "You didn't call to tell me this," he said. "What's wrong?"

"She's failing," Dr. Pope said. "Her vital signs aren't good."

Shock spiraled, sending Ben into a panic. After all of this, surely God wouldn't let her die.

"This doesn't make sense. If everything else is as you said, then why is this happening?" Ben asked.

"I suppose there could be all sorts of explanations," Dr. Pope said. "But my personal opinion is, I don't think she wants to live."

Ben groaned. "I'm on my way."

"What's wrong?" Red asked.

Ben bolted inside the elevator before the door was completely open and quickly punched the Close Door button, then the one for the lobby. Red made it, barely, snatching his coattail before it got caught.

"Come on, partner, talk to me."

It was all Ben could do to say the words aloud. "They're losing China Brown."

"That's too bad," Red said. "We lose her, we lose our only witness."

Ben snapped. "She's more than just a witness, damn it."

Red grabbed Ben's arm. "That's just the problem, buddy. She's not. Whatever you think you're feeling is all in your mind. She doesn't know you exist."

"Shut up. Just shut up and get me to the hospital, and then you're on your own for the rest of the day. I'm not leaving her until I know she's going to be all right."

The elevator stopped. The doors opened. Ben strode out into the lobby of the office building and began moving toward the entrance at a jog.

Red caught up with him at the curb. "Wait! Ben, wait!"

Ben turned. "What?"

"What if she doesn't pull out of this?"

Ben took a deep breath, then another, trying to answer without making a fool of himself, then realized he'd already done that a hundred times over since this whole thing had begun. His shoulders slumped, and for a moment he looked away. Then he lifted his head and gave Red a cool look.

"Are you driving, or am I?"

"I will," Red muttered. "I want to get there in one piece."

China was drifting. There was a place between cognizance and oblivion that let her hide without effort.

All she had to do was focus on the dark and everything else would fade—even the muscle-racking pain that dug into her sleep. It was a place of safety—a place where reality did not exist. When she thought about it, which was rare, she knew she was in a hospital. Now and then there were even flashes of ugly memories that reminded her of why she was there. Those were the times when she felt herself slipping, and slipping was something she longed for, more and more. Remembering was a pain worse than anything physical.

And she would have gone long ago except for that voice that kept pulling at her to stay. In a way, she was reluctant to turn loose of the connection. The tenderness in his voice and the gentleness of his touch were things she'd once longed for. But it was too late—too late to care, too late for everything of this earth. Nothing mattered but finding peace, and when China Brown had faced the barrel of that gun and felt the bullet that ripped her child from her body, she'd accepted the fact that her peace would not be on earth. Now all she wanted to do was go home.

Ben was out of the car and running before Red had come to a complete stop. All the way into the hospital, he'd been unable to think past his panic. His breath came in short anxious gasps as he entered the elevator, and when it stopped, he found himself running down the hall to the ICU.

At the sound of his footsteps, the nurse on duty looked up.

"Dr. Pope called me," Ben gasped.

"Yes, sir, he's inside waiting for you."

Ben dropped his coat and gloves on a nearby chair and kept walking, knowing that if he stopped, he wouldn't be able to move.

Dr. Pope was standing at the foot of China's bed. He looked up when the doors opened and motioned for Ben to come.

God, don't let this be happening. He nodded to Dr. Pope. "Thank you for calling me."

"It seemed important to you. I was glad to do it." Pope looked at China and then down at her chart before moving to her bedside.

"Talk to me," Ben said. "Why is this happening?"

The doctor took Ben by the arm and pulled him aside so that their voices could not be heard by any of the patients.

"The human mind is a powerful and mysterious thing. We know very little about the intricacies of how it works, but basically, I would say she's just not fighting it any longer."

Ben's belly rolled. "She wants to die?"

Pope glanced at China and then shrugged. "It amounts to the same thing."

Ben looked at her then, absorbing the delicate perfection of her face. He moved to the bed, touching her arm, then her wrist, barely able to feel the thin, thready pulse. His voice was shaking, his gaze begging Ross Pope to change his prognosis.

"Don't let this happen."

"It's out of my hands," Pope said.

"And there's nothing you can give her?"

"Medically, I've done all I can. The rest is up to the lady." Then he patted China's leg and gave Ben a sad smile. "I've got to finish rounds. If I'm needed, they'll page me."

Ben suddenly realized that the allotted five-minute ICU visit was not going to be enough. How could he reach China if she couldn't hear his voice?

"I'm not leaving," he said.

Ross Pope nodded. "I didn't think you would. I've already given orders that you be allowed to stay for as long as you want. But you have to be very quiet. There are other patients whose care depends on it."

"Yes, I promise."

"Well…goodbye then," Dr. Pope said, but Bennett English's focus had already shifted to the woman in the bed.

"It's me," Ben said softly, and stroked her cheek from temple to chin with the tip of his finger. "I told you I'd be back."

The only answer he got was a slow but steady beeping from the monitor hooked up to her heart.

"I saw a robin today in a tree outside my apartment. Soon winter will be a thing of the past. I can help you, honey, but you have to wake up."

Beep. Beep. Beep.

Ben bowed his head and closed his eyes. *God give me the right words to say before it's too late.* He took her hand and then inhaled slowly.

"China. China Brown. Can you hear me? If you can, then squeeze my hand."

Beep. Beep. Beep.

"I know it's difficult. You've been very, very sick, but you're getting better now. I know you can hear my voice." He gave her fingers a gentle squeeze. "That was me, squeezing your hand. All you have to do is move a finger, just one finger, and I'll know you're listening."

Beep… Beep…

There was a long pause before the beeps resumed, and the fear that shot through Ben's body left him weak and shaky. He was losing her, and he didn't know what to do. His voice was trembling when he began to speak.

"There are doctors and nurses who have worked very, very hard to make you well. There are policemen who are working day and night, trying to find the man who hurt you. You think you're all alone, but you're not. You're not alone, China. You have me. I'm here. All you have to do is squeeze my hand."

He clasped her fingers, willing his warmth into her hand.

Beep. Beep. Beep. Beep…

Again the monitor skipped the count of two heart-beats before resuming a steady rhythm. Ben could feel her life slipping away before his eyes, and the thought of never seeing her smile made him crazy. He leaned down until his mouth was only inches from her ear, his voice harsh and ragged with fear.

"Damn you, don't you quit on me, woman! Do you hear me? I haven't quit on you. You at least owe me the courtesy of doing the same."

Beep-beep. Beep-beep. Beep-beep.

He didn't know whether the irregularity was a good sign or a bad one, but either way, he'd committed himself.

"That's all right," he said. "Get mad. I'd like nothing better than for you to open those eyes of yours and tell me to take a hike. If that's what it takes, then get mad. Do anything but quit."

Beep-beep. Beep. Beep. Beep.

Ben breathed a little easier. Needing to touch her, wanting her to feel him, he began stroking her hair with his other hand as he searched for a way to reach her. As he stood, racking his brain for something wise to say, he saw tears welling at the corners of her eyes. The breath slid out of his body as quickly as if he'd been punched. All at once he understood.

"Oh, honey." He gave her fingers another gentle squeeze. "You know, don't you? You know your baby is dead."

The monitor beeped erratically a couple of times. Ben was so focused on the sounds that he missed the movement of her fingers against the palm of his hand.

"I'm sorry," he whispered, and without thinking, leaned down again, this time kissing the side of her cheek. "I'm so, so sorry."

Beep… Beep.. Beep.

The length of time between the sounds seemed to

Ben like slow sobs. It wasn't until he straightened that he felt a tremble in her hand. His gaze slid to the delicate length of her fingers against his palm.

"China? Can you hear me? If you can, move your fingers for me."

At first he saw nothing, and then ever so slowly, one finger rose, followed by the one beside it.

"Thank you, God," he muttered, as she rubbed the tips of two fingers against his skin.

"That's it!" he cried. "I knew you could do it! I knew you weren't a quitter."

Instantly the motion stopped, and the message was as clear as her silence had been before.

"You aren't!" he argued. "No one who's fought this long to stay alive would be a quitter. Move again for me, China. Prove it to me."

Beep-beep. Beep-beep. Beep-beep.

"Damn it, no!" he growled. "You don't do this! You don't do this to me! If you quit now, you're letting a man get away with murder. Is that what you want? Is it, China?"

Beep-beep-beep. Beep-beep-beep.

"I don't believe it! I don't believe you. You loved that baby you were carrying. Now help me find the man who killed her."

China drew a slow breath and Ben held his as he waited for her to exhale. If she didn't, he wasn't certain but that he would die right here and now, with her.

Then she exhaled, and it sounded to Ben like a sigh.

As she did, her fingers curled ever so slightly around the palm of his hand, as if grasping to hold on to life. Quick tears blurred his view of her face.

"That's what I wanted to hear," he said softly. "You just hold on, honey, until you feel strong enough on your own to let go. After that, I'm making you a promise that, together, we'll bring your baby's killer to justice."

Beep. Beep. Beep. Beep. And so the monitor danced, slow and steady, all through the night.

Sometime later, a nurse brought him a chair and scooted it beside China's bed. Gingerly, he sat without breaking his hold on her hand. Hours passed and his eyes became heavy. He laid his head down on his arm—just to rest, just for a minute.

He woke at daybreak and for a moment lay without moving, listening to the sounds of the changing shift and the footsteps coming and going as a new set of nurses checked patients' vitals, dispensing gentleness and kind words with the medicine. It took a moment for him to realize that China Brown was no longer holding his hand. Instead, sometime during the night, she'd thrust her fingers into his hair.

Even after he lifted his head to check the monitor by her bed, he imagined he could still feel the imprint of her fingers against his scalp. The strong, steady beep of the heart monitor was a welcome sound. He stood and stretched, raising his arms stiffly above his head and then arching his back before laying a hand against her cheek.

"Good morning, sweetheart. Just for the record, I got your message. You're going to be okay, and so am I. I'll be back, and when I come, I promise to shave. I don't want to look like a wild man the first time you see my face."

Then he leaned over and kissed her again, feeling the warmth of her cheek against his lips. Just as he started to raise his head, he hesitated. With no more than an inch of space separating their faces, Ben moved a bit to the right and kissed her again. This time, right on her mouth.

When he left the ICU, he was smiling.

Bobby Lee tossed the morning paper down onto the dining room table, took a slow, satisfying sip of his favorite coffee, then leaned back in his chair, surveying all that was his.

The opulence of his home was evident, but tasteful, a perfect backdrop for a man who would be king. The festive red and green of Christmas hung from every corner, evidence of the expensive decorator Mona had hired. Bobby Lee had the poor-boy-makes-good syndrome going for him, as well as being a certifiable war hero. His eyes narrowed as he thought back to his years in Vietnam. At the time, he wouldn't have given a plug nickel for his chances of coming home alive, never mind in one piece. If anyone had asked him about the notion of using those years as a springboard into politics, he would have laughed in their face and called them crazy.

He chuckled beneath his breath and then shook his head as he took another sip of coffee. Life could be a bitch, but it could also be beautiful, and right now, his world was full of beauty and light.

"Bobby Lee! Where are you?"

The bubble of perfection popped as the screech of his mother's elevated voice echoed throughout the halls. Goddamn it! Wouldn't that woman ever learn? Ladies did not shout. He bolted from his chair and stalked to the doorway. Mona was standing in the hall, pulling on a pair of elbow-length gloves and preparing to let loose with another shout when he spoke.

"Must you shout?" he snapped.

"If I wanna be heard," she drawled, and sauntered toward him on three-inch heels.

His eyes narrowed with disdain as he absorbed the outfit she was wearing. It was velvet, red and short, with a faux fox collar framing her neck and face. Her gloves were longer than her skirt, and her buxom torso was zippered into the jacket so tightly that one sneeze could prove a disaster.

"Where are you going?"

"Out."

"Not good enough," he said.

She rolled her eyes. "Shopping?"

"Is that a statement or a question?"

She tapped a finger against his chest, angrily punctuating her words with each impact.

"I am your mother, not your child. You do not tell me what to do or where to go, is that understood?"

He grabbed her finger in the midst of a tap and then, ever so slowly, began bending it back toward her hand.

"You are a walking time bomb. I will do what it takes to keep your ass out of trouble, even if that means locking you in your room. Is that understood?"

Pain shafted up her arm as she screamed and yanked away.

"You're hurting me!" she cried. "How dare you?"

Bobby Lee moved closer—so close that he could smell the peppermint flavor of her mouthwash.

"I'll do more than hurt you if you fuck up again, Mother dear."

Mona blanched. "What the hell do you mean?"

Bobby Lee smiled, and in that moment he had no way of knowing how like his mother he looked.

"You think you're so smart. You figure it out."

Mona pivoted angrily. Unwilling for him to see how his words had rattled her, she stalked toward the door, her legs pumping beneath the tight red velvet like well-oiled pistons. When she got to the door, she turned and shouted, "You son of a bitch!"

He grinned. "You should know."

The door slammed behind her with a solid thud, rattling a picture on a nearby wall. Bobby Lee stood for a moment, thoughtfully staring after her exit, then shrugged and went back to his coffee. He had a meeting to attend and no more time to dwell on the over-sexed woman who'd given him life.

Six

Ben English was in good spirits as he and his partner pulled up to the gates of Ariel Simmons's estate on the south edge of Dallas. Red pointed to the massive iron angels on either side of the entrance.

"Unless she's got one hell of an explanation for the picture of her that we found in Finelli's apartment, she's going to be needing more than two of those fellows," he said.

Ben shrugged as he pressed the button on the call box.

"Maybe it was just a poor choice of Halloween costumes."

Red grinned. "Black leather, a whip and iron spikes, maybe…but I don't think that man in manacles was part of the costume."

Ben nodded. "Yeah, and if Finelli hadn't written her name on the back of the photo, chances are we would never have been able to identify her. Looks a damn sight different than the slender blond angel who appears on television four nights a week."

The iron gates swung open.

"So let's go talk to the angel and see what she has to say for herself," Red said.

Ben put the car in gear and drove through. Yet when they were ushered into Ariel Simmons's living room by a uniformed maid, their perception of her changed again. The room was all crystal and steel, with sharp angles in the furniture and freeform sculptures that made no sense.

"Man," Red muttered. "What do you make of this?"

Ben stood with his hands in his pockets as his gaze jumped from one corner of the room to the other, and while he would have been the first person to agree that taste was subjective, the first word that came to mind was, *wasteland*.

"It looks like the set of a bad sci-fi movie," Ben said.

"Gentlemen, how may I help you?"

The woman's voice was startling in its clarity and power. They turned toward the sound, facing the tall, angular woman silhouetted in the doorway. Her white-blond hair was shorter than Red's. Pale-blue leggings accentuated her shapely legs, while the embroidery at the hem of her poet's shirt brushed the tops of her knees. Blue ballerina shoes covered her feet, and a bulky gold chain served as a belt, molding the shirt to a very small waist.

Ben flashed his badge. "Detective Bennett English, Homicide. This is my partner, Detective Fisher." Red offered his badge as identification, too.

As Ariel walked toward them, Ben tried to super-impose the woman in Chaz Finelli's picture onto her face and couldn't quite make the connection. Had they made a mistake?

"So, Detectives, to what do I owe the pleasure?"

"Maybe you'd like to sit," Ben said. "This may take a while."

Ariel smiled and glided past them, moving like a dancer across a stage. When she sat, Ben was aware that, once again, she seemed to be playing a part.

"All right, I'm sitting," she said. "Now, how can I help you?"

Ben sat on the sofa directly across from her chair and then laid the picture on the table between them.

"Explain this."

If he hadn't been watching her so closely, he might have missed the look of shock that came and went in her eyes, because when she looked up, her expression was suitably disgusted.

"A woman in need of God," Ariel said, and touched the picture with the flat of her hand. "Tell me her name, Detective English, and I will pray for her."

Red shifted nervously beside Ben and gave him a questioning glance, but Ben knew her poise had been shaken.

"According to Charles Finelli's files, her name is Ariel Simmons."

Ariel gasped and clasped both hand to the sides of her face. "Have mercy!" she cried. "Surely you gentlemen could not believe that lascivious woman is me? You know my truth. You know God is love.''

"Actually, Miss Simmons, we don't know your truth, which is why we're here. Now can you tell us where you were around 10:00 p.m. on December 11?"

"I was on television. Check your listings," Ariel said, then stood abruptly and sailed past them to a phone on a nearby table. Angrily, she punched in a series of numbers. As she waited for someone to answer, she turned toward the men, giving them a fairly good rendition of a woman wronged.

"Look, Ben," Red muttered, "the captain will have our hides if we tick off the religious right on this case. Maybe it isn't her. After all, that woman in the picture has dark hair."

But Ben didn't answer. He was too busy watching Ariel Simmons's face.

"Langley, I need you," Ariel said. "It's an emergency. Something terrible is happening—just terrible. I'm about to be slandered, and I want protection. Yes, just get over here as soon as you can."

She hung up with a flourish and then pointed toward the door, something Scarlett O'Hara might have done in banishing Rhett Butler from her life. It was all a little too exaggerated for Ben to believe.

"Gentlemen, I believe you can find your way out."

Ben shook his head. "Not until you answer a couple more questions."

"I don't have to answer anything. I know my rights, and I will not be blackmailed by some—"

Ben moved, pinning Ariel between his glare and the front of her desk. He kept thinking of the woman who'd come so close to death last night, and of the baby she'd lost. Even Charles Finelli, as low as he was, hadn't deserved to be gunned down in the street like a gutter rat.

"This isn't blackmail, lady, it's murder," Ben said. "Now you can talk to us here, or you can come down to the station. Either way, you *will* talk to us until we're satisfied with your answers or we decide you're lying. In which case you *will* be needing that lawyer you called when we read you your rights."

Ariel paled. Her eyes darted from one man to the other. Ben imagined he could see the wheels turning as she decided how to play her next scene. Suddenly she became teary-eyed and bowed her head as if humiliated and shamed, then staggered back to her chair before sinking into its depths.

"I'm sorry, so sorry, but you must understand. This was such a shock. Of course that sinful woman is not me. I preach God's message, not Satan's. I'll help you if I can."

"You're quite different in person from the woman on TV," Ben said. "Your hair is short, and your clothes are nothing like the gowns that you wear on your show."

Ariel gave him a tremulous smile. "Praise God, dear sir. If you've seen my broadcasts, then you have heard the Word. Of course, my image is all important. But I make so many public appearances that it becomes difficult to maintain a perfect coiffure, so I wear wigs. I have several, you know. As for the gowns, well..." She shrugged.

"All part of the image, right?" Ben said.

She nodded and sighed, then leaned over and pulled a tissue from a box before using it to blot her tears.

"Did you know Charles Finelli?" Red asked.

Ariel was a little startled when the question came at her from another source, and again Ben saw her composure slip, but it was so fleeting it almost escaped him.

"I'm sorry...what was that name?"

"Finelli. Charles Finelli."

"No, I can't say that I do," Ariel said. "But I meet so many people in my ministry. If you had a picture..."

Ben pulled one out of his pocket and dropped it in her lap.

"Dear Lord!" Ariel gasped, and covered her eyes.

It was the one of Finelli lying in the street after he'd been shot.

"The poor man. And you say he was murdered?"

"He was also a blackmailer," Ben added. "According to the files he kept, a very successful one. How much did you pay him for the pictures he took of you?"

Ariel's eyes narrowed as, once again, her saintly countenance began to fade.

"Again I tell you that woman is not me, nor did I pay any money to Chaz Finelli."

Ben went still. He could feel Red looking at him, but he wouldn't take his eyes off Ariel's face. He leaned down, bracing himself with a hand on either arm of her chair. Her breath was warm against his face as he spoke.

"A few more questions, and then we'll be gone," he said.

She looked up, meeting his gaze head-on.

"I thought you didn't know the murder victim," he said.

"That's right, I don't."

"But you called him Chaz. Only the people who knew him best called him by that name, and since I didn't tell you that little bit of information, I'm inclined to believe you've been lying."

All the blood drained from Ariel Simmons's face. Her eyes widened in fear as her lips went slack.

"And there's something else you should know," Ben said softly.

"Wh-wh-what?"

"I don't like being lied to. Did you have Charles Finelli killed?"

"No, and I don't care what you like," she blustered. "Now get away from me before I call the police."

Ben smiled, and it was not a pretty smile as he waved the picture of Finelli beneath her nose. "We *are* the police, and if I find out you're responsible for this, all the prayers in heaven will not save your lying ass. Do we understand each other?"

"Get out," she muttered.

Ben straightened. "Don't leave town," he said. "Don't bother to get up. We'll see ourselves out."

Once they were outside, Red took a deep breath and then scratched his head as he looked at Ben's angry face.

"I think that went well," he said.

"Just get in the car," Ben muttered.

For the first time in days, China was physically aware of her surroundings. She felt pain. She felt cold. She felt the nurses' hands as they ministered to her needs. Sometimes she even understood what they were saying, but the flashes of cognizance didn't last. Her awareness would fade with the onset of a fresh wave of pain, or from the contents of a hypodermic syringe being administered intravenously. Each time she started going under, there was a part of her that resisted. She kept remembering that voice promising to help find her baby's killer, and all she had to do was wake up. If she didn't, the man behind the voice might forget, and if he did, it would be the end of any hope of justice. She knew they would never find the person responsible for the shootings, because they were looking for a man.

She struggled with the thought, but the sedative was too strong and her pain was too sharp, so she let herself slide into oblivion—one more time.

"Where in hell did you get that?"

Ben put the picture he'd just shown country singer

Larry Dee Jackson back in his coat pocket.

"Why? Did you think you'd bought them all?"

Larry Dee wiped a shaky hand across his face and then dropped to the side of his bed.

"I paid the son of a bitch more for it than I did for the Renoir hanging in my house back in Nashville."

"Then I take it the blonde in the picture isn't your wife?"

Larry groaned beneath his breath. "No." He grabbed Ben's arm. "You've got to keep this under wraps. If my wife finds out, it'll be the end of my marriage." Then he covered his face with his hands. "I can't lose my wife and kids. I love them."

"Should have thought of that before you got naked with another woman," Ben said.

"Oh, man," Larry muttered, and stood abruptly. "I need a drink."

"Not until you answer some questions," Ben said. "Where were you around 10:00 p.m. on December 11?"

"What day was that?" Larry asked.

"Last Friday."

"I was in the hotel having an early night. My flight came in around 3:30 p.m. and I was tired."

"Can anyone vouch for that?"

Larry Dee began to sweat. "Hell, I don't know. I had room service about six. Made a couple of calls, then watched a movie on pay-per-view."

"Any late-night visitors, like maybe the lady in the picture?"

Larry Dee looked away and then shrugged. "I'm not saying."

"You do know that Texas has the death penalty?" Ben asked.

Larry Dee turned pale and then shuddered.

"I swear to God I didn't have anything to do with that man's murder."

"I need more than your word," Ben said. "So, how about it? Did you have any visitors?"

Larry shook his head. "Sorry, I don't kiss and tell."

"Look, Jackson, the time to play gentleman would have been when you had the option of keeping your pants zipped and going home to your wife. You made a choice. Now you face the consequences. Either you tell me now, or we'll take this discussion down to the station."

"Christ almighty, Connie's gonna kill me."

Ben's interest peaked. "Is this Connie capable of murder?"

Larry looked like someone had just goosed him in the butt.

"Oh! No! Hell, no! That was just a figure of speech."

"Poor choice of words," Ben said.

Larry Dee poured himself a generous belt of whiskey, downed it neat, and then turned to the two detectives.

"It's Connie Marx."

Red stopped writing in the middle of a word and looked up.

"*The* Connie Marx, WFAL anchorwoman on the evening news?"

He nodded.

Red whistled beneath his breath and made a couple more notes as Ben shifted his line of questioning.

"Did Miss Marx know that Charles Finelli blackmailed you?"

"Yeah. He got the both of us, actually. Took me for double what she had to pay, though. Said I had more to lose than she did."

"Was he right?" Ben asked.

Larry sighed. "Oh, yeah." Then he added, "What are you going to do?"

"Find a killer, Mr. Jackson."

"Can you keep this under wraps—I mean about the picture?"

"We aren't advertising the names on this list. But if it were me, I think I'd play it safe and confess my sins to my wife and hope for the best. I'd say you have a better chance of coming out on the good side if you do that than if she reads about this mess in the papers."

"Oh, man," Larry muttered, and poured himself another drink as the detectives left.

Once Ben and Red exited the hotel room where Jackson was staying, Ben slipped his notebook into his pocket and pulled out the picture of Larry and the blonde.

"Let's see if we can catch her at the television station and then call it a day, what do you say?" he asked.

Red nodded. "I'm all for that. I could go for a steak and a hot shower. Rita was making apple cobbler when I called her at noon. Want to come over? We can always throw another steak on the grill."

Ben shook his head. "No, but thanks for asking. I'm going to swing by the hospital before I head for home. I didn't get much sleep last night."

"You're moving into dangerous territory with her, you know that," Red said.

Ben started to argue, then nodded instead. "Yes, I know, but it's too late to pull back now. I made promises to her."

Red frowned. "What are you going to do if you can't keep those promises?"

"One thing at a time, buddy. One thing at a time. She's alive, and for now, that's enough."

"Miss Marx, there are two detectives asking for you."

Connie Marx looked up from the script of the night's broadcast and frowned. She didn't know the short, redheaded man, but she recognized the tall one on sight. English. Ben English. He'd been the primary detective on the Whitman kidnapping last year. She stood, then went to meet them.

"Detective English, it's been a while," she said, offering him her hand.

"Miss Marx. This is Detective Fisher, my partner. We need to ask you some questions."

She smiled wryly. "That sounds serious. And here I thought you'd come by to invite me to the policemen's ball."

The fact that Ben didn't return her smile was warning enough that she wasn't going to like what they'd come to say.

"So, what's up?"

Ben took the picture of her and Jackson out of his pocket.

Her expression froze as she stared in disbelief. When she looked up, her eyes were filled with fury.

"I didn't think you were the voyeuristic type," she snapped. "Where did you get that?"

"From Charles Finelli's apartment," Ben said.

"That sorry, lying little bastard," she muttered. "Someone should have shot him sooner and saved us all a lot of trouble."

"So you know he's dead," Ben said.

She rolled her eyes and then waved her script beneath his nose.

"Yes, I know he's dead," she said. "It's what I do for a living."

"Where were you on December 11 at 10:00 p.m.?"

"Home. Nursing a case of the flu."

"That's not what Larry Jackson said."

Ben could tell she was shocked. But her shock soon turned to anger, and she exploded in a fit of rage.

"We have nothing more to say to each other, and

you get the hell out of my face. I've got a show to do. If you have any other questions, you can contact me through my lawyer, is that understood?''

Red glanced at Ben. ''Didn't take that well, did she?'' he asked as she sailed out of the room in high gear.

Ben put the picture back in his pocket. ''No, she didn't, but it's about what I expected of her. She's a real bulldog. Doesn't give an inch.''

Red nodded. ''Would she have someone killed?''

Ben hesitated, trying to imagine Connie Marx hiring a hit man, then shrugged. ''Last month, I would have said no. But after seeing the picture, I couldn't hazard a guess. I know that if the picture gets out, she's probably unemployed.''

''Would you kill to keep your job?'' Red asked.

''People have killed for a whole lot less, and we both know it,'' Ben said. ''Let's get out of here.''

''Sure I can't talk you into coming home with me tonight? Rita would love to have you.''

''No, but thanks anyway, okay?''

Red sighed. ''Tell China Brown I said hello.''

''I will.'' Then he added, ''Hey, Red?''

''Yeah?''

''Don't worry, okay? Everything's under control.''

Music rocked the walls inside the secluded cabin on Lake Texoma. The tall, leggy blonde sat before her mirror, putting the finishing touches on her makeup. Just a last brush of blush, then one more touch of eyeliner at the corner of her left eye. When she had finished, she leaned back, giving herself a final assessment, then slowly smiled. Yes, she was beautiful, but makeup was an art, accentuating that which was already pleasing to the eye.

''Honey, you are a knockout,'' she murmured, then stood and danced her way to the closet and the white, beaded dress hanging on a blue silk hanger.

As she lifted the dress from the hanger, she shivered in sudden ecstasy. God, but she loved the feel of silk between her fingers, and on her body—and between her legs. She stepped into the dress, then pulled it over her hips, slowly sliding her arms into the sleeves. Just the feel of that fabric against her skin turned her on.

The words to the Rod Stewart classic, ''Do Ya Think I'm Sexy?'' were her anthem. She sang along with the CD as she zipped up her dress and stepped into the matching heels.

A quick glance at the clock told her it wouldn't be long before her date would be here. A shiver ran up the back of her spine as she thought about his hands touching her. God, but she loved the feel of a man's hands on her body as much as she loved the feel of silk. It made her sick to her stomach, thinking how close she'd come to losing all of this. She had no misgivings about what she'd done to Chaz Finelli. The little bastard never did know when to quit. Besides, the game he was playing was dangerous. What happened to him was nothing more than a job hazard. She did regret having to shoot an innocent bystander, but not enough to lose any sleep. This was a tough world, and she was as tough as they came. Survival of the fittest was her motto, and to hell with anyone who got in her way.

The song rocked its way to silence, and for one blessed moment she closed her eyes, savoring all that was her world. Secrets were dangerous, but danger also added another frisson of excitement to the game.

Suddenly the sound of tires rolling on gravel became apparent. She moved to the window. Although it was dark, the cat's-eyes headlights on the sports car were a signal that her date had arrived. She'd heard about his predilection for...how could she put it? Unusual sex? All it had taken was one phone call and he was hers. Through the window, she saw him get out of the car. He paused, smoothing back his hair and brushing something from the front of his coat before moving toward the door. She smiled to herself as the doorbell began to ring. The stupid bastard. He might be rich and kinky, but before the night was over, he would know her in a very special way.

Captain Aaron Floyd was nursing a headache and the beginnings of what felt like the flu when Detectives English and Fisher knocked on his door.

"Come in," he said, and then winced at the sound of his own voice. "Give me some good news," he said, as he opened a drawer and took out a bottle of cough medicine.

"China Brown is getting better," Ben said.

"That's good, but not the news I was referring to," he said, then tilted the bottle to his mouth, rather than use the little plastic cup that also served as a lid. He swallowed and shuddered as he replaced the lid and put the bottle back in the drawer. "God, I hate winter and everything that comes with it."

Both detectives wisely chose not to comment and waited for him to continue.

"Okay," Floyd said. "Tell me where we are on this investigation. I'm getting some flack from up above."

"Dang, Captain, you mean even God's in on the case?"

Floyd rolled his eyes and then blew his nose. "Shut up, Fisher. I don't feel good enough to put up with your crap."

Red grinned.

Ben leaned forward, his elbows on his knees. "We've been as discreet as possible without undermining our investigation. Beyond that, I don't give a good damn. Between the adultery, the drugs and the perversions, the people involved brought it on themselves."

"Amen," Red echoed. "And what sticks in my craw is the fact that not a damn one of them even blinked about the money they paid Finelli. It was getting caught that pissed them all off."

Floyd nodded. "Yeah, but when the mayor's involved, it puts a lot of heat on a lot of people. So, what do we know?"

Ben handed the captain a list of names. "The ones

that aren't crossed out are the only people who don't have iron-clad alibis. The ones with a red mark beside them are the ones who have no one to corroborate where they were. The others had people who could vouch for them part of the night, but not all of it.''

Floyd scanned the list. ''Ariel Simmons? Wasn't she on television that night?''

''Taped show,'' Red said. ''Which she forgot to mention when we asked.''

Floyd moved to the next name. ''Connie Marx?''

''Said she was home with the flu,'' Ben offered. ''Turns out Larry Dee Jackson says she was in his hotel room with him. Either way, one of them is lying, maybe both.''

''What about Bo Milam, the real estate developer?''

''In a jet on his way to Las Vegas. It checked out.''

''And the others?'' Floyd asked.

''About the same story, but we're still working on these two.'' Red pointed to the bottom of the page. ''One's a banker. One's a plastic surgeon. Neither one has an alibi worth a damn, and we've got a couple of guys checking them out.''

Floyd looked up. ''Okay, keep at it,'' he said. ''Let me know as soon as something breaks.''

''Captain, about the guard we put on China Brown...''

''What about it?'' Floyd asked.

''I'd like to continue it 24-7 until we know who we're looking for. If word gets out that we've got a live witness to this, her life won't be worth a damn.''

"How are you handling that, by the way?" Floyd asked.

"With a little deception. The newspaper account said two people were killed. Finelli and someone whose name wasn't being released until notification of kin. We're counting on the shooter to assume that China was the other death, since she's the one who got shot. The fact that it was her child instead of her might not occur to him, and as long as he thinks she's dead, she's safe."

"Okay, I'll back you on this," Floyd said. "Continue the guard. But after she's released, that's another story. She was homeless, right? We don't have the budget to put her up in a hotel with round-the-clock guards until we bring in the perp."

Ben was already ahead of the issue. "There won't be any problems. I'm taking her home with me."

Floyd forgot the headache and every other ache in his body as he bolted up out of his seat.

"The hell you will," he said. "You're already over the line with this."

"I'm not planning to kidnap her. I'm just offering her a safe place to stay."

"That's a conflict of interest. I won't allow it."

Ben stood his ground. "I'm not a lawyer. I'm a cop. What I do on my own time is my business as long as it's not illegal."

"I don't like it," Floyd said.

"Objection noted," Ben said. "Is there anything else?"

Floyd glared at Ben English. Ben returned the stare without comment. Floyd was the first to look away.

"You mess this up and I'll have your ass," he warned.

"It's already messed up, Captain. I'm just trying to do something right. It's the least she deserves."

"Then go catch me a killer," Floyd said.

Seven

It was noon the next day when they got their first break in the case, and then it was just by chance. A man named Tommy Fairheart had been booked into jail the previous night on a drunk and disorderly. Ben weighed the odds on how many men would have the same name and not be the man who'd walked out on China, then decided to see for himself. He grabbed Red on the way out of the men's room and together they headed toward the city jail.

A short while later Ben stood outside the interrogation room, staring through a one-way mirror at the man inside. His clothes were fashionable but rumpled. His sandy-blond hair was just a little too long, and, except for a weak chin, Ben had to admit women probably found him handsome. Even though he'd spent the night in jail, he seemed unfazed by his situation. He was smiling and laughing and playing his con, even while Red was interrogating him. Ben wanted to hurt him—to make him suffer the way China was suffering.

When Red turned and stared directly toward the mirror, nodding slightly, Ben's muscles tensed. It was their prearranged signal for Ben to appear. Red had

Fairheart at ease. It was time for Ben to nail his ass to the wall.

When the door opened, Fairheart looked up, a smile still on his face. Compared to the trouble he'd been in before, a drunk and disorderly was nothing. The fact that they were interrogating him made no sense, because no crime had been committed against the bar owner. However, he was willing to go along with their game, as long as it got him released.

But the detective who entered didn't return Tommy's smile, nor did he seem inclined to do so at a later date. Tommy shrugged it off and leaned back in his chair, waiting to see what came next.

Ben walked up behind Fairheart, then stopped. Fairheart looked up into the mirror at the man standing behind him. Their gazes met and locked. After a moment, Fairheart's smile began to slip.

"What's going on here?" he said, and looked at Red for an answer.

"My partner doesn't have anything else to say to you," Ben said. "But I do."

"Oh…I get it," Fairheart said and then smirked. "This is good cop-bad cop, and you're Satan himself, right?"

Ben spoke, his voice low and angry. "Shut up, Fairheart. I'm the one asking questions, understand?"

Fairheart shrugged, although he was beginning to get nervous.

"So ask," he blustered, and leaned back in the chair, balancing it on the back two legs.

"Sit up!" Ben ordered, and pushed the man into an upright position. The chair hit the floor with a thump.

"Where were you at 10:00 p.m. on December 11?"

Fairheart's belly began to knot. Fuck! How had they found out? He would have sworn there was no way they could trace him to the robbery in Dallas Heights.

"I don't remember," he said. "What day was that?"

"Friday."

"Oh, yeah, I guess I was at the movies."

"What did you see?"

"I forget."

Ben circled the table to face him, then leaned down, bracing his hands on the surface.

"You've got to do better than that. Do you own a gun?"

"No," Fairheart blustered, thinking of the 9 mm semiautomatic back in his apartment. "Besides, what does this have to do with having a little too much to drink? All I did was break a couple of chairs."

"Not a damn thing, actually," Ben said. "This is about the two people who were murdered down in Oakcliff on December 11. You *have* heard of the area, right?"

Now they had his attention. Fairheart would have been the first to admit he was a con man, but a killer? Never. Yet he also knew that plenty of men went to prison for things they didn't do.

"Oakcliff is a pretty big area. Where did the murders take place?" Fairheart asked.

"The Blue Parrot sound familiar?" Ben asked.

Fairheart shook his head. "I've heard of it, but I haven't ever been there. Look, Detective, I didn't have anything to do with any killings, and I don't hang out in places like that. I don't swing that way, if you know what I mean."

"You saying The Blue Parrot is a gay bar?"

"All I'm saying is, you go in there, you better be careful who you come out with. You get it? There's a little bit of everything going on in there."

"Yeah, I get it," Ben said. "And we both know you like women, don't you, Fairheart?"

Tommy shrugged and then grinned. "What's not to like about them? I'm all man and then some."

"Oh, we know what kind of man you are," Ben said. "You're a liar and a thief. You use women, and when they don't have anything left to give, you walk out on them, leaving them to deal with the mess you've left behind. Is that a fair assessment?"

Fairheart shrugged again.

Ben slapped the table with the flats of both hands. "Answer me, you son of a bitch, or I swear I'll—"

Red laid a hand on Ben's shoulder. For the moment, it was enough to steady Ben's anger.

"So I'm not the marrying kind, so what?" Fairheart asked. "Since when is that a crime?"

Ben leaned forward until there was less than a foot between their faces.

"For starters, since you stole money from China Brown."

Fairheart sighed with relief. "Is that what this is all about? Well, it's her word against mine. Besides, she's gone."

Ben's heart skipped a beat. The information he had from China's landlord had Fairheart skipping out about a week before she was evicted. How could he know she was gone unless he'd seen her afterward—like maybe on the street, in front of The Blue Parrot?

"Gone where?" Ben snapped.

"She's not at the apartment anymore, that's all I know."

"And you know why, don't you? She's not there because maybe she went looking for you after she got evicted. She was six months pregnant with your kid and needed a place to stay. She got all the way to the South Side, didn't she? Only you didn't want to be found. You got into an argument on the street in front of The Blue Parrot, and you shot her—twice. And then someone started taking pictures of what you'd done, and you shot him, too."

Fairheart needed to throw up. "No! God, no! I didn't shoot China. I didn't even know she got shot. I don't kill people, man. I drink too much, and I don't like to be tied to one woman, but I'm not a killer. I swear to God, I'm not a killer. I'm not the one who killed China, and I don't know anything about another man. As for the kid being dead, so what? At least the system won't be hounding me for the next eighteen years to pay child support for some brat."

Before Red could react, Ben had taken Fairheart by

the neck, yanked him out of his chair and slammed him against the wall.

"Help!" Fairheart screamed. "Get him off me!"

Red grabbed Ben's wrist before he threw the first punch, but it was all he could do to hang on.

"Ben! Ben! Don't ruin your career over this piece of shit!" he cried.

Ben cursed, turning loose of Fairheart as if he'd suddenly ignited and stalked to the other side of the room.

"That's police brutality!" Fairheart shouted. "You're looking at a lawsuit that will—"

Red put his hand against Fairheart's chest, and the quiet tone of his voice was more frightening than any threat he might have made.

"You're not going to sue anybody, because there's not a mark on you, and you are going to sit down and be quiet," Red said. "And while you're there, you need to think about all the dangers a pretty boy like you faces behind bars."

Tommy Fairheart had a sudden urge to urinate. He'd been in jail before, but never for any length of time and never in a maximum security prison. If they nailed him for murder, he wouldn't survive inside, and he knew it.

"I didn't kill anybody," he repeated.

Ben turned, and the look on his face was deadly.

"Then prove it," he said.

Fairheart sighed. Copping to a B and E, breaking and entering, was a hell of a lot better than being sent up for murder. With any luck, he would be out within a year. Besides, it wouldn't be so bad, being inside during the winter months. A warm bed, three squares a day and clean clothes. It was beginning to sound better and better.

"I can prove where I was," he said.

Ben shoved his fists in his pockets to keep from putting them in Fairheart's face.

"Keep talking."

"There's this house over in Highland Park. You can check with Robbery. They'll tell you. I was there on December 11 around nine-thirty in the evening. I pawned the take at Frankie's Gun and Pawn Shop the next morning. There isn't any way I could have been on the south side if I was robbing a house in Highland Park, right?"

At that moment Ben knew he was telling the truth, and the knowledge made him sick. Even if they were going to put Fairheart behind bars, they were back to square one with the murders. He couldn't get Fairheart for murder, but he *could* get him for money.

"I noticed on your booking sheet that you had a little over twelve hundred dollars on you when you were picked up."

Fairheart shrugged. "So?"

"So I'm thinking that you've just gotten an attack of conscience over the way things have turned out." Ben looked up at his partner. "Hey, Red, didn't I just hear Fairheart say he was planning to give that money to the county to pay for burying his child?"

Red grinned. "Yeah, that's what I heard."

Tommy Fairheart bolted to his feet. "Hey, man, you can't do that to me. I need that money for my bail and I—"

Ben took one step toward him.

Fairheart began to back up, holding his hands in front of him like a shield.

"Wait…wait…yeah, that's fine with me. After all, I can always get more." He couldn't resist bragging. "There are plenty of lonely women. China Brown was an easy mark. I didn't hit her. I never hit my women. I treated her good when I was with her."

"And when you left, you destroyed her," Ben said. He pointed at Red. "Call Robbery. Get someone over here to take him to booking, and don't forget to have lover boy here write a letter of intent about the money before he leaves."

Now that everything was beginning to calm down, Fairheart began to regain his bluster.

"You don't scare me," he said, as Ben opened the door.

Ben turned. "You should be afraid," he said softly. "Very afraid. Stay away from China Brown. If you come near her again, I will bury you so deep in the paperwork of the Texas justice system that you'll never see daylight again." He walked away, not trusting himself to stay any longer.

Fairheart glared after the man's back, then turned his fury toward Red.

"That was another threat. You heard him," Fairheart argued as Red began to handcuff him for transport.

"I didn't hear a damned thing," Red said.

Ben walked all the way back to Homicide by himself. He needed to put distance between himself and that man before he did something he couldn't take back. But when he got to his desk, the note by the phone darkened his mood even more.

Call the coroner.

He punched in the numbers, although he suspected what the message would be. Red walked into the room just as he disconnected. He grabbed his coat from the back of his chair and slipped his cell phone in his pocket.

"What's up?" Red asked.

Ben paused. "China Brown's baby…the coroner just released the body to the next of kin."

"I thought she didn't have any kin," Red said.

"She doesn't," Ben muttered, and headed for the door.

"Where are you going?"

"To talk to China. I need to ask her where she wants the baby buried."

"She can't talk," Red argued. "Besides that, you can't just waltz in there and ask her something like that. She doesn't know about the baby. The news could kill her."

"She does know," Ben said. "And she can talk. She just hasn't wanted to yet. I'm taking the rest of the afternoon off, okay? If the captain needs to get in touch with me, he has my number.''

Before Red could argue, Ben was gone.

Someone was washing China's face and brushing her hair, and she wanted to tell them they'd just gotten soap in her eyes, but she couldn't summon enough initiative to argue. Early that morning she'd heard a man—a doctor, she thought—giving orders regarding her care. They had upped the antibiotic and lowered the pain medication. She wanted to tell them they were crazy. If they hurt in as many places as she did, they would shoot themselves full of painkillers and never stop.

A loud noise sounded in the hallway outside, and China jumped. The reflex was instinctive—the sound too much like a gunshot.

"I'm sorry, dear," the nurse said, and patted China's arm in an effort to calm her. "You're in a hospital. You're safe. Don't be afraid. There's a policeman on guard outside the ward, and you're doing just fine."

She struggled with a sigh. Safe? She would never feel safe again. Her mind gave up the struggle to stay awake, and she drifted off to sleep. Sometime later she awoke but could not bring herself to the point of opening her eyes. The last thing she'd seen was that woman pointing a gun at her, and then the snow falling into her eyes. She was afraid to look—afraid of what she might see. So she lay without moving, listening to the murmur of nurses' voices and the occasional moan from a patient nearby.

She was drifting again, lost in a place between reality and denial, when she heard another sound—that of footsteps coming toward her at a steady pace. Her heart skipped a beat. She knew those steps. She knew his voice. It was the promise man.

The adrenaline rush of wanting to wring Tommy Fairheart's neck was subsiding as Ben exited the elevator and started down the hall to the ICU. Normally he looked forward to these visits, but not this afternoon. Instead, he felt sick to his stomach. There was so much he needed to know, and she was the only one who could help them. Guilt had a good foothold in his conscience as the nurse at the desk waved him into the ward. What if Red was right? What if this visit made things worse instead of better? He shrugged off the thought. This woman was a fighter. She deserved the right to be a part of these decisions. For all he knew, it was the only thing keeping her alive.

Then he saw her face, and the tension begin to ease from his body. Just a few more steps. Finally he was there.

"Hello, China."

He stroked the length of her arm, testing the warmth of her skin as he touched her.

Although her eyes were closed, there was something different about her. It had to do with the posture of her body, or maybe the tilt of her head upon the pillow, almost as if she were listening. He slipped his hand beneath her fingers, letting them rest on his palm, and then gave them a gentle squeeze of hello.

"It's me. Ben. It's been a few hours since we last talked, and a lot has happened that I knew you would want to know. We found your friend, Tommy Fairheart."

She inhaled slowly. Ben looked up just in time to see a muscle twitch in her jaw.

"Okay, maybe he's not your friend anymore, but we found him, just the same. At first we thought he was the one who shot you, but he has a pretty good alibi. Just don't give up on us, okay? The investigation is still going strong."

She sighed, then seemed to be waiting for him to continue.

"There's something we need to talk about."

He hesitated, uncertain of how to begin. She was so small and so hurt, and the thought of causing her more pain of any kind was abhorrent. Yet it was her child, and she was the one on whom the decision should rest.

He cupped the side of her face, tracing the curve of her cheek with his thumb.

"China, you do understand me, don't you?"

Within seconds, she nodded slightly. The communication, scant though it was, was beautiful to Ben. He wanted to laugh, then he wanted to cry. Instead, he patted her cheek and then brushed a few strands of hair from her forehead.

"That's good, honey, so good. Now, do you think you can do something for me?"

She didn't move, but he could feel her pulse jumping.

"Will you open your eyes for me?"

China's heart was pounding inside her chest so hard that it felt like it might explode. Her fear was so great that she couldn't find the words to say no.

"Please," Ben begged. "I promise it will be okay."

She sighed. The promise man—back with another promise. Did she dare to trust him? Did she dare to trust herself?"

"I need your help," Ben said softly. "We need to bury your baby. I don't know what you want me to do."

A moan slid out from between her lips, followed by the onset of tears. Both the sound and the sight broke Ben's heart. He didn't know whether to apologize and leave, or cry along with her.

"I know, honey…I know," Ben whispered. "I'm sorry. Do you want me to leave?"

When her fingers curled around his wrist, he took it as a no.

"Okay, then," he said. "I'm here. You just take your time. When you're ready, we'll talk."

He looked around for a chair, but before he could move, he heard her take a slow breath. He looked down. Her eyelids were fluttering, then opening to accommodate only the briefest of glances, as if the lights were too bright for her eyes.

"Here, China. I'm here."

She turned to the sound of his voice and then stilled. Ben felt as if he'd been waiting all his life to look into her eyes.

China's memory quickened. Light. She'd almost forgotten there was a world beyond the darkness of her mind. Shadows danced before her eyes, coupled with intermittent flashes of brilliance. Her eyelids were dry against the corneas, and she blinked several times until it was no longer painful. She could feel his breath on her face and the rock-steady beat of his heart beneath her fingers.

"Mama," she said, and didn't even recognize the sound of her own voice.

Ben frowned. Was she more confused than he'd imagined? Her mother was dead. Surely she wasn't asking for her.

"I'm sorry, China, but your mother can't be here."

She licked her lips and then slowly shook her head no.

Ben was even more confused. "I don't understand," he said. "What are you trying to tell me?"

"Baby…with Mama."

Suddenly Ben understood. "You want the baby buried beside your mother?"

Immediately the tension in her body relaxed and she managed a nod.

"Can you tell me where she's buried?" Ben asked.

"Rest…"

At first Ben didn't understand as his mind raced toward a dozen different conclusions.

"I know she's at rest, honey. But I need to know where she's buried. Is she in Dallas?"

Her eyes opened a little bit more, and then she was looking at Ben English's face. Ben caught himself holding his breath. Her eyes were blue—a deep, stormy blue—and her gaze reflected such sorrow he couldn't find the strength to speak. He waited, naked before her gaze.

"Restland."

"Oh…Restland Cemetery on the north side of Dallas?"

She nodded, then closed her eyes.

"I understand. You're mother is buried there, and you want the baby with her."

China's answer came out in whisper.

"Yes."

"Will you trust me to do this for you? Will you do that, honey? I promise to make it special."

Tears welled, coming all the way from a broken heart to China's eyes. The promise man—so full of promises. Why couldn't she have met a man like this before it was too late?

"Ah, God," Ben murmured. "I didn't mean to make you cry any more. Forgive me?"

She curled her fingers around his wrist and then sighed. She was tired—so very tired. She wanted to sleep, but there was something she needed to tell him, only she couldn't remember what.

Ben could tell her endurance was just about gone,

but he didn't regret a moment of his visit. Today was the first day since he'd seen her lying on the sidewalk in front of that bar that he felt positive she would recover.

"I'm going to let you sleep now," Ben said. "You did good today, really good. I'm so proud of you, China. Just remember, we're still hard at work on your case, and we will find the man who shot you. It's just a matter of time."

Suddenly China's eyes flew open. She remembered what it was that she'd been wanting to say.

"No," she muttered, and dug her fingers into his wrist.

Startled by her vehemence, Ben frowned.

"No? You don't believe we'll find him?"

"No," China said, her voice little more than a whisper. "Not a him."

Ben froze. What she'd just said was something they'd never considered.

"China, are you saying the person who shot you was a woman?"

China's eyes were drooping. She was fighting an overwhelming urge to sleep, but he had to understand that they were looking in the wrong places. Her head lolled to the side. She could hear the promise man's voice, calling to her from far away.

Ben was frantic. "China…sweetheart…just one more time. You can do it, I know you can. Are you telling me that the person who shot you was a woman?"

He saw her take a breath. Her lips parted. He stared

at her mouth, waiting for the word to emerge. Finally a whisper came, so faint that he had to bend down to hear.

"Yes."

His eyes narrowed as shock shot through his body.

"I heard you, honey. I understand. Now rest. I'll be back tomorrow. I promise."

When China heard the words "I promise" she smiled in her mind, though the smile never reached her face.

Ben straightened abruptly. Satisfied that his visit had done China no harm, he touched the side of her cheek one last time and then walked away. This changed everything, and Red and Captain Floyd needed to know as soon as possible.

"Senator Wakefield, you'd better turn on your television and take a look at this."

Bobby Lee glanced up as his aide, Duffy Melton, entered his office, then picked up the remote and hit the Power button.

"What channel?" he asked.

"Breaking story on all channels, I think," Duffy said.

As the picture began to emerge, Bobby Lee could see news crews and an ambulance, as well as about a dozen of Dallas's finest cordoning off what appeared to be a crime scene.

"What's the big deal?" Bobby Lee asked.

"Tashi Yamamoto was found dead in his car in a bank parking lot. They think it was a robbery. His wallet and jewelry are missing, and they're saying he died of a gunshot to the head.''

Bobby Lee frowned. ''Tashi Yamamoto of Yamamoto Industries?''

Duffy nodded. ''One and the same. This is going to play hell in South Dallas. That factory employs over a thousand of your constituents. If they close down that plant, we've got a whole lot of people out of a job, and in this economy, that's not good.''

''I never met the man,'' Bobby Lee muttered.

''No, sir, but you know the rumors about him. He didn't come to Texas often, but when he did, he was almost a recluse. People said he was into a lot of weird stuff...perversion...things like that.''

Bobby Lee shrugged. ''I was taught never to speak ill of the dead, so just drop it. By the way, where's that EPA file on the Ellis Fishery? Damn agency, always meddling into hardworking people's business. Find it for me, will you? I promised Edward Ellis that I'd see to it they didn't shut him down.''

''Yes, sir,'' Duffy said. ''I'll be right back with it.''

As Duffy left, Bobby Lee's frown deepened as he glanced back at the television screen. He hated surprises, but he hated turmoil more. With a muffled curse, he aimed the remote at the television. When the screen went black, he tossed the remote aside and stalked to the sideboard to pour himself a drink.

Eight

The information Ben received from China set Homicide into an uproar. Now the forty-five names on the original list had to be looked at from another angle, and within the space of three days, the investigation had Dallas society into an uproar. The media had been told nothing, but it was inevitable from the number of people involved that something would eventually leak. China Brown had been moved from the ICU into a private room with a guard posted outside her door. No one went in or out who wasn't on the list, and Ben's anxiety grew. The longer it took to find the killer, the more difficult it would be. And if word got out that the Dallas police had an eyewitness, China's life wouldn't be worth a dime.

The men who'd been eliminated earlier were still in the clear, but now their wives were not. Before, the women in Finelli's pictures who were without good alibis had been put more or less in the background of the investigation. Now they were prime suspects. Four teams of detectives from Homicide were working the list, going from one household to the next and raising more hell in Dallas than the annual rivalry of the Texas A and M–Oklahoma University football game.

High on the list of suspects were anchorwoman Connie Marx, Shelly Milam, a local real estate developer's wife, and televangelist Ariel Simmons. Their alibis were vague, and they had no one to corroborate their whereabouts on the night of the shootings.

After learning she was a suspect in a double homicide, Connie Marx had been put on temporary leave by her boss. She was so angry at the Dallas P.D. that she was threatening to hire a lawyer. The fact that Larry Jackson claimed she was with him was tainted by the fact that there was no one else to verify their story. In the eyes of the police, being lovers *and* suspects more or less negated whatever truth there might be between them.

Two other detectives were trying to find Shelly Milam, who'd served her husband with divorce papers after he'd been interviewed the first time around. All they knew at this point was that she'd flown to Alabama to be with her family and wouldn't be back in Texas until next week. They were in the process of notifying the Selma, Alabama, police department that Mrs. Milam was wanted for questioning in two murders and asking their help in locating her.

Since Ariel Simmons's earlier claim that she was broadcasting her show had been disproved, Red and Ben descended upon the woman's home with renewed fervor. Only this time, Ariel's lawyer was present.

*   *   *

"Looks like she's got company," Red said, as he parked in front of Ariel Simmons's door.

The black Jaguar already in the driveway spelled money, and the vanity plate below the bumper, ILUV2SUE, was a mobile advertisement for the lawyer who owned it.

"More like reinforcements," Ben said. "Let's get this over with. I promised China I'd come by this evening before I drove out to the ranch."

"Going to see Mattie?" Red asked.

Ben nodded, then grinned. "Yeah, tomorrow's my day off, and Mom's been giving me heck about how long it's been since I've been home. Thought I'd better check on her and the place while I've got a chance."

He rang the doorbell.

Within seconds, a man answered. From the cut of his suit and the Rolex on his wrist, Ben assumed this would be the lawyer.

"Detectives English and Fisher to see Miss Simmons," Ben said.

"This way, gentlemen. And for the record, I'm Herb Langley, Miss Simmons's lawyer."

"For the record, she's going to need one," Ben replied, and was satisfied to see the back of Langley's neck turning red as he escorted them down the hall.

As they entered the library, it was obvious that Ariel had been awaiting their arrival. She was in character, from the long blond hair to a soft, white flowing dress. At their approach, she looked up from the chair where she was sitting and laid her hand on her Bible, as if to hold her place while she greeted them.

"Do sit down," she said softly, and then bent her head and closed her eyes as she murmured a quick, silent prayer.

When she looked up, her face seemed illuminated, her eyes wide and bright with unshed tears. She sighed, then closed her Bible and laid it aside, giving them her full attention.

"I was told you have some more questions for me, so I've asked my lawyer, Herbert Langley, to sit in. I'm sure you understand."

Neither detective seemed impressed with her change of manner or appearance, and it aggravated Ariel greatly, but she didn't let it show.

"Now, what can I do for you gentlemen?"

Ben pulled out his notebook and went straight to the point.

"When we where here before, you told us that on the night Finelli was murdered, you were doing a live broadcast. We have since found out that the show that night was taped at an earlier date."

Ariel's hands fluttered up from her lap in an awkward sort of way, as if they were connected to the strings of an apprentice puppeteer.

"You are so right, and I apologize for the mistake. You see, I rarely air anything that's not live, and I suppose in my shock at that horrible photograph you showed me, I just forgot. Of course, when I checked my calendar, I realized what I'd done and told Langley immediately. Didn't I, Langley?''

''Yes, you certainly did,'' he said. ''And, as you know, before I could contact the police department and inform them of the error, your people contacted my client instead. The accusation that she is in any way connected to that horrible woman in the photograph, or to the murders, is absurd.''

''That's all well and good,'' Ben said. ''But we need more than an apology from Ms. Simmons. We still need to know where she was that night.''

Ariel smiled, although in truth she wanted to scream. This was all Finelli's fault. If the stupid little bastard hadn't chosen to meddle in things that were not his business, none of this would be happening.

''I was here, in my home,'' she said, and then the tears that were glittering in her eyes began to slide soundlessly down her face. ''I was preparing my sermon for the Sunday broadcast, and I'm afraid my only witness was God.'' She leaned forward. ''Will you take God's word, Detective English?''

''Of course,'' Ben said. ''Tell him I'm listening.''

A dark flush spread across her cheeks. ''You jest about God's word? How dare you?'' She looked to her lawyer, holding out her hands in supplication. ''Langley, how am I to deal with unbelievers?''

Ben's patience had been thin when they started this conversation, but it snapped when she started to emote.

''Look, lady, can the drama, okay? My religious beliefs are not on trial, but you very well could be if you don't come up with a better alibi than that."

Ariel stood abruptly, her saintly persona gone. "I have nothing more to say to you. Either arrest me or get out of my home. And be warned, I intend to go on the air and tell the world of the evil that is trying to drag me down." She was in full swing now, beginning to pace back and forth in front of them the way she did onstage. "That picture you have of me is a fake. Someone has put my face on another's body. Langley says it's a simple matter to do such a thing nowadays, and I won't be railroaded into submission. God is my strength. I accept this as a trial of my faith. God will be with me through the wilderness of this horror, and I will prevail."

Ben stood. "Sit down, Miss Simmons. We're not through until I say we're through. Yes, faking photographs is easy, but it's also easy for an expert to detect, and so far, our experts haven't found any discrepancies. The only abnormalities are what the pictures depict."

Ariel sat, her fury evident. "Langley, do something," she muttered.

"Are you going to arrest her?" Langley asked.

Ariel shrieked. "You're supposed to be helping me, not them!"

"Shut up, Ariel, you've said enough," Langley said. The woman's shock was evident, but she hushed. Langley looked up. "Okay, men, we've all got our cards on the table. Miss Simmons was in her home preparing her sermon. She can't prove it, but can you prove otherwise? Do you have any witnesses who say they saw her in Oakcliff that night? No, you don't, or she would already be under arrest. So where does that leave us? In the clear, that's where.'' He stood. ''Now, my client has cooperated fully with you people, and if you aren't going to arrest her, then I suggest it's time you take your leave.''

Both men stood. Ben gave the preacher a calculated look, then left her with a parting shot.

''We're going, but I want you to remember something, lady. Lies have a way of coming back and biting you on the ass, so you better watch where you sit.''

When Langley got up to follow them out, Ben stopped. ''Don't bother,'' he said. ''We can find our own way.''

Ariel Simmons was arguing with her lawyer before they got out the door, and when they were halfway down the hall, they heard her starting to shout.

Red grinned. ''Right about now, old Langley's earning every penny she pays him.''

Ben shook his head. ''There isn't enough money on earth to pay me to work for a woman like her. She's lying, Red. But how in hell can we prove it?''

''Do you think she did it?'' Red said.

''I don't know,'' Ben answered. ''Only China can help us with that one. Yesterday, when I went to see her, she talked to me for almost five minutes before she went back to sleep. I keep wanting to push her for answers, but then I remember how she looked that night, all pale and still, with the snow falling on her face.'' He shuddered. ''I thought she was dead.''

''She came close,'' Red said. ''But that's the operative word. *Close* is not the same as *over*. You said it yourself, she's getting better every day. When she's ready to do more, you'll know it. Right now, be grateful for small favors. At least we know the shooter was a woman. Now all we need is a name.''

China was awake when Ben came into her room. The sight of his smile did things to her heart that she would rather not face. No use wasting time caring about a man ever again. They were full of pretty words—until they were through with you.

''Hey, there,'' Ben said, as he reached her bedside and set a little Santa Claus doll on her table. ''It's just a feel-good thing,'' he said, pointing to the doll. ''Good to see you awake. How have you been doing?''

''All right,'' she said, and when he touched the side of her face with the back of his hand, she told herself he was only feeling for fever. But when his hand turned and he cupped her cheek, she didn't know what to think.

Ben was elated that she was recovering, but there was a drawback he hadn't expected. Before, he'd touched her without thought. Now she was obviously not receptive to the notion and while he understood her distrust, it hurt him just the same.

''That's good,'' Ben said, and took off his coat and laid it at the foot of her bed.

China wiggled her toes beneath the weight and decided it felt comfortable after all.

"Do you feel up to taking a look at a few pictures?" he asked.

"Of what?" China asked.

"Possible suspects."

China's eyes widened as she stared at the pictures he took out of his jacket pocket. She wanted the woman found, but the thought of seeing her again made her sick with fear.

Ben saw the look and instantly understood. "It will be okay, honey. They're only pictures."

China bit her lip and then reached for them. "Yes, I'll look at them."

"Good."

He laid them in her lap, spreading them out until she could clearly see all six. Almost immediately, she pointed to three of them.

"Not her, or her, or her," she said.

Ben picked them up and put them back in his pocket.

"What about the other three?"

China picked them up one at a time, looking intently. One was of Shelly Milam. There was a resemblance, but she couldn't be sure. Twice, she went back to two of them—one of Ariel Simmons, one of Connie Marx. Finally shook her head.

"I can't be sure. There's something about these two that looks familiar, yet not exactly right."

Ben knew that a lawyer would have a field day with

that remark. Both women were recognizable in their own right, which could be why China was confused.

"Take your time," he said. "Try to remember what she—"

She looked up. "I don't have to try. That woman's face is forever etched in my mind."

"Sorry," Ben said, and then picked up the pictures and put them back in his pocket. "It was worth a try."

"No, I'm sorry," she said. "But their hair is different, and it was dark, and the woman was wearing some kind of evening dress under a full-length fur coat."

Ben took Ariel's and Connie's pictures out of his pocket again and laid them back in her lap.

"Picture them wearing a wig like the woman who shot you and then tell me if the features fit."

China looked again, fingering one, then the other. Finally, she shook her head.

"I just can't be sure."

Ben's hopes fell, but he didn't let on. "That's all right. Don't think this brings anything to a halt, okay?"

"Okay."

"Well, I'd better get back to work. Red's at the dentist. I promised to pick him up before noon, and he reminded me earlier that it's my day to buy lunch."

China listened intently but without comment. It would seem that Ben English kept his promises to everyone, not just to her.

"You going to be all right?" Ben asked. "Is there anything you need?"

"No, thank you, I don't need anything." *Except peace.*

Ben hesitated, wanting to hug her goodbye, but having to settle for a smile and a wave instead.

"We'll talk soon."

She nodded, glanced once at the smiling Santa doll, then drifted off to sleep.

Outside, the holiday spirit was in full swing. Nurses went about their duties wearing Santa Claus hats, and a group of children from a private elementary school sang carols out in the hall.

China awoke just as a little boy began his solo verse. His voice was clear, a pure tenor that would one day give way to maturity, but for now it wrapped around a verse with such purity that she felt shattered all the way to her soul.

Away in a manger,
No crib for a bed,
The little lord Jesus,
Lay down His sweet head.
The stars in the bright sky
Looked down where He lay.
The little lord Jesus,
Asleep on the hay.

The image of a baby—any baby—was too much for China to bear.

"Oh God," she whispered, and then she started to cry.

Two days later, China was sitting up when Ben walked into her room. When the door opened, she flinched, relaxing only after she recognized who it was.

"You startled me."

"Sorry," Ben said, and strode quickly to her bedside. "Should you be sitting up like that? You don't want to—"

"I walked from the bed to the bathroom today."

Without thinking, he cupped the side of her face. "Oh, honey, that's wonderful news!"

The familiarity of his palm against her cheek made China nervous. It wasn't the first time he'd touched her in this way, but today it felt different—less impersonal. She looked at him, frightened by the power in his gaze, and caught herself holding her breath.

For a moment, neither of them moved. China was the first to look away, and she shivered as she fidgeted with her sheets. This was something she wasn't ready to handle—might never be able to handle again. Right now, any intimacy with a man, no matter how innocent, was impossible. There was nothing left inside her but the need to get well and the need for revenge.

Ben saw the look on her face. At that moment, if Tommy Fairheart had been within reach, he would have beaten him senseless. Damn that man to hell and back for what he'd done to China Brown. He decided that a change of subject was in order.

"Has your doctor been in today?"

To his surprise, she hesitated, then began to tremble.

"China?"

"What?"

"What did Dr. Pope tell you?"

"That he will release me in two or three days."

Ben frowned. "And that bothers you?"

She shrugged.

He eased down on the side of her bed and laid his hand on the covers. Her legs were shaking beneath them as if she'd gotten a chill, but he knew she wasn't cold.

"China, we've come too far in this together for you to quit trusting me now. What's wrong?"

She bit her lip and then looked up at him. "After all this time and no notice, I know I've lost my job. I have no money or home. When they release me from the hospital, I will have no place to go."

He wanted to take her in his arms and kiss away all the pain, but it would only make things more complicated than they already were.

"I'm sorry. I should have told you sooner," he said. "That's already taken care of. I'm taking you to my mother's until I'm certain you're safe."

"Oh, but I couldn't impose on—"

Ben shook his head and patted her leg. "If you knew my mother, you'd know better than to say that. She's a widow, and I suspect she's often lonely. She lives by herself in a great big house out in the country and will welcome the company, trust me."

She shook her head, still not convinced. "What if that woman—the woman who shot me—what if she comes looking for me?"

"You'll be fine. I have someone who's going to play bodyguard for the both of you. He's an ex-cop and an old friend of the family. He'll be happy to have an excuse to hang around my mother, anyway."

China was intrigued in spite of herself. "He's in love with her?"

Ben grinned. "Probably, but I'm staying out of that. Now don't worry. You just concentrate on getting well. I'll have Mom call you before you leave the hospital. You can say hello over the phone, and maybe you won't feel like such strangers when you do finally meet."

She hesitated, then sighed. "It shames me to admit that I don't really have a choice."

Ben tilted her chin to meet his gaze.

"We all have choices, China. Some are better than others, but none of them are wrong, they're just choices, okay?"

She nodded, and when he moved his finger from her chin, she felt as if her gravity shifted. The thought made her angry, but only with herself. He didn't really mean anything to her except a means to an end. He was a cop. He was sworn to protect her. The fact that he was willing to go a few steps farther was good for her. As her mother used to say, she shouldn't look a gift horse in the mouth.

"Then tell your mother I'm grateful," she said.

"Tell her yourself when she calls," Ben said. "Now I'd better let you get some rest. I'll see you the day after tomorrow."

Her heart skipped a beat. A whole day without seeing him? In spite of her unwillingness to admit he mattered to her, he'd become her safety net.

"Okay, sure," she muttered, and willed herself not to cry.

Ben started to leave, but there was something about her silence and posture that bothered him.

"Is there anything you want to tell me—anything you need?"

She didn't answer.

"China."

She looked up.

"You can trust me. I promise," he said.

Tears welled anew. The promise man. He had yet to let her down.

"No, nothing is wrong. I've been crying a lot the last couple of days for no reason. Dr. Pope said it's my body readjusting." She bit her lip and then met his gaze. "You know, after the baby and all. I guess my hormones are all messed up."

If she'd punched him in the belly, he couldn't have been more dismayed. What the hell had he been thinking? Of course something was wrong. She was grieving for her child.

"Another thing I should have told you. I found where your mother is buried. Tomorrow your daughter will be beside her."

China started to shake. "Thank you," she mumbled. "I—" And then she covered her face with her hands. "Please let this be a nightmare and please let me wake up."

Ben groaned. Seconds later he was at her bedside and cradling her in his arms.

"Ah God, honey, your grief is breaking my heart. You might not need to be held, but right now, I need to hold you."

She cried herself to sleep in Bennett's arms.

Ben stood on the porch of the ranch house where he'd been raised, listening to the occasional bawl of a cow searching for her calf and the sound of the big rigs shifting gears on the highway a few miles east. Last night had been great. His mother had been so happy to have him, cooking all his favorite foods and dragging out picture albums and talking about his childhood as if it were yesterday. He'd waited too long to come visit and wouldn't do it to her again.

Tomorrow he would report back to work, which also meant that he would see China again. Although he was less than an hour from Dallas, he could easily imagine himself in another world.

He folded his arms across his chest and then leaned against the porch post as he looked up at the sky. The night was cold, but the sky was clear. The lights from the house behind him made patches on the floor of the porch like cold pats of butter on dry toast. The television was on in the other room, and he could hear his mother chuckling at the antics of the situation comedy she was watching.

A fresh wave of guilt hit him gut first. His mother laughed alone every night. He should be in there sharing the laughter with her. But there was a loneliness inside him that not even a mother's love could heal. He would crawl into his bed tonight and sleep alone, as he slept every night. He was thirty-six years old and had been engaged only once, twelve years ago. The engagement had lasted six weeks. To this day, he couldn't remember who'd broken up with whom. All he knew was, it was the smartest thing he'd ever done. He wanted a family, but with the right woman, not just because he was lonely. He wanted a marriage like the one his parents had shared.

Immediately, his thoughts moved to China. He didn't know a damn thing about her except that she'd put her faith in someone who'd let her down. He didn't know if she liked to dance. He didn't know her favorite color or what she liked to eat, and yet he'd bonded with her in a way he'd never done with any woman before. However, what he felt—or thought he felt—for her was moot.

"Bennett, darling, you're going to freeze."

He turned. His mother was standing in the doorway with a worried expression on her face.

"You're right, it's colder than I thought," he said, and followed her back inside.

Mattie English paused in the hallway to look at her son. There were shadows beneath his eyes and a grimness to his mouth she couldn't remember ever seeing before.

"Son?"

"What?"

"Is everything all right?"

"I'm fine, Mom. Sorry I'm not better company. I've got a lot on my mind."

She slipped a hand beneath his elbow and walked him back into the living room.

"Put another log on the fire, will you, honey?"

"Sure," he said, glad to have something concrete to do. He moved the fire screen aside and dropped another log on the fire. When he turned, his mother was on the sofa. She patted the cushion beside her.

"Come sit with me," she said.

He sat.

"Is it work?" Mattie asked.

Ben hesitated, but he knew better than to lie to her.

"Yes."

"Are you in trouble?"

"No, no, Mom, nothing like that. I'm sorry if I worried you."

"I've just never seen you so distracted. Do you want to talk about it?"

He looked at her and almost smiled.

"I think I'd better," he said. "Especially since I've more or less involved you in the problem."

Mattie grinned. "As long as it has nothing to do with a bake sale, we're in business."

He laughed aloud. It was an old family joke, dating

back to a time when he'd volunteered her baking prowess for a bake sale his Cub Scout pack was having, and at the time, Mattie had had one arm in a sling and the other in a cast.

"No bake sales," he said. "I promise."

"Then talk to me," she said.

Ben took a breath. How to explain? There was only one way—from the beginning.

"It started two weeks ago, with a shooting in Oakcliff. A man was murdered, and a woman was shot and left for dead."

He glanced at his mother, aware that this could get touchy, because she had miscarried and lost the only child she would ever carry. The fact that they'd adopted him when he was only days old rarely crossed his mind. But if China was to stay here, this had to be said. His mother needed to know what she was going through.

"The woman was pregnant. The baby died."

"Oh, Ben," Mattie said, and then leaned over and took him by the hands. "It's all right, sweetie. I'm not that fragile, you know. Losing your father was the hardest thing I've ever had to bear, and I survived that. Keep talking."

"Okay, but remember, you asked for it."

She nodded. "So, this case…it's one of yours?"

"Yes."

"The woman who was shot…will she live?"

"For a while it was touch and go, but she's doing great now. In fact, that's part of what's been bothering me. The day she was shot, she'd just been evicted from her home. Long story short, her boyfriend dumped her, stole all her money and left her flat. She's now the only witness to a murder that is becoming a bigger mess with each passing day, and in a few days she's going to be released, but with nowhere to go. I need to keep her safe.'' Then he added, ''I care what happens to her, Mom, and I'm about to ask a very big favor of you.''

Mattie could see what was coming. ''Is she nice…you know…decent?''

''As far as we can tell, she's an innocent. She's distrusting of men, but Mom, she's so tiny…I guess *fragile* is a better word. And she's beautiful, only the oddest thing about that is, I don't think she knows it.''

Mattie knew her son. She'd never heard him speak of a woman in this way. The last thing she wanted was to see Ben get mixed up with someone sordid. In her opinion, the best way to oversee the situation was to be in the middle of it. Ben might be smitten, but she would reserve judgment until she'd seen for herself.

''Bring her to me,'' Mattie said.

''You'll have to put up with Dave being around, too,'' he warned.

Mattie felt herself flushing. ''Oh, Ben, he makes me nervous,'' she muttered. ''Always fiddling around, trying to help me do stuff. I've been taking care of myself for years. I don't need him to do anything for me.''

''She's a witness to a crime, Mom. The guard is necessary. Dave Lambert is a retired cop. He's nearby.

He's volunteered. If China comes, he has to be part of the deal.''

"China? Surely that's not her real name?'' Mattie asked, envisioning some tawdry stage name for a stripper act.

He grinned. "Yes, ma'am, it is. China Brown. Her mother, Mae, is deceased, or you could take the name business up with her.''

Mattie frowned. "I didn't mean there was something wrong with it. It's just different, that's all.''

"And so is she,'' Ben said. "So it's all right? I can tell her you said it's okay?''

"I'll tell her myself tomorrow. What hospital is she in?''

"Parkland.''

"I'll call her room. We'll talk.''

Ben's grin spread. "Come here to me,'' he said, and held out his arms, giving her a hug when she scooted nearer. "I know what you're thinking, but you'll see for yourself. She's about the least dangerous woman you'll ever meet.'' Then his mood shifted, and his smile slipped. "I buried her baby today before I drove to the ranch. There was no one there but me and a preacher I didn't know. Help her, Mom, because I damn sure don't know how.''

In that moment, Mattie felt a connection with the woman she had yet to meet.

"It will be all right, son,'' she said softly. "Time heals a lot. Maybe we'll heal each other. Who knows?''

Nine

"**B**obby Lee! Bobby Lee! We'll vote for you!"

Bobby Lee smiled and waved at the trio of giggling women across the street from the television station as he and Ainsley Been got out of his car. WFAL Channel 7 was doing a special interview on him and his recent announcement to run for president, and he was running late.

"I'll hold you to that," he called out as he entered the station.

A harried producer was waiting for him at the door.

"Senator Wakefield, thank goodness! You're on in five minutes," he said, and began miking Bobby Lee as they walked.

"Well, now," Bobby Lee said. "And here I thought I was late." Then he added. "This is my campaign manager, Ainsley Been."

The producer nodded a quick hello and then hustled the men into the studio, where Ronnie Boyle, the evening anchorman, was winding up the national news.

"Just have a seat," the producer said quietly.

Ainsley Been handed the producer a sheet of paper.

"This is a list of questions the senator will respond to."

"You're restricting us as to what we can discuss?"

Bobby Lee frowned at Ainsley, then patted the young man on the back.

"Hell no, boy! I'm an open book. You just tell Boyle to ask away, you hear?"

"Thank you," he said. "Now step this way. We need to get you seated."

Ainsley started to argue, but Bobby Lee shook his head, then strode onto the set, taking a chair as if it were a throne and he the reigning king.

Granted, there weren't any real time bombs in Bobby Lee's past—except possibly his mother, and most everyone in Texas knew Mona Wakefield, or at least knew of her and accepted her as the colorful character she was. Bobby Lee's past *was* his ticket to stardom. His war record, his football prowess, his dedication to government from an early age—he was a man's man in every sense of the word, yet wealthy, unattached and handsome enough to set every woman's heart aflutter. However, it could not be forgotten that the senator was no longer just a Texas boy made good. He had moved into the national arena, and it remained to be seen how Mona Wakefield would fare.

Normally Connie Marx would have been doing the interview, but since her suspension from the network, her coanchor, Ronnie Boyle, was sitting in as host on the guest segment of the broadcast.

"Good evening, Senator," Boyle said, and shook Bobby Lee's hand as he took a seat opposite his guest.

Bobby Lee nodded and smiled.

"You're on in two," someone said.

Boyle nodded without taking his eyes from Bobby Lee.

"Are you comfortable, Senator Wakefield?"

"Yes, I'm fine," Bobby Lee said.

Boyle nodded again and began readjusting his mike, then glanced down in his lap to refer to some notes he was holding.

Again nerves twitched in the pit of Ainsley's belly, but he told himself to stay calm. After all, what the hell could happen?

In the background, someone began counting down the time.

"Five…four…three…two…"

Ronnie Boyle looked up and smiled straight into the camera.

"Welcome back. We have a special guest in the studio this evening. One of Texas's finest, our very own Senator Bobby Lee Wakefield." Boyle turned his smile to Bobby Lee. "Senator, you recently announced your candidacy for president of the United States. What was it that led you to the decision to run?"

Bobby Lee leaned forward just a fraction, giving the impression that he was imparting confidential information. The expression on his face was warm but serious.

On the sidelines, Ainsley breathed a sigh of relief.

He should have known better than to worry. When it came to the media, Bobby Lee was a consummate professional.

"Well now, Ronnie...you don't mind if I call you Ronnie, do you?" Bobby Lee asked.

"Of course not," Boyle said. "We're all among friends here."

"That's what I want to hear," Bobby Lee said, and began to talk.

On the other side of the city, Mona sat cross-legged in the middle of her bed, her gaze fixed on the television screen. She was listening to her son with an absent air. Most of her attention was focused on what he was wearing and how he looked. After a couple of moments, she began to relax. He looked just fine, and that Boyle fellow didn't know it yet, but Bobby Lee was guiding the interview right where he wanted it to go.

Minutes passed as Mona's mind wandered to the future and a much more momentous occasion than a local television interview. She leaned back against the headboard of her bed and closed her eyes, picturing her son standing on the steps of the White House and taking the oath of office while she stood at his side. She would wear white—no, maybe she would wear red. It would show up better on national TV. And she would wear a hat. She looked good in hats, and it was cold in the capitol in January.

Then her thoughts refocused on the show, and she glanced back at the screen just in time to hear Boyle changing the subject from national platforms to local politics.

"Senator, I'm sure you're aware of the recent death of Tashi Yamamoto. There's a rumor that the company he owned here in Dallas will fold. If it does, a lot of your constituents will be out of a job. Do you have any information that might alleviate the worry for all those families?"

Bobby Lee tilted his head sideways just a bit, giving himself a thoughtful appearance. He knew it made him look good. He'd practiced just that very pose for years to get it right.

"That was a tragedy, for sure," Bobby Lee said. "Unfortunately, I've not been contacted directly regarding any decisions from Mr. Yamamoto's company, but my sympathies go out to his family, and to the people who might be affected by the company's closing." Then he looked straight into Boyle's eyes, well aware that the camera would make it appear as if he were talking to the viewers themselves. "This is proof of how violence in this country affects us all, even indirectly. If I'm elected president, I intend to do everything in my power to change this country's thinking on capital punishment. Too many repeat offenders are released back into our society."

Boyle glanced ruefully at the producer, who was indicating that time was up, then skillfully wrapped up the interview. When it was over, Bobby Lee stood and took off his mike, dropping it into the chair in which he'd been sitting.

"Fine job, Mr. Boyle," he said, and shook the man's hand.

Ronnie Boyle nodded and smiled. "You made it easy."

Bobby Lee smiled. He never tired of having his ego stroked.

"We covered a lot of bases in five minutes," Boyle said.

"There's a lot going on in this country."

"You're right about that," Boyle said. "Especially here in Dallas."

Bobby Lee looked confused. "Are you referring to Yamamoto's death?"

"That and the Finelli scandal."

Bobby Lee's expression blanked. "Yes, well, I have another appointment in a few minutes. I must be going."

Boyle followed him off the set. "How do you think Dallas is going to come out of the mess?" he asked, and then lowered his voice a bit as he continued. "I mean, after all, this thing goes all the way to the top of the city's business and social ladder."

Bobby Lee's heart began to pound. He'd heard all about the police interrogations and the pictures they'd found in the murdered man's apartment. He'd lost sleep wondering if his mother would show up in any of them, then wondering how many people he would have to buy off to make sure the pictures disappeared if she did.

"Yes, I suppose it does, although I'd rather not

comment." He grabbed Boyle's hand and gave it a vigorous shake. "Thank you again, son, for a fine interview." Then he looked at Ainsley. "Have the driver bring the car around. We're through here."

He walked away without looking back, leaving Ronnie Boyle to wonder why the senator's jovial manner had so suddenly disappeared.

The television on the wall was on, but the sound had been muted. A plate of congealing chicken and noodles was on the table near China's bed. The bowl of Jell-O was half-eaten and most of her milk was gone. She'd eaten because they'd insisted, not because she was hungry. Her appetite for everything except revenge was gone. Ever since Ben English had challenged her to get well, she'd focused all her energies on doing that very thing, and for one reason only. She wanted the woman who'd shot her to pay. Maybe then she would learn how to live with some measure of peace.

As she lay there, someone suddenly laughed aloud outside her door, and the sound hurt her heart. It seemed obscene that the world still turned when hers had all but stopped. She felt caught in a vacuum without any way out. Everything seemed pointless and frightening. During rounds this evening, Dr. Pope had told her that if she continued to progress, she would be released the day after tomorrow. The idea of moving beyond the safety of this small room and the guard at her door was horrifying. What if the moment she stepped outside the hospital door the killer shot her again? It could happen easily enough, and the killer certainly had good reason to want her dead. After all, she was the only person who could identify her.

"Oh, God, help me get through this," China whispered, and turned her face to the wall.

Within moments, the phone beside her bed began to ring. Her heart jerked with fright. Who could be calling her? No one even knew she was here. And then she thought of Ben. She hadn't seen him since the day before yesterday. Maybe he was calling to check on her. Wincing as she extended her arm, she picked up the receiver and held it to her ear.

"Hello?"

Mattie English took a deep breath. The soft, broken sound of the word was not what she'd been expecting.

"Is this China Brown?"

Suddenly the face of the woman who'd shot her flashed before her eyes. What if it was her? Frightened, China hung up, then pulled the covers up to her chin, as if the simple act would keep her safe.

A few seconds later the phone rang again, shattering her nerves and sending her into a panic. She opened her mouth to scream for help, but nothing came out. All she could do was lie there in fear. On the fifth ring, a nurse entered.

"Honey, your phone's ringing off the wall. Can't you reach it?"

Without waiting for China to speak, she picked up the receiver.

"Miss Brown's room. May I help you?"

China was holding her breath when the nurse handed her the phone.

"It's Mattie English. Says she's Detective English's mother. Do you want to talk to her?"

"Oh, my God," China muttered, and started to shake. She'd forgotten that Ben's mother was going to call. She'd hung up on Ben's mother. She reached for the phone.

"Hello?"

Mattie started talking before China could hang up again. "I should have identified myself. I know you've been through a terrible ordeal, but I'm told you're making wonderful progress."

"Yes, ma'am," China said.

"Ben tells me you're going to be released soon."

"Yes, ma'am."

Some of Mattie's doubts began to slip. *Ma'am.* At least the girl had been raised to respect her elders.

"The reason I'm calling is to second the offer Ben made to have you come stay with me for a while—at least until an arrest can be made."

China hesitated. "He said something to me about it, but it's such an imposition for you, having a complete stranger in your home."

Mattie smiled to herself and relaxed even more.

"Oh, honey, these days I'm lonesome more than I care to remember. It will be good to have another voice in this house besides my own."

Tears unexpectedly filled China's eyes. It had been

so long since she'd felt welcome anywhere that the empathy got to her.

"I suppose Ben told you I had nowhere else to go."

When the girl's voice began to shake, Mattie's empathy changed to sympathy.

"Yes, he did, and he told me the reasons why. I'm so sorry for your loss," she said softly.

Tears spilled down China's face. All she could do was nod, even though she knew Mattie could not see her.

When Mattie thought she heard a choked sob, her last bit of reserve disappeared.

"You go ahead and cry all you want to," she said. "I know the pain of what you're going through. I miscarried my only baby two months before he was due and I wanted to die. I think I tried to die." Her voice shook with remembered pain. "But the damnedest thing happened."

"What?" Mattie managed to ask, intrigued in spite of herself.

"First, I discovered that it's impossible to die from holding your own breath."

China almost smiled.

"And," Mattie continued, "I'd worked too hard on the nursery to take it all down. I wanted to be a mother more than anything on this earth, so my husband and I adopted a baby boy. It took a couple of years, but my Ben was worth the wait."

"Ben is adopted?"

Mattie smiled. Even though China's voice was still shaking, she could hear true interest in the question.

"Yes. Turned out pretty well, considering how much my husband and I spoiled him, don't you think?"

China closed her eyes, trying to picture the big man she knew as a baby someone hadn't wanted. The image hurt her heart.

"Yes, ma'am."

"Well, now, if you're going to be sleeping under my roof, you need to know one thing right now. I won't answer to anything but Mattie. None of that ma'am stuff, you hear?"

This time, China did smile. "Yes, ma'—I mean, yes, Mattie."

"That's better," she said. "Now, don't you worry about another thing. Just get well. I'll see you soon."

"All right," China said. "And thank you."

"You're welcome, honey," Mattie said. "Oh... almost forgot. Do you have any allergies, or any horrible dislikes to foods?"

"No allergies, and the only thing I dislike about food is not having any."

Mattie's laugh tickled China's ear, making her smile widen.

"Good," Mattie said. "You've got a sense of humor. I can tell we're going to get along just fine. Get some rest. I'll see you soon."

China hung up the phone, the smile still on her face. Sometime during her conversation the nurse had gone, taking the tray of uneaten food with her. China glanced up at the television and the muted screen, then toward the window. The skyline looked the same, but there was an intangible difference in how she felt. She closed her eyes, willing herself to sleep, but the longer she lay there, the more restless she became. If only…

The door opened. She heard the swift intake of someone's breath, and she turned her head.

Ben. It was Ben. Once again her promise man had come through.

"You came," she said.

The door closed behind him as he moved toward her bed.

"I said I would."

China almost smiled. "Yes, I know."

They stared at each other without speaking. Ben felt as if he'd been away for a week instead of only one day. He wanted to take her in his arms and feel the warmth of her skin against his face, but he couldn't. Whatever he was feeling for her had nothing to do with reality.

China was silent, uneasy with her feelings. She kept staring at his face and the tenderness there—remembering how safe she'd felt within the shelter of his arms.

Suddenly he moved, and she panicked. If he came any closer, she might do something stupid, like throw herself into his arms.

"Your mother called me."

Ben stopped at the foot of her bed and then shed his coat, tossing it on a nearby chair.

"So, what did you think?"

"That she's very nice."

Ben breathed a quiet sigh of relief. "Yeah, she's that, all right."

China hesitated, then added, "She told me about her miscarriage."

Ben was surprised but didn't show it. He managed a nod. When China gave him another speculative look, he would have bet his next month's wages he knew what she was thinking.

"She said you were adopted."

And he would have been right.

"Yep, when I was about a week old. I was given up for adoption when I was born. That's about all I know."

"Does it matter to you…not knowing?"

He shook his head. "Being a cop, I've seen just about every sordid aspect of life that people can bring upon themselves. I feel thankful my mother didn't have me aborted and, if there was trouble in her life, had the good sense to give me up to shelter me from it. My adoptive parents couldn't have been any better. I consider myself blessed."

"My mother loved me very much," China said. "She left my stepfather because he was mean to me. She protected me from everything bad up until the day she died." China sighed. "That was almost five years ago, just after my twenty-first birthday, and there isn't a day goes by that I don't think of her. When I died…she was there, waiting for me,'' China said, and then looked away, shocked that she'd revealed something so personal.

For a moment Ben couldn't speak. China had spoken so casually about dying that it took him aback.

"When you died?"

China shrugged and looked away.

Ben scooted onto the edge of her bed and took both her hands in his.

"I'm not making fun of you. I just didn't know."

China looked up, her eyes swimming with tears. "I knew what had happened, but it didn't seem to matter. My baby was with me. I could hear voices welcoming me, then I saw people. My mother was there, smiling and calling my name." She took a deep breath and then shuddered. "Oh, Ben, He made me come back, said it wasn't my time. Only He sent me back alone."

Ben groaned and then took her in his arms, cradling her gently against his chest.

"But you're not alone anymore. I'm here for you. I'll always be here for you. I promise."

Her promise man had done it again. China closed her eyes and gave herself up to him—just for a moment, just long enough to remember what being safe felt like.

They sat without moving—him testing the boundaries of his emotions while China absorbed the scent of his aftershave and the feel of his hands cupping the back of her head.

And then she moved.

Ben found himself staring at her eyes, then the slight flare of her nostrils, then the curve of her lips.

The next thing he knew, he was kissing her.

Gently.

Slowly.

Imprinting the shape and texture of her mouth onto his brain.

Then again.

Urgently.

Desperately.

Wanting more than she was ready to offer.

He was the first to break away.

"China, I—"

She put her fingers on his mouth, then shook her head.

"Don't. Don't say anything…please."

He stood abruptly and shoved his hands in his pockets as he strode to the window, needing to put space between them before he made a complete fool of himself. Had he frightened her? He was almost afraid to turn around and look. Would she change her mind about staying with his mother? Ah God, not that. The killer was still out there, and he had to know she was safe.

He turned, intent on offering an apology, but she was looking away. Although he knew he'd embarrassed her, he saw something on her face that stopped him cold. He stared, trying to figure out what was different about her. And then his heart skipped a beat.

Her cheeks were pink. Her eyes were flashing. And by God, she was almost smiling.

"You going to be all right about staying with my mother?"

She looked up. "Will you be there?"

He hesitated, then nodded. "As often as I can."

Satisfied with his answer, China folded her hands in her lap.

"Then yes, if you're there, I will be all right."

Moved by the simplicity of her answer, for a moment he couldn't bring himself to speak. Suddenly he knew if he didn't leave now, he was going to make an even bigger fool of himself. He grabbed his coat and began putting it on.

"I'll see you tomorrow," he said. "Call if you need me."

China nodded, her gaze following his every movement. He was almost at the door when he stopped and turned.

"Why?" he asked.

"Why what?"

"After what Fairheart did to you, why do you trust me?"

"Promises," she said.

Ben wondered if he looked as confused as he felt. "Promises?"

"You're a smart man. You figure it out," China said. "Would you turn out the lights when you leave?"

"What? Oh…yeah, sure," Ben said, and flipped the

switch as he opened the door. Then he looked at her again. She had rolled onto her side and closed her eyes. Just for a moment, before his eyes adjusted to the dark, he thought he saw someone standing beside her bed. Then he blinked, and the image was gone.

"Sleep tight, honey. I'll see you tomorrow."

Her voice reached for him from across the room.

"Do you promise?"

"Absolutely," he said.

He was still smiling as he started down the hall. It wasn't until he reached the elevator that it hit him. Day by day she'd been judging him on the promises he made against the promises he kept. A shudder racked him as the thought slid through his mind. *Please, God, I don't ever want to let her down.*

That night, despite the underlying, inevitable noise of a hospital, China slept—without nightmares, without fear—just like she'd slept as a child, knowing her mother was near.

She woke the next morning as a nurse barged into the room with a tray of pills and carrying a sprig of mistletoe, which she promptly pinned on China's pillow.

"Something to dream on, honey," she said, and then poured some water and handed China her pills to take.

"They'll be bringing your breakfast soon," the nurse said. "Do you need help getting up and getting to the bathroom?"

"No, I can do it," China said.

"Fine, then," the nurse said. "Ring if you need me."

China made her way to the bathroom and back, ever conscious of the light-headed feeling she always had when she first stood. She hated being weak and depending on others for her care. But she was alive, which was something, and she would recover fully, Dr. Pope had promised her.

Before she got back into bed, she vaguely remembered Ben leaving one of his cards and dug through the stuff in the table drawer until she found it. Her legs were shaky, so she got back in bed before reaching for the phone, but her intent was strong. Last night, in a dream, she'd seen the woman's face again—so clearly that she'd imagined the warmth of her breath upon her own face. She'd watched her expression change from rage to a complete disregard for human life, and there was something she had to do while the image was fresh in her mind.

She glanced at the clock. It was a little before seven. Maybe she should try the home number first. She punched in the numbers, then waited, counting the rings.

Ben was just getting out of the shower when the phone began to ring.

"Well damn," he muttered, then grabbed a towel and wrapped it around his waist as he made a run for the phone.

"Hello," he said, a little breathless from the dash through the apartment.

China hesitated. He sounded out of breath and busy, and it suddenly occurred to her that his personal life might include a woman. Her mind went from that to picturing her phone call disturbing them in the act of making love.

"I'm sorry...I shouldn't have called so early. I'll call you later when you—"

"China...honey...is that you?"

"Uh, yes, but I've obviously caught you at a bad time and I can—"

"I was in the shower, that's all," he said quickly. "What's wrong?"

Her fingers curled around the receiver as she tried to picture him wet and naked. The image came through all too quickly and clearly, and she immediately bit her lip in order to focus on the pain instead of Ben.

"Nothing's wrong," she said. "But I had a dream about the woman last night, and in the dream, I saw her face so clearly. Does your department have an artist? You know, someone who can draw faces of people from a description?"

"Yes, and that's a good idea. In fact, Red and I had discussed it before, but I didn't think you were up to it."

"I want to do it," China said.

"Then it will be done. Give me a couple of hours to get everything worked out, and then we'll come to your room."

China began to relax. "All right. Uh…Ben?"

"What, honey?"

"Thank you."

"No, honey. Thank you. See you later, okay?"

"Yes, later."

She hung up and then sat quietly, contemplating what she'd just done. For the first time since the incident, she didn't feel so much like a victim, and it felt good—damn good.

Ten

China was sitting up in a wheelchair when Ben and Red arrived. Another officer was right behind them, his arms full of computer equipment.

Ben went straight to where she was sitting. He wanted to hug her but had to settle for a smile.

"Good morning, China. This is Officer Matt Avery. Just as soon as he gets set up, we'll start recreating the shooter's face."

China had expected an artist with a sketch pad, not a laptop. "You do it with a computer?" she asked.

The officer looked at China and grinned. "Just wait until you see what I can do with this thing," he said.

Ben shed his coat and began helping Avery set up his equipment, while Red sidled toward her breakfast tray.

"Good morning, Miss Brown," Red Fisher said, and then pointed to her tray. "You didn't eat your toast."

"I got full."

"Do you mind?" he asked, and picked up the toast, as well as a packet of jelly, and gave it a liberal smear before taking a bite.

Ben rolled his eyes. "For God's sake, Red, if you could see yourself."

Red shrugged and then took another bite.

"So, we can assume Rita still has you on that diet," Ben muttered.

"Yeah, but the damned thing doesn't work," he muttered around his last bite of toast.

"I wonder why?" Ben drawled, and then looked at China. "As you can see, I can't take him anywhere."

China laughed and then almost immediately was flooded with guilt. How could she be laughing at a time like this? She looked down at her hands and then at a hairline crack in the corner of the room near the window, making herself focus on anything to keep from crying.

Ben moved away from Avery and then squatted down before China's wheelchair.

"Don't," he said softly.

She wouldn't look at him. "Don't what?"

"Don't play that game with yourself. It's wrong."

"I don't know what you're talking about."

"Survivor's guilt. I've seen it time and time again." He turned her chair, making her face him. "What happened was not your fault. You weren't on the streets by choice, and you didn't pull the trigger. The fact that you didn't also die when everyone else did is a miracle, not something of which to be ashamed."

Her chin was quivering, her eyes blinded with unshed tears. In her mind, she knew he was right, but it was her heart that was having difficulties in letting go of the guilt.

"China?"

"Yes, I know," she said. "Hand me some tissues, will you?"

He handed her the box from the table and then walked away, giving her time to wipe her eyes and compose herself again.

A spoon clinked against a bowl. They all turned to look at Red.

"What?" he mumbled. "It's perfectly good oatmeal. Oatmeal is healthy. Give it a rest."

This time, when China laughed, it was easier, and when the last echo of the sound was gone, a large measure of her guilt had gone with it.

"I'm up and running, Detective English."

"Are you ready, China?" Ben asked.

She nodded.

"Good," he said, then wheeled her over to the table where Avery was waiting.

"The program Officer Avery works with has literally thousands and thousands of combinations of facial features from which to draw. You tell him what you saw, and he'll start with a face similar in structure. Between the two of you, you'll fine-tune the features individually until you're satisfied with the composite of the perpetrator's face. Understand?"

"I think so," China said.

"Anytime you get tired or want to stop for any reason, you just say so. The last thing we want to do is endanger your health.''

''Okay.''

He laid his hand on the back of her head and then allowed himself one stroke of the thick, dark length of her hair.

''Just relax, honey, and do the best you can.''

The feel of his hand on her head and then the back of her neck was distracting, but when he moved away, she felt abandoned.

''Miss Brown?''

China turned. ''Sorry,'' she told Avery. ''What do I do?''

Avery smiled. ''Talk to me. You'll see how this works as we go. We're going to start with the shape of her face and an approximate age.''

China frowned, trying to remember exactly. ''The street was almost deserted. There were lots of dark places and shadows, but we were standing in front of a bar, and there were so many Christmas lights that I got a pretty good look at her—twice. Once when we bumped into each other and then when she aimed the gun at—''

She stopped and shuddered.

''Take your time,'' Avery said. ''I know this is hard.''

''I'm fine,'' China said. ''As for her age, it would be a guess, but I will say she wasn't young.''

''By that, do you mean she was middle-aged?'' Avery asked.

"I mean she wasn't a twenty-something, or, for that matter, a thirty-something, either. She was a very beautiful but mature woman. Maybe in her late forties. Her face was oval, I think, with a strong chin and a straight nose. Very regular features."

Ben stood aside, watching the screen as a face began to take shape.

"Hey, partner, I'm going to run down to the gift shop a minute," Red said. "I need some antacids."

"Just don't come back here with chocolate on your breath or I'm telling Rita."

"Jeez, can't a man have a simple snack without starting a revolution?"

He ambled out of the room, leaving Ben to watch over the proceedings.

Ten minutes passed. Red returned and took a silent stance beside his partner. Soon a half hour had gone by. Avery's quiet but persistent questions were pulling things from China's memory that she hadn't known were there.

One eyebrow that arched slightly higher than the other.

Lips that were less than voluptuous.

By the time an hour had passed, she was pale and shaking. When she suddenly slumped forward, Ben called a halt.

"That's enough," he said, and started to push her wheelchair back toward her bed. But China grabbed his arm.

"No, wait," she said. "I need to finish this, and it

just isn't right. There's something wrong.'' She stared at the screen, taking apart the woman's face one feature at a time.

''Maybe her forehead was higher,'' Avery suggested. He typed in a series of commands, and the forehead of the face on the screen morphed into another face altogether.

''No, go back to the way it was,'' China said. ''It's not above the nose. It's something around her mouth, but I can't—'' She gasped. ''Her upper lip. That's it. Her upper lip. Make it longer and add a deep indentation. The way it is now makes her face too soft.''

Avery's fingers flew over the keyboard, and a new feature was added to the face.

''Yes!'' China cried. ''Yes. That's her! That's the woman who shot me.'' Her voice broke. ''That's the woman who killed my baby girl!'' She covered her face and started to cry.

''Wrap it up,'' Ben ordered.

Avery did as he was told. Whatever else had to be done could now be done at headquarters. Red began helping pack up the equipment, while Ben wheeled China back to her bed. Within moments they were alone. She started to stand, but Ben stopped her.

''Let me,'' he said softly, and lifted her out of the chair and then into bed.

She was limp with exhaustion and so tired of crying. ''I did it, didn't I, Ben?''

Ben straightened her legs and then pulled the covers up past her waist. There was a knot in his throat and rage in his heart. God would have to have mercy on the shooter, because he never would. He smoothed her hair away from her face and took a deep, calming breath before he trusted himself to talk.

"Yes, honey, you did it, but are you all right? Should I call a nurse? Are you in pain?"

He was reaching for the buzzer when she grabbed his wrist.

"No. No nurse."

"You're sure?"

She nodded. "I just need to rest."

"Then close your eyes."

Her eyelids fluttered, then fell, as she took a deep breath. Within moments, her breathing had slowed. Ben watched until he was certain she was falling asleep; then he turned out the light over her bed and leaned down and kissed the side of her cheek.

"Sleep tight, China. Sleep tight, and don't let the bedbugs bite."

He looked back as he reached the door, assuring himself that she was all right, then made a quiet exit. But his goodbye had slipped deep into China's subconscious, dredging up an old, but sweet memory from her youth.

"But, Mommy, I don't want to go to bed."

"School tomorrow, China Mae. Now close your eyes and think sweet dreams."

China wiggled beneath the covers and closed her eyes, but sleep wouldn't come.

"Sing to me, Mommy. Sing me one song and then I can sleep."

Mae Shubert smiled. "If I do, will you promise to be quiet?"

"Yes, Mommy, yes, I promise."

The sweet sound of Mae's voice filled the room.

"'Amazing grace, how sweet the sound. That saved a wretch like me. I once was lost, but now am found. Was blind, but now I see.'"

She sang one verse and was halfway through the second when she realized China was asleep. She stopped, leaned down and pressed a kiss on her daughter's forehead.

"Sleep tight, China doll. Sleep tight and don't let the bedbugs bite."

China smiled in her sleep. It was good to see her mother again.

Mona Wakefield paid the cab driver and then hurried into the Galleria to get out of the cold. Her pantsuit was fashionable but less than suitable for the December weather. The fabric was too thin to protect her from the piercing wind gusts, and while she could have worn any one of the dozen or more coats that she owned, she hadn't wanted to be burdened with hiding what she'd worked so hard to present—namely herself. The smug expression on her face was partly due to the fact that she was about to embark upon her favorite thing, which was shopping, and also due to the fact that she'd eluded Bobby Lee's watchful eye. She shifted the strap of her purse to a more comfortable position on her shoulder and set off down the mall with purposeful strides. The aroma of cinnamon and popcorn filled the air, reminiscent of the upcoming holiday. As she strolled from store to store, she took great pleasure in the surprised glances and second looks her appearance was eliciting. God, but she loved the fame, even if it was secondhand.

Bobby Lee slammed down the receiver and then turned with a jerk and pointed a finger at Ainsley Been.

"Delia says my mother is not at home. You told me she was taking a nap."

Ainsley paled. "But that's what she told me she was going to do when I stopped by the house to pick up that file I left yesterday. Besides, I'm not her keeper, and what's the big deal? Maybe she decided to go out. She's a grown woman. Surely she doesn't need your approval before she makes a move."

"Big deal? What's the big deal, you say?" He grabbed Ainsley by the lapels of his suit and pulled him to within inches of his face. "If you want to ride my coattails all the way to the White House, then you'd better learn to become her keeper. You don't know what hell Mona is capable of, and by God, you better hope you never find out."

Ainsley's eyes bugged and his mouth dropped. He'd never seen Bobby Lee so upset.

"Okay, okay," he muttered, and peeled himself out

of Bobby Lee's grasp. "I'll see what I can find out. Meantime, you settle down now, you hear? You wouldn't want the media to get wind of the fact that you think your mother needs a keeper."

He escaped without further comment, thanking his lucky stars that all he'd gotten were new orders. For a minute there he'd thought Bobby Lee was going to hit him.

Bobby Lee strode to the window overlooking downtown Dallas. This should have been a time of regrouping. The senate was not in session, and the family business more or less ran itself, although he showed up at the office now and then, as he was doing today. The oil business wasn't as profitable as it had once been, but Wakefield Industries had diversified years ago. The Wakefields might not be old money, but they had a whole hell of a lot of the new stuff. Yet for Bobby Lee, it was never enough. It wasn't about money; it was about power. He liked to play games, like buying industries on the brink of bankruptcy and then selling them for huge profits. In the old days, before he'd become Senator, his peers had called him a shark. The fact that he made money was almost incidental to the joy he received in being in control. Now he'd embarked upon the ultimate power trip, and God help anyone who got in his way—including his mother.

It wasn't even noon, and Connie Marx was pouring herself another drink. She tossed it back with a grimace and then poured herself another as she resumed her pacing between the wet bar in her living room and the computer she kept in her bedroom. The blinking screen mocked her, as did the text she'd typed days before. It was a letter of resignation that she had yet to hand in, and therein lay her dilemma. Delay could mean the end of her career. If she quit, she could begin that book she'd always been going to write. Then later, when things cooled off, which they were bound to do, she could wend her way back into broadcasting, maybe with a bestseller under her belt. But if she waited and wound up getting fired, she would never work in the business again.

"Goddamn it," she muttered, and downed her drink, then spun and threw the empty shot glass at the wall, hitting the picture of Larry Dee Jackson right between the eyes. "It's all your fault, you amorous jackass. If you'd kept your big mouth shut, none of this would be happening."

Within seconds the phone rang. Startled, she spun and ran to answer. It had been days since she'd talked to anyone, including Larry Dee.

"Hello?"

"Hey, Connie, it's me, Ronnie Boyle."

The familiar voice of her coanchor was surprising. He had never called her at home. In fact, they didn't even like each other. At least, she damn sure didn't like him.

"Ronnie."

Boyle caught the cautious tone in her voice and

knew he was going to have to play loose to make this work.

"Just thought I'd check in and see how you're doing. We miss you, you know."

"Really?"

He grimaced and tried another tack. "Look, Connie, I want you to know I think you're getting a raw deal. No one believes you had anything to do with the shootings. I mean…hell, you report stories like that, not cause them, right?"

"Look, Ronnie, I appreciate the call, but I'm kinda busy. Thanks for—"

"Wait!"

She sighed. "What?"

"How about an exclusive? Are you really having an affair with Larry Jackson? He's news, Connie, and we both know it. The public has a right to—"

"Who the fucking hell are you working for—Channel 7 or the tabloids? As for the public, they can go straight to hell with you."

She hung up the phone and then yanked the jack from the wall and threw the phone across the room.

"Damn you, Boyle, damn Larry Dee, and damn you Chaz Finelli for starting this mess. I hope you're in hell, because it's where you belong."

Ariel Simmons took a deep breath and then exited her dressing room, making her way from backstage toward the podium and the awaiting crowd. Tonight the congregation had spilled out into the parking lot of the amphitheater where her broadcast was being held. Many of those in attendance were regulars—people who believed in her ministry—and then there were the others who'd come to see the woman who was under suspicion for murder. She'd heard the gossip. Everyone knew about the picture of her in leather and brandishing a whip. They'd come to see the woman who preached the word on Sundays and played with the devil on Saturday nights. Damn Chaz Finelli. She still didn't know how he'd gotten that picture, but there was nothing she could do but bluff her way through. Commandment or not, she would gladly shoot Chaz Finelli a thousand times over if it would make this all go away.

"Sister Simmons, are you ready?"

She turned. Her producer was watching her. Even he was treating her differently. The rage that had been bubbling within her began to boil over. She'd come too far from the backwoods of Mississippi to be stopped now.

"Yes, I'm ready," she said, and strode onto the stage, her pale-blue gown floating about her ankles like clouds too low to the ground.

The murmuring crowd was suddenly silent as Ariel thrust her hands upward, as if beseeching God to hear.

"I am being tested!" she cried, and before anyone could react, she doubled up her fists and shook them toward the crowd. "Satan is trying to silence the Word. He's poisoned the minds of the law and the media and all of you who doubt me now. He's putting evil in my path at every turn, but hear me now!'' Her voice rose to a scream. ''I will not be overcome! God is my sword. He is my shield. I am an innocent lamb, but I will not be slaughtered in Satan's name.''

Then she fell to her knees, her long blond hair falling over her shoulders and onto the stage as she prostrated herself before the crowd.

They came to their feet as one, crying and shouting. The people began wailing and praying aloud, shamed that they'd believed, even for a minute, that this delicate angel of God could be guilty of even one measure of the gossip being spread.

Ariel lay immobile, her face hidden beneath her arms. When she felt the floor shaking from the thousands of stomping feet and heard the wailing of the crowd, she smiled.

Rod Stewart music rocked the walls of the cabin as the woman strutted before the cheval mirror standing in the corner. The red silk against her skin and the long blond hair brushing against her neck were aphrodisiacs. But the music was her anthem—her high. And there was only one thing she needed now to complete the mood. She paused before the mirror to stare at the picture she'd taped to the surface. Dark eyes stared back at her from a chocolate-brown face. It didn't matter to her what color a man's skin was as long as he had what it took to set her on fire, and from everything she'd been told about this man, he was a walking flame and none too picky about who or what turned him on.

She liked that in a man—someone who was willing to experiment.

"Hurry, my darling," she whispered, then touched herself lightly, fondling her breasts, sliding her hands between her legs.

The loose silk of the caftan wrapped around her hands as she pressed them against her body, and she closed her eyes and let her head fall back, playing out the sexual fantasy of a man's hands upon her. It felt good—so good. The blood began to pulse within her to the beat of the music. She opened her eyes, watching her own face as she began to pleasure herself.

Suddenly the lights of a car swept across the wall behind her, and she stilled, her heart pounding, still cupping herself. A slow sigh slid from between her lips, and then she smiled.

"Just in time," she whispered, and headed for the door.

Just after daybreak, the nude and lifeless body of LaShon Fontana was found near a Dumpster in Garland. The media arrived at the same time the coroner's car pulled up.

"Christ almighty," someone said. "Tell me it isn't so. Tell me that's not Fancy Feet Fontana."

But it was. All six feet five inches of pure muscled perfection—pride of the Dallas Slickers and the best running back in the league for three years straight—with a bullet through the back of his head. Four hours later they found his abandoned car at a convenience

mart with all his clothes inside. A few hundred work-
ers had mourned the death of Tashi Yamamoto, and
only then because of losing their jobs, but the state of
Texas and the nation had gone into mourning over
Fontana's death. The Garland police department was
overwhelmed with media camping on their doorstep.
But it wasn't until late that afternoon that the real shit
hit the fan. Someone in the Dallas crime lab got curious and ran a test on the bullet that killed Fontana
to see if it matched the bullet that killed Yamamoto.
It did, and not only that, they also got a match on one
of the bullets they had dug out of Chaz Finelli. The
police commissioner then ordered a series of tests to
be run on all the unsolved murders in the Dallas-Fort
Worth area with similar profiles. By nightfall, there
were six matches.

Ronnie Boyle broke the story on the 10:00 p.m.
news. Even the death of Fancy Feet Fontana took second place to the fact that there was a serial killer in
their midst.

Connie Marx sat on her living room sofa with a
bottle of Scotch between her legs, a shot glass in her
hand and tears streaming down her face. Last month,
this would have been her story. She would have been
the one covering the updates. But thanks to Chaz
Finelli, she was part of the sordid affair. She poured
herself another drink and then tossed it back as if she
were taking medicine. With each passing minute, her
rage and sense of injustice grew. If Chaz Finelli hadn't

already been dead, she would willingly have killed him.

Homicide was in an uproar at the Dallas P.D. The governor had called the commissioner, expressing his concerns over the recent revelations. A tactical meeting had just taken place in which Captain Floyd had established a task force on the Finelli and Yamamoto murders, with Ben English as the primary and Red Fisher as second in command. Everyone who wasn't already tied up on serious cases had been ordered to give this top priority. All information was to be shared with both the Garland police department and the Arlington police departments, since they, too, had open cases that were now connected to the whole.

The picture that Avery and China had made the day before was being distributed to every police department in the area and had also been released to all the media. By morning, that face would be in every newspaper and on every television station in the area.

That was the good news.

The bad news was that, inevitably, someone would ask who'd given them the ID.

China was no longer safe.

Eleven

Mattie English alternated between pacing the floor and staring out the window. The sun was setting, and she still hadn't heard from Ben, although she'd left two messages for him to call. Ever since she'd heard last night's news, she hadn't been able to get China Brown out of her mind. The poor girl had to be terrified, knowing that she was the only witness to a serial killer. It also occurred to Mattie that by having China stay with her, she was putting her own life in danger, but she couldn't bring herself to say no. The memory of the heartbreak she'd heard in China Brown's voice was stronger than her fear.

Just as she was passed the phone, it rang. Startled, she jumped, then grabbed the receiver.

"English residence."

"Mom, it's me."

"Ben, what on earth is going on? Is China all right? Has the media gotten wind of her identity?"

"She's fine, and thank God, no. Look, Mom, I think maybe we need to rethink this visit. Having her on the ranch could put both of you in danger."

"We'll be fine," she said. "Dave will be here, remember? Besides, I've lived in the shadow of life for too long. A little excitement might be just what I need.''

Ben snorted lightly beneath his breath. ''Mother, we're not talking about a trip to Six Flags, we're talking about a serial killer. I love you. I don't want you hurt.''

''What about China? How do you feel about her?'' Mattie countered.

There was a moment of total silence, and then Ben completely ignored both her questions.

''The only way this is happening is if the both of you are under twenty-four hour watch. Dave will watch you during the day. I'm staying there at night.''

''That's quite a drive to make each morning,'' she said, reminding him that it was more than half an hour from the ranch to the city.

''I think you're worth it,'' he said. ''Both of you.''

Mattie pursed her lips. She'd been right all along. There *was* more to Ben's feelings for China than duty.

''That's it, then,'' she said. ''When can I expect you?''

''As soon as it gets dark. I don't want to take a chance on some snoopy journalist recognizing me, then seeing me with a convalescing woman and putting two and two together.''

''I'll be waiting,'' Mattie said. ''Drive safely, Bennie. I love you.''

''I love you, too, Mom,'' he said.

He was frowning when he hung up the phone. Bennie. Hell. She hadn't called him that in years. She must really be worried. Well, it was his job to make sure she didn't have anything to worry about. He put on his coat, then picked up a handful of files and dropped them on another detective's desk as he walked by.

"Merry Christmas," he said. "The captain has taken me off everything except the Finelli case. If you have any questions about my notes, just yell."

The detective rolled his eyes and then grinned. "How loud?"

"At least let me get out of the station," Ben said, and then added, "Thanks. I owe you big time."

"I won't let you forget it," the second detective said.

But Ben already had. His thoughts were on China and getting her out of Parkland Hospital unobserved. He also needed to talk to her doctor and make sure that everything about China Brown's stay at that hospital ceased to exist—at least for the time being.

China was dressed and waiting for Ben to arrive. Tonight she was leaving the sanctity of the hospital, and she was more than a little bit scared. After all the hospital gowns, it felt strange to be wearing her own clothes again, even though they'd been in the closet in her room since she'd been moved out of the ICU. It had been a battle of wills not to cry as she'd pulled up her sweats. The last time she'd worn these clothes, they'd been tight across her tummy. Now there was no baby, only a long, healing scar. She'd managed her pants, but had to ring for help from a nurse to get her sweatshirt over her head. She had several months of rehabilitation ahead of her before her arm would be back to normal, but Dr. Pope had assured her that it would eventually heal. Until then, her infirmities would be constant reminders of the ordeal she so badly wanted to forget.

She walked to the door and peeked out, hoping to see Ben coming down the hall, but all she got was a polite nod from the guard stationed outside her door.

"You'd best keep the door closed, miss," he said quietly.

China sighed as she let it shut. How long would this enforced imprisonment last? What if they never caught the killer? Would she have to stay in hiding for the rest of her life? Overwhelmed by the thought of the troubles ahead of her, she crawled back into bed. Wincing a bit, she rolled over on her side and closed her eyes, but sleep wouldn't come. Her thoughts were full of what lay ahead. Not only was she going into hiding, but she would be doing it with strangers. Trust had always come easy to China—too easy. But that was before. Now, everyone was a threat. Except for Ben English. So far, he'd proved himself trustworthy in every way. Ben. Her promise man.

And with the thought, in he came, carrying a sack and striding through the door with purposeful intent and flanked by three uniformed officers, her doctor and a nurse pushing a wheelchair.

"It's time," Ben said.

China started to sit up and then groaned. Immediately Ben was at her side.

"Here, honey, let me," he said, and scooted his arm beneath her shoulder and lifted her to a sitting position. "Okay?"

She nodded.

Dr. Pope stepped forward and put a hand on her knee. "You're a remarkable woman, Miss Brown. I'm sorry we met under these circumstances, but I can truthfully say that it would have been my loss had I never known you."

"Thank you, Dr. Pope, for everything you've done for me."

Ross Pope smiled, then glanced at Ben. "They're ready for you now, and you're ready to go. If you have any concerns, you know how to reach me. Continue the pain medicine I gave you, and I'll call in a prescription for you, which Detective English has assured me he will see that you get. Take care and God bless."

Impulsively, China wrapped her arms around the doctor's neck.

"You saved my life," she said softly. "I won't waste it."

"Let's get you in the wheelchair," the nurse said.

"I can walk," China said.

The nurse shook her head. "Hospital rules."

"It's cold outside," Ben said, and handed her the sack.

She looked inside, and then her eyes filled. It was a new coat. She hadn't thought once of the condition of her old one, but it dawned on her that it had probably been ruined by bullet holes and blood.

"Oh, Ben."

He took it out and held it up for her to put on.

She put one arm in and then the other, enveloped by the weight and warmth of the blue wool. When she stood, the hem of it reached the backs of her knees.

Ben reached for the edges and buttoned it up.

"Good, it fits," he said, and let the hood hang down her back. He added quietly, so only she could hear, "It's the color of your eyes."

While she was still digesting the fact that he'd been thoughtful enough to provide her with a coat, she had to accept the fact that he'd also picked one out that matched her eyes.

She sat down in the wheelchair. Ben picked up her bag, then set it in her lap as the nurse began pushing her toward the door.

"Just a minute," Ben said, and opened the door and stepped out into the hall, looking first one way and then the other. "Okay," he said. "Bring her out."

Everything seemed to move past her in a blur. Flanked by the uniformed officers, with Ben taking the lead, they headed for the service elevator at a fast pace. China's last few impressions were the scent of antiseptic, the sound of someone laughing, and a television playing too loudly in a room somewhere down the hall, and then they were in the elevator. All too soon they'd reached the ground floor.

Again Ben was the first to step out, and as he did,

China realized he had taken his gun out of his holster. The sight of it in his hand made her sick. The urge to bolt and run was strong, but where would she go? Then sanity returned, and she closed her eyes and took a deep breath. These people weren't the enemy. They were here to protect her.

"Okay," Ben said shortly. "Bring her out."

Seconds later they were in a parking garage and headed toward a light-gray sedan. A cold wind whipped through the area, and China was grateful for the warmth of the coat.

"Easy, honey," Ben said, as he helped her into his car.

The absurdity of the moment seemed surreal. The wind on her face. The scent of leather from the interior of his car. The satiny comfort of the coat lining. The uniformed officers outside the car with weapons drawn. She wasn't just being released from the hospital. She was going into hiding.

She had settled in her seat and was buckling the seat belt across her lap when Ben got inside. Almost immediately the car seemed smaller. His presence beside her seemed threatening until she happened to catch him looking at her for assurance. When she gave him a tentative smile, he seemed to relax.

"I know this is tough for you," Ben said. "But in my business, there's no such thing as being too cautious."

"It's all right. After all, you're doing this for my benefit."

"Good," he said. "Now here's the deal. I'm taking you straight to Mom's. It's already dark, so we won't be spotted. The ranch is isolated enough that you can pretty much move about as you feel like it. You just won't be leaving the ranch until we've caught the killer. So far, your identity is protected, but we can't take any chances, understand?"

She bit her lower lip and then nodded.

"Are you feeling all right?" Ben asked. "If you're uncomfortable, you can lie down in the back or—"

China laid her hand on his arm. "I'm fine."

"I won't let anything happen to you, China. I promise."

"I know."

The trust in her eyes humbled him and, at the same time, scared him to death. As she leaned back in her seat and folded her hands in her lap, he started the car, waved off the officers and drove out of the parking garage into the night.

Within the hour Ben was pulling into the yard of his childhood home. He killed the engine, then glanced over at his passenger. She'd fallen asleep before they'd cleared the streets of Dallas, and he'd played a game with himself all the way to the ranch, pretending that they had been together for years and had been out on the town, and then, on the way home, she had just fallen asleep. It was frightening to accept that this woman was stealing his heart.

As he sat, she began to stir, then slowly opened her eyes.

"Are we here?"

"We're here. Welcome home."

He got out and circled the car, intent on helping her inside. But China was still trying to absorb the sweetness of the invitation he'd given her.

Home.

He'd welcomed her home.

What would it be like to have a home with this man, to never know uncertainty or hunger again—to feel safe and loved?

China shuddered. Loved? Where had that come from?

Ben opened the car door and slipped a hand under her elbow.

"Easy does it, honey. I'll get you in the house and come back for your bag."

"All right," China said, and scooted to the edge of the seat before allowing herself to stand.

Stiff muscles protested as she braced herself against the sharp bite of the wind. Almost immediately, Ben put himself between her and the blast, and then slipped an arm around her shoulder.

"Lean on me," he said, as they started toward the house.

China wouldn't look at him or let herself comment. She was too taken aback by the notion of doing that very thing. She was only here because she was valuable to them as a witness. Leaning on Bennett English would be all too easy to do, but she had to remember that one day this would be over, and when it was, his duty to her would be over, as well.

As they reached the porch, the front door swung open. China had a moment's impression of a gray-haired woman in blue jeans and a red flannel shirt, a Christmas wreath hanging on the front door, and then she was whisked inside.

"Mother, this is China Brown. China, this is my mother, Mattie English."

In typical Mattie fashion, she held out her hand. "Welcome to my home. You look chilled. Let's get that coat off you and come in by the fire."

"Thank you, ma'am," China said.

Mattie stopped. "No *ma'am,* remember? Call me Mattie." She looked at Ben. "Well, what are you waiting for…Christmas? Go get her bag and take it to her room. I put her in the east room."

"Yes, ma'am," Ben said, then winked at China. "I swear her bark is worse than her bite."

"Get," Mattie said. "And don't dawdle in the doorway. You let in too much cold air." She took China's coat, hung it on a rack in the hall and took her by the elbow. "Can you walk all right, dear? We'll go slow."

"I'm okay," China said. "Just a little stiff. The pain is pretty manageable now. Not like before."

Mattie hesitated, giving the young woman a careful look. She wasn't very tall, probably no more than four or five inches over five feet. Her hair was thick and dark and looked as if she'd been cutting it herself for years. Her face had a fragile, delicate beauty that made her seem weak until Mattie looked in her eyes. That was where her strength shone through.

"You're a tough one, aren't you, girl?" Mattie murmured.

"I've had to be." Then she looked a bit nervous. "At least, I have been up until now. Ben thinks I'm in danger."

"Ben is a good man and a good cop. He will see that you're protected."

"Yes," China said. "He promised not to let anything happen to me. He's a man who keeps his promises."

Mattie nodded, for the moment satisfied with her houseguest.

"Now, let's get you a chair by the fire. I made some hot chocolate earlier. Would you care for a cup?"

A pensive smile broke the somberness of China's face. "Mother used to make hot chocolate for us on cold nights."

Mattie nodded. "Sounds like a smart woman."

"Yes, ma'am, that she was."

"Mattie! Not ma'am. Now put your feet up on this stool and close your eyes. I'll be back in a bit with the chocolate."

China did as she was told, thankful she wasn't having to make any decisions.

The warmth of the fire and the peacefulness of the house lulled her. Once again, she dozed. When she woke, Ben was coming into the room carrying a tray with the mugs of hot chocolate. Mattie was right behind him with a plate of cookies.

"Smells wonderful," China said, as Ben handed her a cup.

"One lump or two?" Ben asked, holding out a bowl of miniature marshmallows, rather than cubes of sugar.

Surprised by his playfulness, China slipped into similar character as she peered into the bowl. "They're rather small."

Ben grinned. "Then allow me," he said, and dropped a handful into her mug, then handed her a spoon. "Knock yourself out, kid."

Mattie sat on the sofa sipping her chocolate and watching them spar, wondering if they knew how obvious they were—wondering if they knew they were falling in love.

Within the hour, China caught herself nodding off. Ben saw her and got to his feet.

"You're done for, honey," he said softly, and lifted her out of the chair and into his arms.

China woke abruptly. Embarrassed that Ben was doing this in front of his mother, she began to argue.

"I can walk."

"Humor me," Ben said, and headed down the hall toward her room.

Mattie watched, again without comment. But she'd seen enough to know that her son was in over his head. This woman was part of a case—a witness to a murder—and he was falling in love.

Ben carried China into the room she'd been given and then set her down on the edge of the bed.

"Your things are on that chair," Ben said. "There's a new toothbrush in the bathroom drawer and fresh towels in the cabinet beneath, although I laid one out for you for tonight. Do you want to shower tonight, or in the morning?"

"I'll shower in the morning," China said.

"Don't try to do it by yourself," Ben said. "When you're ready, give us a yell. Mom will be glad to help."

China nodded. "She's really nice—your mom."

Ben smiled. "Yeah, she's pretty great."

"I think she wishes I wasn't here," China said; then, embarrassed that she'd even brought it up, she added, "Not that I blame her."

Ben's smile stopped. "Why would you say that?"

China's face flamed, and she looked away, unable to meet his gaze. "I think she wishes...I mean, I think she believes that I...that we..."

Ben turned her head, making her look at him.

"And that would be bad?" he asked.

China shook her head. "Yes...no...well, from her point of view, yes. But it's okay...I mean, I don't blame her for being concerned. You're her son. Of course she would want the best for you."

"And why would that exclude you?"

China's chin quivered once, and then she shrugged.

"Get real, Detective. I'm homeless and involved in a very ugly crime. I'm obviously not too smart or I would never have involved myself with someone like Tommy Fairheart and I'm not much to look at.''

Ben was flabbergasted. He didn't know what to respond to first, but the most obvious was her reference to her looks.

''Who told you that?'' he snapped.

''Told me what?'' China asked.

''That you weren't much to look at? Was it Fairheart, because if it was, I can—''

''Oh, no,'' China said. ''I've known that all my life.''

Ben couldn't believe what he was hearing. She wasn't kidding. She really believed she was homely.

''Who told you that?'' he repeated.

China looked up at him then, a little surprised by his anger.

''Clyde.''

''And who in hell is this Clyde?''

''He was my stepfather, until my mother divorced him.''

Ben stood abruptly. ''Was he blind? For that matter, honey, are you? Don't you know how beautiful you are?''

China was stunned. All she could do was shake her head.

''Well, you are,'' Ben said shortly. ''Now get in bed before I say something we'll both regret, and remember, if you need anything during the night, just call out. My room is right across the hall.''

He strode out of her room, leaving his anger behind him.

China sat without moving, reliving the last moments of their conversation over and over until her mind was reeling. Finally she made her way to the adjoining bathroom and started to undress. As she did, she caught a glimpse of herself in the mirror and stopped to look, then abruptly looked away.

Ben had lied. There wasn't anything pretty about her, and she could prove it. If she was beautiful, as he'd claimed, then why did men treat her as they did? From her earliest memory, men had ridiculed her, beaten her and lied to her. It would take more than words to make her change her mind.

She got her nightgown from her bag and then began to undress. Painfully, she managed to get her sweat-shirt over her head. She laid it on the side of the tub and was reaching for a washcloth when she caught another glimpse of herself in the full-length mirror hanging on the back of the door. Her eyes widened in quiet horror as she touched her breast and the red puckering scar above it. Then her gaze slid lower, to the beginning of the scar that showed just above the waistband of her sweats. With shaking hands, she pushed the elastic down, then down some more, finally stepping out of her clothes until it had been completely revealed. Her tummy was almost flat again—a painful reminder of what she'd lost. But it was the fiery scar down her belly that put everything into perspective.

Damaged goods. In every way that counted, she was damaged goods.

In a rush of panic, she grabbed her nightgown and yanked it over her head. Ignoring the pain of sudden movement, she wouldn't look at herself again until she was completely covered. Only after she felt the night-gown brushing against her ankles and had buttoned the last button would she turn and face herself in the mirror.

The look on her face was not unlike that of a deer caught in the headlights of a car—frightened, but rather fatalistic. She reached for her washcloth again and let the water run until it was warm. Methodically she washed her face, brushed her teeth, then her hair and then turned out the light. Carefully she made her way to the bed and crawled between the covers. The pillow was soft, the mattress and fresh bed linens smelling of springtime—nothing like the antiseptic smell of the hospital. A strong gust of wind rattled the windows on the other side of the room. She pulled the covers up to her chin and closed her eyes. Down the hall, she could just hear the murmur of voices as mother and son continued to talk. Somewhere outside these walls, a killer was waiting for another chance to finish what she had started.

In the back of China's mind, she could almost hear her mother calling out to her.

Sleep tight, China doll. Sleep tight and don't let the bedbugs bite.

She started to cry, and once the tears began to fall,

they just wouldn't stop. She had survived thus far, and even if she somehow managed to survive the rest of this horrible mess, there was nothing in her future but loneliness. And right now, it was the loneliness that was hardest to bear.

Betty, Ariel Simmons's maid, was just coming into her bedroom with some tea when Ariel sneezed several times in succession and then moaned softly as she reached for some fresh tissues and tossed the others into the trash.

Betty quickly set the tea tray aside and rushed to Ariel's bed.

"Miss Simmons, do you want me to call your doctor? You sound just awful."

Ariel managed a pitiful smile and shook her head. "No, dear, I will be fine. A good night's sleep will help, I'm sure."

"But you look feverish."

Ariel put a hand against her own forehead and sank back against the bank of pillows behind her.

"I suppose I am, a little, but this past week has been draining on my spirit. Satan always comes at you when you're at your weakest, you know. Just put the tea here by my bed where I can reach it and hand me my Bible. I'll read a bit before I go to sleep. It will be better medicine than any pills the doctor could bring."

Betty's eyes teared. "Yes, ma'am. You're right. Will there be anything else?"

"No, dear. You go on to bed now, you hear?"

"Yes, ma'am."

She exited the room, closing the door quietly behind her.

The moment she was gone, Ariel sat straight up in bed and checked the time. It was five minutes to ten. Betty's routine was set in stone. She would sneak her three shots of whiskey that she thought no one knew about, and by ten-thirty she would be out like a light. And that was what Ariel was counting on.

She flung her handful of tissues into the trash and jumped out of bed, her "illness" disappearing as miraculously as it had appeared. Dressing quickly in dark clothing and tennis shoes, she pulled a black stocking cap over her hair and made her way downstairs. The grandfather clock in the hallway began to strike as she reached the last step.

Perfect. Betty would be sound asleep. But just to make sure, Ariel made a quick sweep through the kitchen and down the hall to the servants' quarters. She could hear Betty's snores before she reached the door. Pivoting sharply, she retraced her steps, disarmed the security system and slipped out the front door. Her car was too recognizable to take, so she slipped through the hedge to the garage in back and quietly rolled a small black motorbike out onto the street before she started it up. The power of the engine between her legs made her shudder with want, but this was no time to give in to her lust. She sped off into the night.

Hours later, on the other side of the city, a small fire suddenly sprang to life inside an abandoned warehouse. Within minutes a wall of flames was devouring the guts of it, destroying everything in its path. The first fire trucks arrived on the scene with a noisy blast of sirens, drowning out the sounds of the motorbike's exit.

It was 3:00 a.m. when Ariel Simmons slipped back into her house. She reset the security alarm, double-checked Betty's room to make sure she was still asleep and then sauntered up her stairs. She stripped off her clothes and tossed them in a bag of clothing that was going to Goodwill, took a shower to wash the scent of smoke from her body and crawled into bed.

Without saying her prayers, she closed her eyes and fell fast asleep, secure in the knowledge that she could never be linked to that picture again. The leather, the chains, even the black silk and whips, had just gone up in smoke.

Twelve

"Good morning, Senator. How would you like your eggs?"

"Morning, Delia," Bobby Lee said. "I'm thinking I'll have my hen fruit poached today, and bring me some bacon and toast, too."

"Yes, sir," Delia said, as she poured him a cup of freshly brewed coffee. "You just sit yourself down and enjoy your paper. I'll be back shortly."

"Thank you, Delia," Bobby Lee said, as he reached for his cup.

"Oh, Senator…is your mama awake?"

"I don't think so," he said. "Just go on and tell cook to fix my food. If Mother comes down before I'm through, I'll ring."

"Yes, sir," Delia said, then set the coffeepot down and left.

Bobby Lee took a careful sip of the brew, then leaned back in his chair and opened the paper. A woman's face was centered right below the headline which read "Serial Killer at Large." The coffee hung at the back of his throat as he forgot to swallow. When he gasped in shock, the coffee rerouted itself through his nose. The paper fell to the floor as he grabbed for his napkin, saving his clean shirt and suit from stains as the scalding liquid seared the hairs inside his nose.

"Jesus Christ!" he yelped, and dabbed at himself until he was certain all the coffee had been blotted.

He picked up the paper again, his horrified gaze fixed upon the woman's face. How could this be? In the midst of panic, his mother walked in.

"I heard you cussin' all the way down the hall. What's got you riled up so early in the morning?"

"Burned my mouth on hot coffee," he muttered.

"Poor baby," she said, and sauntered toward the sideboard to pour herself a cup.

The fact that she was actually dressed this morning should have been a relief. But her clothes or lack thereof were the least of Bobby Lee's worries. He stared at her then as if he'd never seen her before—at the long blond hair falling over one shoulder, at the mouth a shade too thin to be truly sexy, at her large, puppy dog eyes and the thrust of her chin. Feature by feature, her face would have been unremarkable, but together, somehow they were a thing of beauty—and a damn sight too close to the woman in the paper for his peace of mind.

He knew that it was only a stroke of luck that his mother had never been implicated in the Finelli investigation. By her own words, she had not been recognizable in the picture that Finelli had used in his blackmail. And it had been another stroke of luck that John Woodley had come up with a fail-safe alibi for the night of the murders. The fact that Woodley had known enough to keep his mouth shut about the woman he'd been with had been entirely due to a phone call from Bobby Lee himself. This, however, was another kettle of fish.

Mona flashed him a smile as she sat down. In that moment, Bobby Lee knew what to do. He laid the paper aside and then reached for her hand.

"Mother, I want to tell you something."

Mona was surprised but pleased by the tenderness of his gesture. More times than not they were fighting, and she did love her son more than life.

"What is it, Bobby Lee?"

"Lately, with the stress of the announcement and all the stuff that goes with it, I confess I haven't been myself. I feel I've been short-tempered with you, and I regret it and want to make it up to you."

Mona beamed. "Now, honey, you don't have to do any such thing. Mothers understand about things like that. You know you're my pride and joy. I would do *anything* for you. *Anything*."

It was the *anything* that made him nervous.

"I know, and I for you," he said. "I have a surprise."

Mona clapped her hands. "Oh, Bobby Lee, you know how I like surprises."

He grinned. "Yes, ma'am, that I do."

"What is it, Bobby Lee?"

"I know Christmas is still a few days away, but I want to give you your Christmas present early. How would you like a two-week vacation at the spa of your choice? Have daily massages, go shopping at all the best places, play tennis or even lie around a pool all day if that's what you want?''

Mona was ecstatic. Next to shopping, pleasuring herself was her favorite thing.

"Oooh, Bobby Lee, it sounds perfect. To get away from this awful·old cold weather—I can't think of anything I'd like better.''

"Wonderful,'' he said. "Then it's decided. When I get to the office, I'll have Duffy get your reservation. How about L.A.? You can do Hollywood. Shop on Rodeo Drive, do the town up right.''

Mona squealed.

He grinned and then gave her a casual glance, as if assessing her features.

"You know what else you should do while you're down there?''

"What?''

"Have yourself one of those makeovers. If I'm going to be the next president, I want you shining by my side.''

Mona began to frown, uncomfortable with the idea that she didn't look perfect. But Bobby Lee had been ready for that. He wasn't through piling on the bull.

"You're such a beautiful woman, Mother. I want your best qualities accentuated, and where better to do it than in Hollywood, where perfection is a business? What do you think?''

When she looked at it from that angle, it made perfect sense.

''I think you're the best son a woman could have,'' she said.

Bobby Lee leaned back in his chair, his scalded nose forgotten. When his mother came back, she would look nothing like that woman in the paper, and that would be that.

China had been awake for some time when she heard the sounds of people stirring outside her door. Although she could not distinguish what they were saying, she could tell that there was great love between mother and son. The tone of Mattie's voice was teasing yet gentle, and Ben's laughter proved the camaraderie between the two was comfortable. It made her homesick for her mother. They'd laughed like that—before Mae had died.

Footsteps faded. She supposed they had moved to the kitchen. Ben would soon be leaving for Dallas. The thought of not seeing him again until nightfall had her rolling out of bed. As she stood, it dawned on her that she wasn't as sore as she'd been the day before. So Dr. Pope had been right. Her body was healing. She sighed. If only it were that easy to heal a spirit.

She made her way to the bathroom, taking time to pick out some clothes to wear for the day. There was a shower to take and hair to brush—things she'd once taken for granted and dashed through without thought.

Now she had to plan her moves so as not to cause herself pain.

The warm water felt good on her body. The light, peppering spray was like a body massage, loosening tight muscles as well as her nerves. By the time she emerged, she was feeling much better. When she reached for a towel, she realized that the full-length mirror had fogged over. So much the better, she thought. At least she wouldn't have to face the hideousness of her physical self.

A few minutes later she emerged from the bathroom wearing an old shirt and jeans. The last time she'd worn the jeans was back in the spring, before her belly had started to grow. They were loose on her frame, evidence of the weight that she'd lost during her hospital stay. The shirt had seen better days, but the snaps were what sold her. They were easier to fasten than pulling another sweatshirt over her head. Carrying her socks and a band for her ponytail, she left the anonymity of her room.

Although her entrance was silent, Ben seemed to sense her arrival before she spoke. He looked up. China braced herself.

"Good morning," he said. "How did you sleep?"

Mattie turned around, a pancake turner in her hand.

"Welcome. I hope you brought your appetite," she said. "Breakfast is almost ready."

"The bed was very comfortable, thank you. Something smells good."

"Good," Ben said, although he noted she hadn't

really answered his question. A comfortable bed did not necessarily make for a good night's sleep. Then he noticed she was carrying her socks and shoes. "Need some help?" he asked, and was up before she could answer.

She hesitated, then handed them over. "Yes, I'm sorry to have to ask, but—"

Ben's voice was almost angry. "Don't apologize for something that's not your fault."

She took a seat at the table as he knelt before her. Once she glanced up at Mattie, a little nervous as to how the woman would construe her son on his knees before her. But Mattie seemed focused on taking eggs out of a skillet. China looked down at Ben, watching the gentle way in which he pulled up her socks, then reached for her shoes. As he turned, she noticed a backward swirl in his hair right at the crown. Without thinking, she touched it.

"I'll bet you had a time keeping that combed when you were a little boy."

The touch of her hand in his hair gave Ben the shivers. To his relief, his mother spoke, saving him from making a fool of himself.

"That cowlick, you mean? I'll show you some pictures later. You should have seen it. Are you familiar with the little boy who played Alfalfa on *The Little Rascals?*"

China smiled. "The one with the freckles across his nose and the piece of hair that stood up like a flagpole?"

Mattie chuckled. "That's the one. Well, Bennie's hair was a little like that, only it didn't stand up stiff and straight, it was a great big curl."

Ben finally found his voice. "Yeah, and I gave Pete Farmer a black eye for calling me a sissy."

Mattie laughed aloud. "I remember. That summer your daddy took you and got your hair cut so short we didn't even have to comb it."

China grinned. By that time, the awkwardness had passed.

"Did I tie them too tight?" Ben asked.

China wiggled her feet inside her tennis shoes, then shook her head, and as she did, the heavy fall of her hair slid across her forehead.

"Mattie, when you've finished there and before we eat, would you mind doing my ponytail? My arm is still a bit too stiff to do it right."

"I can do that," Ben said, and took the ponytail band from her hand before either one of them could argue.

China was a bit startled. She hadn't expected him to volunteer for such a girlie thing.

"I...um, you don't have to."

"Don't get all sexist on me, woman. Just because I'm a man, doesn't mean I can't do this right."

"I didn't mean...I just thought that..."

Mattie grinned. "Don't you apologize to that man, dear. He's just teasing." Then she waved her finger at Ben. "Be nice. You'll scare her off before we've had a chance to make friends."

Ben snorted lightly. "Just what I need. Two women instead of one to make me dance through hoops."

"But, Bennie, you dance so well," Mattie said, and began serving the food that she'd cooked.

"Are you tender-headed?" Ben asked.

"No," China said.

"Good," he said, and thrust his hands into the thickness of her hair and began combing it back with his fingers.

Instead of feeling awkward, the rhythm of his hands against her scalp was oddly soothing. She closed her eyes and gave herself up to the pleasure.

"At the back of your neck or up higher?" he asked.

"The back is fine," China said.

A few quick twists and he was through.

"Breakfast is ready," Mattie said, as she carried the plates to the table. "I hope you like your eggs fried hard. Can't stand to look at a runny yolk."

China hid a smile. Mattie was outspoken, but somehow, it suited her.

"They look good," China said.

"You get choices around here," Ben drawled. "But food isn't one of them."

Mattie arched an eyebrow at her son. "You've managed to survive on my cooking all these years."

"And it's good cooking, too," he countered. "Now, may I have my food so I can eat and get to work?"

Mattie plunked his plate in front of him and then kissed his cheek. Ben grinned and then glanced up at China, who was looking as if she didn't know whether to laugh or pretend she wasn't there. He winked. Almost immediately, he saw her relax. As soon as he was satisfied that their teasing hadn't upset her, he dug into his food.

China picked up her fork, then realized Mattie had yet to sit down. She laid down her fork and folded her hands in her lap just as Mattie turned toward the table with a platter of toast.

"Aren't you hungry?" Mattie asked.

"I'm waiting for you," China said.

Touched by the girl's thoughtfulness, Mattie hurried to the table and set the platter down.

"Help yourself," she said. "Bennie, pass the jelly."

Ben rolled his eyes as he reached for the jar. "Only if you quit calling me Bennie."

Mattie looked a little startled, then grinned. "Sorry. Was I cramping your style?"

China grabbed the pepper shaker and began peppering her food so she wouldn't have to look at Ben's face. But she could tell by the ensuing silence that he was probably giving his mother a disgusted look.

Soon the mood lightened and the meal commenced.

Ben was at his desk, digging through the mounds of paperwork that seemed to grow on a daily basis. But it was difficult to concentrate, knowing that when he went home, China would be there. Maybe not officially waiting for him, but there just the same.

"Hey, Ben, is Bo Milam's wife officially off the suspect list?" Red asked.

Ben looked up. "Yes, according to China, even with a wig and a lot of makeup, she's about a foot too short to be the shooter, remember?"

"Oh, yeah," Red said, and then laid aside the file. "Good. At least that's one less face to consider." He stretched, then got up from his desk. "I'm going to get some coffee. Want some?"

"Yeah, thanks," Ben said absently, and handed Red his cup without looking up.

A few minutes passed before it occurred to him that Red hadn't come back. He looked up, searching the room for his partner's face, but he was nowhere to be seen. He stood and stretched. He liked being a cop, but not the paperwork that went with it.

Suddenly he saw Red come rushing into the room. Wherever he'd been, he'd left both of their coffee cups behind.

"Did you have to pick it?" Ben asked.

"Pick what?" Red asked.

"The coffee beans."

"Oh! Yeah, that's right. Dang, where did I leave those cups?" Then he shook his head, as if reminding himself why he'd been hurrying in the first place. "Never mind about the coffee. I ran into Jones in the hall, and you'll never guess what he told me."

"Jones who?" Ben asked.

"Mike Jones—from the bomb squad."

An image of a short bulldog of a man emerged from Ben's memory. "Oh, yeah, that Jones. So, what's the big scoop?"

"He had a call early this morning to go to a big fire down in the warehouse district. At first they thought it might have been started by a bomb, because someone said they heard a loud explosion. But it was later determined that the fire had been burning for some time before it detonated some stored chemicals."

"And how does that impact us?" Ben asked.

"Jones said his buddy with the fire department said it was arson, but that's not the kicker. It's who the warehouse belongs to that he thought might interest us."

"And the winner is…?" Ben drawled.

"One Ariel Simmons, that's who."

Ben jerked. "The hell you say."

"Jones also said that there was some real strange stuff in that fire that didn't burn up."

"Like what?" Ben asked.

"Like a pair of manacles and chains attached to a wall that didn't completely burn, and he said there were also the remnants of what looked like a bed."

"Wouldn't it be interesting to find out what Ariel has to say about this?" Ben asked.

Red was already putting on his coat. "I knew you'd say that," he said. "I already told Captain Floyd we're paying her another visit."

Ariel was playing the role of patient to the hilt. Betty had made two trips to her room since breakfast, bringing honey and lemon tea for Ariel's cough, and then the morning mail as soon as it came. She was fielding all of Ariel's phone calls as she'd been instructed to do, so that if questions arose, there would be no doubt in anyone's mind that Ariel Simmons was ailing.

Just before noon, the doorbell rang. Ariel heard the chimes echoing in the downstairs hall and fluffed her hair just a bit to look mussed, then pinched her nose several times to give it a red, stuffy appearance. She grabbed a handful of tissues and then flopped backward into the nest of pillows behind her, then yanked and kicked the bedclothes to make it look as if she had suffered a long, sleepless night. Satisfied that she was now in character, Ariel waited for the inevitable knock on the door.

"I'm sorry, Miss Simmons, but there are two detectives who insist upon seeing you."

"If they want to risk my contagion, they are welcome to come up, but I'm not feeling well enough to come down."

"Yes, ma'am," Betty said. "I'll go tell them."

Within minutes, another knock came. Ariel smirked. Just like moths to a flame, they obviously couldn't resist seeing if she was really indisposed.

"Come in," she croaked, and then lowered her eyelids to half-mast as the door opened. "Detectives, forgive me for not greeting you properly, but as you can see, I'm a bit under the weather."

Red glanced at Ben, trying to judge his expression to see if his partner was as uncomfortable as he was. But Ben's face gave away nothing of what he was thinking. Red waited for his partner to make the first move.

Ben was quietly judging the scene before him. Granted, Ariel Simmons was in bed, but other than a half-empty cup of tea and a few tossed tissues, he could see no signs of illness. There was no cough medicine in sight, no pill bottle on the table, and there were no signs of illness or fatigue on her face. She didn't appear feverish, although she was playing it to the hilt, and her eyes were clear and glittering with interest. He decided they were being had and refused to comment on her condition.

"We had a few more questions for you," he said.

Ariel frowned. At the least, she had expected a word of apology from them.

"If you must," she said. "But please don't draw this all out. I'm not well."

Ben nodded. "So you said."

Ariel's color rose, but not from fever. She scooted herself up to a sitting position.

"Ask away."

"One of your warehouses burned down last night. The firemen found some interesting items in the fire. Items that relate to the picture Chaz Finelli had of you—items that would punch a lot of holes in your claim that the picture in question was faked."

Ariel's heart skipped a beat. "I'm sorry, but I don't know what you're talking about. I have no business that has need of a warehouse. You must be mistaken about the ownership."

"No, there's no mistake," Ben said. "The deed on

the property states it belongs to the Simmons Ministry.''

Ariel shook her head, still maintaining a perplexed attitude. To throw a little reality into the moment, she managed a sneeze.

''Bless you,'' Red said.

''Why, thank you,'' Ariel said, and gave him a smile.

''About the warehouse?'' Ben persisted.

Ariel shrugged. ''I really don't know,'' she said. ''However, I will tell you that my ministry receives hundreds of property donations during any given year. I suppose it's possible that one of my viewers donated such a building in God's name, but I have no knowledge of it. I will give you my accountant's name and number. He could clarify that for you better than I. I don't bother myself with such things. I'd rather focus my energies on the Word.''

Red wrote down the accountant's name and number as she gave them out, but Ben wouldn't let go.

''Where were you last night?''

Ariel gave them an indignant look. ''Not again!'' she cried. ''Must I constantly prove myself to you people? Don't you have someone else you can harass?'' Then she picked up the phone by her bedside and buzzed for Betty to come up. ''I was in bed last night, suffering from this cold or flu or whatever you call it. Betty was here. Ask her yourself.''

As if on cue, Betty knocked and then entered. ''Yes, ma'am, how can I help you?''

"These men have some questions they want to ask you."

She turned. "Yes?"

For all it was worth, Ben asked the questions, but in his opinion, the woman could easily be lying on her employer's behalf.

"Betty, is it?"

The maid nodded.

"Okay, Betty, can you tell us what time it was when you last saw Miss Simmons last night?"

The maid frowned, trying to remember. "I brought her some honey-lemon tea for her throat just before ten. She was as ill as she is now, so I left her alone to sleep."

"Do you live on the premises?" Ben asked.

"Yes, my rooms are directly off the kitchen downstairs."

"Are you able to hear anyone coming or going?"

"Yes, definitely. My bedroom is next to the garage, and I heard nothing."

Ariel gave both men a triumphant glance. "That will be all, Betty." She waited until her maid was gone; then she glared at both men. "Before you ask, yes, that's my car out front, so if I had driven it, there's the possibility Betty would not have heard it. However, it's been parked out front since the day before yesterday. It has not been moved, and with all your snoopy technology, I'm sure there's some mechanic or something who could verify that. Now, if you gentlemen will let yourselves out, I need to rest."

Ben knew she was lying about the fire. He could

see it in her eyes, which made him suspect she was lying about everything else. With the right wig and makeup, she could be the woman China had seen. He knew she wore wigs, she'd admitted as much, and she had been lying about everything else from the start of their investigation, but at the moment, he didn't have any leverage to make her break.

As they started to leave, he saw she'd been reading the *Dallas Morning News,* which meant she'd seen the picture on the front page. He reached for the paper, then tossed it in her lap with the headlines facing her.

"Interesting likeness, isn't it?

Ariel turned pale. "You can't be serious! That woman doesn't look anything like me."

"I don't know about that," Ben said, then elbowed his partner. "What do you think, Red? Does that look like Miss Simmons?"

Red squinted his eyes, pretending to study her face.

"Well, with the right wig and makeup, I think she could pass."

Ariel's belly lurched, and for the first time since she'd taken to her bed, she really began to feel sick.

"Get out," she moaned. "Just get out and leave me alone."

Then she bolted from her bed and into an adjoining bath, slamming the door behind her. The sounds of retching were too real to be faked.

"What do you think, partner?" Red asked.

"I think we hit a nerve."

Thirteen

Mattie English was all out of sorts, and China had done her best to stay out of her way. The moment Dave Lambert had arrived at the ranch, Mattie's good humor had fled. As an outsider, it seemed obvious to China that they cared for each other, but she didn't know enough about their history to question what kept them at odds.

However, Dave and China had hit it off from the start. The retired cop was gruff but gentle with her. At least she knew where she stood with him. But it would seem that Mattie did not. She couldn't be in the same room with him without making a caustic comment about one thing or another. China went to her room to escape the consequences of both their bad tempers.

By noon, Mattie was frazzled and snapping constantly at Dave. Finally China overheard the confrontation as Dave's patience ended.

"Damn it to hell, Mattie, I know you don't want me here. You've made that blatantly clear. But this isn't about you. It's about that young woman in there. I made a promise to your son, and I aim to keep it, which leaves you with two choices. Put up or shut up.''

China held her breath as the silence lengthened. Then she heard a pan bang against the cabinet as Mattie uttered one word.

"Fine."

"Fine what?" Dave asked.

"You figure it out," Mattie said, and that ended that.

China smiled. Although she wasn't really tired, she decided that she would stay in her room rather than get in the middle of their cease-fire. A small bookcase beneath the window held an assortment of books. She knelt before the shelves, searching the titles for something to read. As she looked, she heard an approaching car and pushed aside the curtains to look out.

It wasn't Ben's car, although she hadn't really expected it to be. It was too early for him to come home. With no knowledge of Mattie's daily routine, she watched out of curiosity. The car came to a stop at the end of the walk leading to the house. The sun was glaring on the driver's side of the windshield, so for a moment, she couldn't see who got out. Then the driver moved into her line of vision.

It was a tall, slender woman wearing dark slacks and a knee-length coat, with a fur-lined hood pulled tightly around her face. A large bag hung awkwardly on her shoulder, while sunglasses disguised a good portion of her face. As China watched, the woman ducked her head and started toward the house at a run.

Staggered by a sudden panic, it was all China could do to get up. She bolted out the door, calling Dave's name as she ran.

The fear in China's voice yanked Dave out of his chair. He came around the corner on the run, his gun drawn.

"What?" he yelled.

She pointed toward the door.

"A tall woman—running toward the house. I—"

Mattie was there within seconds. "What's wrong?"

"China said there's a woman running toward the house."

At that moment a series of rapid knocks sounded on the door, and then it flew back against the wall, rattling the ornaments on the Christmas tree standing in front of the picture window.

Dave turned, his gun aimed.

China screamed.

Mattie began to shout as she ran toward the woman. "Don't shoot! Don't shoot. It's the Avon lady."

Almost immediately, Dave recognized his neighbor, Patsy Reynolds.

"Damnation, Patsy. You almost got yourself shot."

Patsy's face mirrored her confusion. "I knocked," she mumbled, as her bag slid to the floor. Her eyes filled with tears as she looked at Mattie. "I was in a hurry. I needed to pee."

Overwhelmed with relief, China started to laugh as Dave began to curse even more.

"Well, you know where the bathroom is," Mattie said.

Patsy shook her head. "I don't need to anymore. Guess I got it scared out of me."

This made China laugh even harder. Patsy didn't know whether to be insulted or glad no one was angry that she'd come in without an invitation.

Mattie stifled a sigh, although it was funny. Dave looked as if he'd swallowed a bug as he holstered his gun and stalked out of the room.

"Have a seat, Patsy. You'll have to excuse us, but we've been under a little stress, and you just got caught in the middle."

Patsy Reynolds sat, but on the edge of the chair, in case she needed to make a quick getaway.

"Ya'll must have really been mad," she said, eyeing the doorway where Dave had disappeared. "He had a gun."

This sent China into convulsions of laughter, and she waved herself out and escaped to her room.

"Who's she?" Patsy asked, as China left.

Mattie rolled her eyes. "Oh…she's family. Distant…but family, just the same."

Back to business, Patsy nodded, then reached into her bag. "Here's the latest brochure. We've got a special on hand cream—the kind you like. And if you buy two tubes, you get the third one free."

The last thing Mattie wanted was to look at Avon products, but considering what could have happened a few moments ago, she decided the least she could do was spend a few dollars for hand cream. It was a whole lot cheaper than flowers for the poor woman's funeral.

Connie Marx stood at the window of her Highland Park apartment, contemplating her life. She'd had her last drink more than two days ago, after accepting the fact that she'd brought every damn thing that was happening to her down on her own head. A Mississippi sharecropper's daughter, she'd spent most of her life dreaming of success, and she'd had it all—until she'd messed around with someone else's husband.

All during her days of self-pity, when she'd stayed lost in the whiskey, an old memory had stayed in her head. Just after her sixth birthday, it had started to rain. It rained for five days straight. The river below their house began to flood, and just before sundown, their house was swept away by the waters. Her daddy had stood on a rise above the river with a look on his face that she had never before seen; then he sat down with his head between his knees and began to cry. Two days later, he hung himself from the rafters of his brother's barn, ending his worries, but exacerbating theirs. In a fit of blind grief, her mother had packed up all five of her children and set out walking. They walked all night and most of the next day before the children began to cry, begging her to stop. So she stopped.

But she never managed to get up. Someone passing by on the road reported a woman and five kids were in some sort of distress. Just before nightfall, a couple of police cars drove up and loaded the kids in one car and Connie's mother in the other. They never saw her again. In later years, she learned that her mother had gone quietly insane and died one night in her sleep. The weakness of both her parents, to just quit on themselves and the children they'd brought in the world, had been something Connie kept to herself. She'd prided herself on being strong and focused, with her eye always on the goal ahead and never on her personal self.

But then she had met Larry Dee Jackson, and the suave, sexy superstar had sweet-talked her right into his bed. In one fit of passion, Connie Marx had traded her dreams for pleasure.

For a while she'd wallowed in self-pity and had even contemplated ending it all herself. But that was before the dream—before she remembered the dark, bloody face of her father as he swung from the rafters, his eyes bulging, his lips slack and swollen, and the puddle of pee on the ground below his feet. She'd come out of her bed with a gasp. In that moment, a plan was born.

Now she paced the living room of her Highland Park apartment, waiting for Detective English to return her call.

A few minutes later, her telephone rang. With a strong sense of déjà vu, she picked up the receiver.

"Hello."

"Miss Marx, this is Ben English. I have a note here that you called."

Connie's fingers tightened around the receiver in her hand.

"Yes. There's something I need you to do for me."

Ben had never had a murder suspect ask him for a favor before. To say he was surprised would have been putting it lightly.

"Yes?"

"I want to take a lie detector test, and I want you to set it up for me. I didn't kill Chaz Finelli, and I want you to prove it."

Ben was stunned. The vehemence in her voice was not faked, nor was her confidence in herself.

"You know that such a test is not admissible in court," he said.

"Yes, but I also know the weight one carries in the public eye, and I will not be dragged through any more of the mud Finelli made of my life. He's dead. I'm not sorry, but I didn't do it."

"When can you come in?"

"Today, tomorrow, you name it."

"It's just after one. Let me make a few calls and I'll get right back to you," he said. "Oh…I suppose I should tell you, you might want your lawyer present."

"No. I just want this over."

A distinct click sounded in Ben's ear. Frowning, he hung up and headed for the captain's office. He knocked once, then opened the door.

Aaron Floyd was on the phone. He waved for Ben to come in and then quickly hung up.

"What's up?" he asked.

"I'm not sure," Ben said. "It could be a ploy, but I think she sounded sincere."

"Who sounded sincere?" Floyd asked.

"Connie Marx. She wants to take a lie detector test—today, if it can be set up. What do you think?"

"Go for it," Floyd said. "Call her back. Tell her three o'clock, and tell her where to go. I'll set it up."

"Yes, sir," Ben said, and backed out of the office.

Five minutes later, the call had been made. Ben left a note on his partner's desk, then made a quick call home. This might make him late, and he wanted to be sure Dave Lambert would be there until he arrived.

His mother answered the phone.

"Hey, Mom, how's everything going?"

"You don't want to know."

The hair rose on the back of Ben's neck. He didn't like the sound of her voice.

"Has there been a problem? Is China okay?"

Mattie snorted. "Oh, she's fine. I can't say the same for Patsy Reynolds, and Dave hasn't spoken to either of us since noon, but other than that, we're just great."

He frowned. "What happened to Dave, and how does Patsy Reynolds come into the scenario?"

"She would be my Avon lady, remember? Dave nearly shot her today. I don't think she'll ever be back, and I do like that hand cream they sell."

Ben almost dropped the phone. "Shot her? Why the hell would Dave want to shoot the Avon lady?"

Mattie sighed. "Looking back, it was sort of funny,

but at the time, no one but China saw the humor in the situation. Anyway, China came out of her room like a scalded cat, said some woman was running toward the house. Dave pulled his gun just as the door flew open. It was Patsy. But she wasn't trying to hurt anyone, she was just in a hurry to use the bathroom. Oh…it was all such a mix-up, and then—''

''China! Is she all right? It didn't frighten her, did it?''

''Frighten her? Oh, hell, no. She laughed herself silly, that's what she did. And the longer it went on, the harder she laughed. Dave is embarrassed and mad, but he's been mad ever since he got here. China has spent the afternoon reading. Every time I go check on her, she grins. It's just been hell. Tomorrow is bound to be better.''

Throughout the story his mother was telling, only one thing stuck in his mind. China had laughed. He would have given a lot to have heard the sound. Then he remembered why he'd called.

''I may be a little late. Tell Dave not to leave until I get there.''

''Oh, fine,'' Mattie said. ''This should finish off the day just right.''

Ben grinned. ''Tell him I'll honk twice when I drive up so he won't shoot me by mistake.''

''We're not talking,'' Mattie said.

Ben's grin faded. He'd expected something like this.

''Somebody better be talking when I get there,'' he said.

"We don't always get what we want, my dear son. Just get yourself home before you completely ruin what is left of my world."

"Yes, ma'am," he said. She hung up in his ear.

Ben sighed as he hung up. That was the second time a woman had hung up on him within the last half hour. He hoped it was not a portent of things to come.

Connie Marx came out of the interrogation room with a defiant stride, her head held high, her shoulders back and soldier straight. Ben was waiting for her at the end of the hall.

"You passed," he said.

"That's because I'm innocent," she said shortly. "Now call off your dogs, or I will get myself a coyote-mean lawyer who'll take you and everyone connected with the Dallas P.D. to the cleaners. Do I make myself clear?"

"There are no dogs on your trail, Miss Marx."

Connie looked startled. "What do you mean?"

"Didn't you see the sketch in today's paper?"

"I haven't read a paper in days," she muttered.

He handed her a copy.

She unfolded it, scanned the headline, then the face below. Her eyes widened in disbelief.

"She doesn't look like me," she said.

"No, ma'am, she doesn't."

She took a deep breath. "You mean you don't consider me a suspect anymore?"

"That's right."

"And you let me rave on about that test, then let me take it, knowing it wasn't necessary?"

"I wasn't aware you hadn't seen the paper, Miss Marx. Look at it this way. You've cleared yourself in the eyes of the world by volunteering to take the test. Passing it was a plus."

Her voice began to shake. "Has anyone called my place of employment to let them know I am no longer a suspect?"

"No, ma'am. It's not something we normally do."

Connie lifted her chin. There was another wall she had yet to climb.

"I have a favor to ask."

Ben hesitated. "You can ask. I can't guarantee anything."

"When all this breaks, I want an exclusive."

Ben had to admire her. "I'll do what I can," he said.

"That's enough," Connie said, and then began to walk away.

"Miss Marx?"

She stopped and turned.

"Where can you be reached in case I need to make that call?"

"At home. I'm not going back to Channel 7 with my tail between my legs. I will go back with the scoop of the year and a raise in salary, or flip burgers for the rest of my life."

Ben gave her a quick salute. She smiled grimly and then headed for home. More than halfway down the hall, she saw the elevator begin to open. When Larry Dee Jackson emerged, a huge smile on his face and his arms open wide, beckoning for her to come in, she couldn't believe her eyes.

"Connie, sweetheart! I saw the paper. Now everyone will know you couldn't be the killer. I've been looking for you all over. Your lawyer told me where you'd gone. It's over, isn't it, baby? It's all over."

She stared at him, trying to figure out what she'd ever seen in the man. Other than a pretty face, he was as shallow as they came. He'd given up her name to the police, then abandoned her when she became a suspect. Now he was back with that take-me-to-bed smirk on his face? She didn't think so.

"Oh, it's over, all right."

She slapped him hard, taking pleasure in the pain against her own palm, then stepped inside the elevator and rode it down alone.

Ben saw it all from a distance and even winced when she slapped Jackson's face, yet he couldn't help thinking the man deserved it. That was one incident when Jackson hadn't been able to pay out to make everything right.

Then Ben thought of China, and of his mother and Dave and the mess waiting for him there. It was time to go home.

Around six in the evening, the scent of something wonderful cooking and guilt that she hadn't offered to help prepare it drew China from her room. As she walked down the hall, she could hear the murmur of voices coming from the kitchen and hesitated, but they didn't sound angry, so she kept on going. Just as she reached the doorway, she heard Mattie laugh. It was a quiet, intimate chuckle between old friends, and she smiled. It would seem that the ruffled feathers had been soothed, at least for the time being.

"Am I too late to help?" she asked.

Both Dave and Mattie looked up. Mattie waved her in.

"Figured we'd scared you out of ever coming out," she said.

China figured she'd laughed enough for one day and just smiled.

"I wasn't scared. I just thought it prudent to stay out of the line of fire."

Dave grinned. "Told you she was a smart one."

Mattie waved a spoon toward the table. "Sit down, honey. There will be time enough for you to work later, when you've recovered some more. This was your first full day home from the hospital. You're bound to be a little bit weak."

"I've rested," China said. "And since you're all about honesty here, I have to tell you that I feel very guilty about invading your lives like this. I know if it wasn't for Ben's insistence, you would not have been forced into this situation."

"No one forces me to do anything," Mattie said. "So sit."

Dave got up and pulled out a chair for her. "You

may as well do as she says," he said. "She won't hush until she has her way."

China sat.

Mattie muttered something beneath her breath as she turned back to her cooking but managed to keep her thoughts to herself.

China glanced at the clock, and Dave saw her.

"Ben called earlier. Said he would be late," he said.

China blushed. "I wasn't…I mean I didn't…"

He chuckled. "You know what they say about protesting too much."

"Now I know why Mattie feels the need to tear a strip off you from time to time," she muttered.

His chuckle deepened.

"David Wayne, leave her alone," Mattie snapped.

Dave hushed, but his eyes were still twinkling as he leaned back in his chair.

An awkward silence rose between them, and China was thinking she should have waited to come out after all when the sound of an approaching car altered the mood. Two short blasts from the car horn followed.

"That's probably Ben," Dave said. "I'll go see."

China's heart skipped a beat. Suddenly the thought of his deep, booming voice and the tenderness of his touch was more than she could bear. She started to bolt when Mattie turned, aiming a spoon at her to punctuate her order.

"You can set the table now," she said. "Silverware is in the top drawer on the left of the sink."

"Yes, ma'am," China said and got up.

Mattie sighed, laid her spoon on the cabinet and then walked over to where China was standing and gave her a hug.

"Honey, I'm sorry I've been so hateful today. It had nothing to do with you. There's old business between Dave and me, and you just got caught up in the middle."

The warmth of Mattie's hug and the sincerity in her voice were enough to make China want to cry. Instead, she swallowed the lump in her throat and managed a smile.

"I figured as much," she said. "And you didn't hurt my feelings."

Mattie grinned and playfully tweaked the end of China's nose. "Good. Then the next time you call me 'ma'am,' I'm going to stuff a sock in your mouth."

China laughed aloud.

And that was the first sound Ben heard as he walked into the house. It stopped him in his tracks, leaving him weak and wanting, and in that moment he had to accept the fact that he was in love with China Brown.

"About time you showed up," Dave said.

Ben blinked. He hadn't even seen Dave standing there.

"Shut the door, boy," Dave said. "You're letting in a whole lot of cold air."

"Oh, yeah, sorry," Ben muttered, and came the rest of the way inside, shedding his coat and gloves as he moved toward the hall closet. "How did everything go today?" he asked.

Dave snorted. "Oh, I'd say pretty good, except for the fact that I almost shot the Avon lady."

Ben grinned. "I heard."

Dave frowned. "Then why the hell did you ask? Just to see if I'd tell you the truth?"

Ben chuckled and then slapped his old friend on the back.

"Confession is good for the soul. You taught me that, remember?"

Dave grinned wryly. "Yeah, but that was because I caught you smoking a cigar behind your daddy's barn. There's a big difference between sneaking a smoke and plugging your neighbor."

"Heard she was in a hurry to use the bathroom," Ben said.

Dave's grin widened. "After I pulled my gun on her, I doubt she made it in time."

"Wish I'd been here," Ben said. "That would have been something to see."

"Wish you'd been here, too," Dave said. "A houseful of women makes me nervous. Now come on, boy, let's go see your mama before she comes looking for us."

"Is China okay?" Ben asked.

The smile slid off Dave Lambert's face. "You're pretty gone on her, aren't you?"

"There you are," Mattie said, as she came into the room. She gave her son a welcoming hug. "Supper is ready. We'll have it on the table in five minutes."

"Smells good," Ben said. "But I want to say hello to China before I change."

"Oh, she's—" Mattie started to say, but Ben walked off before she could finish.

"He's in love with her," Dave said.

Mattie frowned.

"What?" Dave asked. "I thought you liked her?"

Mattie shrugged. "I like what I know about her well enough, but she's only been here a day. I've wanted Ben to settle down for years now. After all, he's in his thirties. But I don't know what I think about a woman like her."

"She seems decent enough," Dave said.

"Only months ago she was living with another man and having his baby without being married. When she got shot, she was homeless. Now she's the only person who's seen this serial killer and lived to tell about it. That's not exactly the kind of woman a mother wants her son to marry."

Dave looked at Mattie and then shook his head. "How soon you forget," he said.

Mattie's color rose and her chin jutted. "I don't know what you're talking about."

Dave took her by the shoulders. His voice was quiet, his grip firm.

"You stayed married to a man you didn't love out of a sense of duty. You cheated yourself and me out of a lifetime of happiness. Your husband hadn't been dead more than a week when we made love, and you've never forgiven me for it. Judging that girl is a little beneath you, don't you think?''

Mattie's face fell. Her eyes glittered with unshed tears. Truth was a hard thing to face.

''I've got to get supper on the table,'' she said. ''Go wash your hands.''

''I think I've been here long enough for one day,'' he said. ''I'm going home.''

''You walk out that door, don't bother to come back,'' she said quietly and then walked away.

Dave stared for a moment, then went to wash his hands.

Fourteen

Ben entered the kitchen and found China at the cutlery drawer.

"Mom put you to work?" he asked.

The deep voice startled and, at the same time, excited her. Reacting normally around this man was becoming a difficult thing to do.

"I offered," she said quietly, and moved toward the table, her steps slow and measured.

Ben watched her through narrowed eyes. She was sore. He could tell by the way she moved.

"You've been up too much today," he said, and took the cutlery out of her hands and began laying it in place around the table.

"I've been in my room almost—"

Ben looked up and grinned. "Yeah, I heard you lit out for parts unknown after Dave tried to shoot the Avon lady."

She grinned in spite of herself. "I shouldn't have laughed."

"Sounded pretty funny to me," Ben said.

"It was all my fault. I panicked. They just reacted to me. It nearly got a woman shot."

Ben shook his head. "Dave's too good a cop to shoot an unarmed suspect, even if she was carrying."

"But she wasn't armed," China said.

"She had her Avon bag."

China giggled. "And I laughed."

Ben couldn't quit staring. Since he'd known her, she'd either been suffering from pain or grief. This playful side was a surprise and a joy.

China straightened a spoon, then moved to another place and switched the knife and fork to opposite sides of the plate while still trying to explain.

"I think it was all just a reaction to my relief...you know...realizing that the woman wasn't here to kill me after all. It was right after she said she needed to pee that I started to fall apart."

Ben chuckled.

China grinned. "I tried to stop laughing, I swear I did. But things kept going from bad to worse, and Dave was so mad, and Mattie was yelling, 'Don't shoot, don't shoot, it's the Avon lady,' and...well, you just had to be there." Then she laughed aloud.

Her laughter stopped him cold.

"Jesus," he whispered.

China froze. Something had changed, and she didn't know what had caused it. When Ben began to circle the table toward her, she started to get nervous.

"What?" she asked. "What did I do?"

He touched her face, tracing the shape of her mouth with his fingers. It was soft, so damned soft.

"The laughter," he mumbled. "It changes you."

Suddenly embarrassed, she tried to turn away, but he wouldn't let her.

"It probably makes me look stupid. My eyes are too big and my mouth is too wide, anyway."

Ever careful of her injuries, he took her by the shoulders and turned her back around to face him.

"Look at me, China."

He had given her no choice.

"Your laughter is beautiful, just like you, and it makes me ache with envy, knowing I wasn't the one who made you smile. I don't know how, but one of these days you'll learn to believe in yourself."

He moved away, knowing that if he stayed this close any longer, he would be kissing her.

China's heart was pounding—her thoughts going crazy. God, how she wanted to believe him, but she'd looked in the mirror, she'd seen the flaws for more years than she cared to count.

And then Mattie came striding into the kitchen with her head up and fire in her eyes, and the moment to question him was lost.

"I'm going to change. Be back in five," Ben said quickly, and left.

China sensed Mattie's mood. Uncomfortable being alone with Ben's mother, she sat down, hoping the silence would make her invisible. But to her surprise, Mattie suddenly turned and smiled.

"Hope you're hungry, dear," Mattie said. "I think I made too much chicken and dumplings."

"Oh! One of my favorite foods," China said. "I haven't had it in years."

It was the perfect thing to say. Mattie began talking companionably, as if they'd been working together all their lives, and by the time the food was on the table and everyone had gathered round, the atmosphere in the room was comfortable and light.

An hour or so later, after the food had been eaten and the dishes were done, Dave left for the night. Mattie moved to the living room, settling in her favorite chair with the remote at her elbow and her knitting in her lap, leaving Ben and China alone in the kitchen.

"Want to take a walk?" he asked.

The idea of getting out, even for a short while, was exciting.

"Yes, very much," she said.

"Get your coat."

She jumped up too quickly and winced.

"Take your time, honey," Ben said. "I won't leave without you."

Excited about doing something normal rather than hiding in fear, she went to the front closet to get her coat. Mattie looked up from her knitting as China slipped her coat from its hanger.

"We're going for a walk," she said.

Mattie nodded approvingly. "It will be good for you," she said. "You'll sleep better after getting some fresh air."

"We won't be long," China said.

''Take as long as you like. Ben won't let you come to harm.''

China hurried back to the kitchen, where Ben was waiting, but with a new sense of peace. Seven little words, but they had made all the difference in her world. *Ben won't let you come to harm.* His mother was right. Ben would take care of her, and not just because he was a cop and it was his job, but because he'd promised.

Ben helped her put on her coat, pulled the hood up close around her face and fastened it beneath her chin.

''Don't want you getting chilled.''

''I'm tough.''

He paused, staring intently at her face. ''Yes, you are, aren't you, honey?''

Pinned by the shadows in his eyes, China shivered, and then the moment passed. He took her by the elbow and led her out the back door. Earlier, the wind had stopped. Now the air was cold and still, and as they stepped off the porch, the grass crunched beneath their feet. She took a deep breath and then looked up at the sky. Only a few stars were showing, which told her the storm front that had been predicted earlier was probably moving in.

''Are you warm enough?'' Ben asked.

She nodded, then remembered it was dark and added a yes.

''Better take my hand,'' Ben said. ''Some of the ground is a little uneven. Above everything else, I don't want you to fall.''

She slipped her hand in his without thinking about the consequences, yet as soon as they touched, the awareness between them came back.

"We'll make this quick," Ben said. "When you're stronger, we'll stay longer, but a short walk to the barn and back should be enough for tonight."

The silence between them was oddly comfortable. As they walked, China became aware of a dark shadow looming in the distance. This had to be the barn. As they neared, a horse suddenly nickered. She jumped.

"It's just Cowboy," Ben said. "He's my horse. He's twenty years old and has never lived anywhere but this ranch."

A sense of poignancy swept over China. How strange that she was homeless but Ben English's horse wasn't. She shrugged off the self-pity and made herself smile.

"Can we see him?" she asked.

"That's a given," Ben said. "He knows we're coming. If we don't show up with a treat or two, he'll sulk for a week."

"Oh, but we didn't bring anything with us."

"I have some sugar cubes in my pocket," Ben said. "I got them while I was waiting for you."

"I've never petted a horse before," China said.

Ben stopped, pretending great surprise. "And how long have you lived in Texas, lady?"

"Almost twenty years."

"Someone has neglected your raising, honey. Allow me to intervene."

China was smiling as they entered the barn, and although the building was open at both ends, there was a sense of warmth and shelter. She shoved the hood away from her face as Ben flipped a switch, flooding the barn with light. Immediately, a big sorrel with a white blaze on his face stuck his head over the door of his stall.

Ben laughed. "Yeah, I see you, fella. We're coming as fast as we can."

China was beside herself with excitement. Before Ben could stop her, she hurried ahead. Ben started to caution her. Cowboy didn't like strangers. But there was something about the silence of the horse and the woman as they took each other's measure that told him this would be different. He stopped and took a deep breath, savoring the rare communication between the pair.

China was entranced. The animal's dark-brown eyes were fixed upon her face, its nostrils slightly flared as it explored her scent. And then Cowboy nickered softly, as if saying hello. China looked to Ben for approval. When he nodded, she extended her hand. The soft, velvety pull of the horse's lips tickled the palm of her hand, in search of the favored treat. Ben slipped her a cube, which she promptly extended.

When the horse took it out of her hand without touching her skin, she sighed with delight.

"His nose…it's so soft," she whispered.

"He likes you," Ben said.

There was childlike excitement in her voice. "He does?"

Ben nodded. "He doesn't let just anyone pet him."

China shivered with delight. "Do you have any more sugar?"

Ben handed her what he'd brought, watching as the big horse daintily nibbled up his treats.

"That's all," China said, when the last one had been eaten.

Just as if he understood, the horse tossed his head and then surprised her by nuzzling the side of her face and then gently pulling at her hair.

When China gasped, Ben thought she was afraid and moved to step between them.

"No," she begged. "He's not hurting me. He's loving me, isn't he?"

Pain twisted his heart. "How can you blame him? You'd be easy to love."

She turned then, her eyes wide with disbelief. "You mean easy prey, don't you? After all, look at what I let Tommy Fairheart do."

"No, that's not what I meant, and don't put words in my mouth. You didn't *let* that heel do anything to you, honey. You were his victim. He's a con man. He looks for innocent young women...lonely women. He feeds them a line and takes them for what he can get and moves on." He moved closer, his voice softening. "It's not a mistake to want happiness. It's not a crime to fall in love, and I'm sorry he hurt you—more than you can know."

She glanced at Ben, then looked away. "Maybe so, but it doesn't make me feel any less stupid."

"Do you still love him?"

"Absolutely not," she said, and moved away. "That part of our relationship had been over for months. Even before he stole my money and left. I just didn't know how to let go of the man who was my baby's father."

Ben couldn't deny the relief he felt. At least he wasn't going to have to fight that, too. And fight he would. He'd already decided that she was worth whatever it took.

"That's good," Ben said. "It makes my job a whole lot easier."

"How does my hating Tommy Fairheart have anything to do with protecting me?"

Ben moved closer then. "I'm not talking about that job," he whispered, as he cupped her face with his hands. "I'm talking about teaching you to trust me. Without trust, there's no love, and, honey, I want you to love me more than I've ever wanted anything in my life."

China's eyes widened, her lips parting in surprise.

It was what Ben had been waiting for. He lowered his head, centering a kiss in the middle of her mouth. Her head fell back against his arm as he cradled her against his chest. He felt her shock, then her lips trembling against his. She was sweet, so sweet, and so damned scared. When she moaned, he instantly pulled back.

"Don't be scared," he begged. "Not of me. I would never hurt you." He nuzzled his lips against the side of her neck. "Never."

She stared up at his face. The tenderness was there. She'd expected it. But there was also a passion she didn't know how to take. Her hands were shaking as she lifted them to her mouth. She felt branded and wondered if the imprint of his lips could be physically felt.

Ben was scared he'd ruined everything by coming on so strong. It had been too soon. What the hell had he been thinking?

"China...honey?"

She shook her head, as if coming out of a daze.

"Never?" she asked.

Ben exhaled on a shaky sigh. "God yes, never ever."

"You promise?"

He nodded. "Have I ever broken a promise to you?"

She bit her lower lip, then shrugged. "Not yet."

At that moment, if Ben could have put his hands around Fairheart's throat, he would have throttled him. He stifled the urge to react in anger, but it came out in his voice anyway.

"China."

"What?"

"Don't make me pay for someone else's mistakes."

"I—"

"You've been out long enough," he said. "It's getting late. Tomorrow's another day."

Their walk back to the house was silent. When they got inside, Ben paused to lock the door behind them. China watched him, wondering if she'd ruined everything between them, then deciding that it was all in her head, because there was nothing to be ruined. He'd kissed her. That was all. No need to wrap herself around a future that couldn't possibly exist.

"Give me your coat," he said. "I'll hang it up for you."

She handed him the coat, then stood, unwilling to end their evening.

"Thank you for the walk…and for Cowboy… and…" Unable to speak of the rest of what had happened, she ended her thanks with a shrug.

The last of his anger faded as he saw the panic on her face. His voice gentled, his smile forgiving.

"You're welcome."

She was on her way out of the kitchen when Ben called out to her.

"China?"

She spun, unaware of the anxiety in her voice. "Yes?"

"Do you need any help getting undressed?"

"No, no, I can manage."

He shoved his hands in his pockets and nodded.

She started to leave again, but there was something inside him that hated to let go. He called to her again, and again she turned.

"Yes?" China said.

"Sleep tight. Don't let the bed bugs bite."

The tension on her face began to fade, replaced by a slow, timid smile.

"Yes. You, too," she said softly, and then left him standing. She couldn't bring herself to look back for fear the look of hunger she'd seen on his face would still be there.

Long after the house was quiet and everyone had gone to bed, China sat in a chair by her window, staring out into the night. Her thoughts were on replay, from the time Ben had tied the hood beneath her chin to the moment he'd told her good-night. She kept remembering the feel of Cowboy's nose on the palm of her hand and Ben English's mouth upon her lips. One had tickled, the other had made her knees go weak. What was she to do? She couldn't be falling in love. She was in enough danger already without giving another man entry into her heart.

But then she reminded herself that Ben wouldn't hurt her. He wasn't that kind. He was a man who kept the promises he made. All she had to do was learn to believe in herself as much as she believed in him.

The woman opened her closet and reached in for a gown, letting her fingers run lightly over the satins and silks before choosing one of red chiffon. She dropped it over her head, sighing in satisfaction as the fabric slid the length of her long, slender body. It hung loose from the decolletage—a diaphanous nightgown that swept the floor as she walked. She stepped into a pair of red mules and then put on the matching robe, tying it beneath her breasts in a neat, dainty bow.

As she passed the stereo, she punched Play. At once, the throbbing bass of a rock-and-roll band reverberated against her skin. She shivered as the sensation went all the way to her bones. Dancing her way toward the dresser in long, sensuous strides, she paused to give herself a critical stare, then reached for the wig on a nearby stand. With a practiced hand, she flipped it over her head, then pulled it down around her ears. The new haircut made it fit a little bit loose, and she tugged on the cap until it finally settled in place. This time, when she swung around to view herself in the full-length mirror, she liked what she saw. The only problem was, no one would see her like this. It was too dangerous to play the game anymore.

She frowned. The music played on, but she wasn't able to respond as she normally did. She kept picturing that woman on the front page of the *Dallas Morning News*. Damn it all to hell, how had they done that? She would have sworn there wasn't a living soul who'd seen her face. She'd been so careful, never leaving a witness to tell about her little games.

A shiver ran up her spine as she remembered Chaz Finelli coming out of nowhere and the flash of his camera as it caught her in disguise. Thank God she'd had her gun with her. She'd made short work of Finelli and his damned camera. The cops would never find it. She'd stripped the film from the camera and set it on fire, then tossed the camera into a Dumpster on the other side of town. It had been unfortunate about that woman—the one with the baby in her belly. Then she shrugged. It was survival of the fittest. She'd worked too hard to get where she was to toss it away on sentimentality.

Suddenly angry, she stomped over to the stereo and turned it off, then began yanking off her clothes and tossing them all around. When she was through, the woman from the mirror was no longer recognizable. She washed her face until it was devoid of any makeup, dressed in the clothes she'd worn to the cabin and turned out the lights as she left. In a week or so, after the New Year had been rung in, she would start a quiet investigation. She had money and power and friends in high places. Somehow she would find out how the police had come up with that picture. There was too much at stake to take any chances of being found.

Christmas Day dawned with a gray, cloudy sky. China buried her nose beneath the covers, reluctant to emerge. This day hadn't meant much to her since her mother's death, but she had looked forward to the Christmases she would have had with a child. Shopping for toys, pretty dresses and bows for a little girl's hair. But the dream was gone now, like everything else she had treasured.

A knock sounded on her door.

"China, are you up?"

"No," she said.

He opened the door. "But you're awake."

"I am now."

"Good," he said. "I wanted to give you your present."

"But I didn't get you anything," she said.

"Of course not," he said. "You're in hiding, remember?"

"So that makes me exempt from giving gifts?"

He tugged at a lock of her hair, then sat on the edge of her bed.

"In this instance, yes." He laid a small box in her lap.

"That doesn't seem right," she said, although she was interested enough to sit up.

"Open it," Ben urged. "Please."

She began to remove the ribbon, then the paper. A few seconds later, she opened the lid and lifted the figurine out.

"Oh, Ben." Her eyes filled with tears.

"I know," he said. "But when I saw it, I knew it was yours."

"It's perfect," she said. "Even though it makes me sad, it's also a reminder of where she's at."

Ben sighed with relief. It was exactly what he'd been trying to convey.

She lifted her arms, then wrapped them around his neck.

"Thank you," she said.

"You're welcome," he whispered, and stole himself

one Christmas kiss. "Mom's making biscuits. Do you feel like getting up to eat?"

"I wouldn't miss it," she said. "Just give me a few minutes to get dressed."

"If you need any help, just holler."

She nodded. He winked and then left, leaving her alone with the gift she'd unwrapped. The porcelain angel was perfect in detail, right down to the folds of fabric on her pale-pink gown, but it was the infant she was holding that broke China's heart.

She picked it up again, holding it to the light coming in through the window. Sadness swept over her in one crashing wave after another as she read the small inscription at the base of the statuette.

Someone to Watch Over Me.

It hit her, as she studied her gift, that this could also be symbolic of her relationship with Ben. In a way, she was the infant, helpless to fight all that was facing her now, and he was the angel, holding her safe to his heart. He was pledging his life to keep her safe.

All through the day, she kept the thought in her heart.

Ben tossed aside a file he'd been working on and then leaned back in his chair, eyeing his partner at the desk opposite his.

"Hey, Red, are you taking Rita out tonight?"

Red looked up and frowned. "No. Why?"

"It's New Year's Eve, for God's sake. This time

tomorrow it will be a whole new year. That's something to celebrate.''

Red looked nervous. ''She hasn't said anything.''

Ben rolled his eyes. ''She shouldn't have to.''

''So you think I'd better come up with a plan?'' Red asked.

Ben grinned. ''If it was me, I would.''

Red folded his arms on his desk and leaned forward.

''So, lover boy, if you're so on the mark, exactly what do you have planned for you and the china doll?''

Ben's grin faded. ''That's different. She just got out of the hospital, and we're not dating. Besides that, I could hardly take her out, even if we were. She's in hiding, remember?''

''Yeah, I guess. But it seems like you could do something. I mean, she's really had a rough month.''

They went back to work, but the seed had been planted in Ben's mind. A short while later, he called home. His mother answered.

''Mom, it's me. Just checking on everyone.''

''We're fine. China is napping, and I'm considering it. Dave is puttering around out in the barn, looking for something to fix a broken shutter.''

''Tell him there's some stuff in the last granary on the right.''

''Okay, I will,'' Mattie said. ''Will you be home late?''

''No, and that's why I'm calling. Have you started anything for supper?''

''Not yet. I don't know why, but I just can't get in

the mood. I'll come up with something before the evening is over.''

"How about if I bring something home? Maybe Chinese? It's New Year's Eve. Thought we might have a little celebration of our own. Tell Dave he's welcome to stay and see the New Year in if he wants.''

Mattie was silent just a moment too long.

"What?'' Ben asked.

"Well, Dave sort of asked me out to eat tonight. I told him I'd see.''

Ben's pulse jumped. A whole night alone with China. He couldn't have asked for anything more.

"For Pete's sake, go, Mom. We don't need baby-sitters. I'll bring Chinese for us, and you and Dave go kick up your heels.''

"He said there was a dance at the Elks lodge, although I probably should say no. I don't have a thing to wear.''

"Mom, for the last time, accept his invitation. If you won't do it for yourself, do it for me. I know you get lonely out there by yourself. Nothing would please me more than to know you had someone in your life.''

He sensed her embarrassment, but to his delight, she finally agreed.

"Good, it's settled then,'' he said. "Tell China what's going on when she wakes up. And if she doesn't like Chinese food, somebody better call me before I get off work. I can always pick up something else.''

"All right, son,'' Mattie said. "And thank you.''

''No, Mom. I should be thanking you for putting up with all of this.''

''You already did. And if the truth be told, I admit that I'm enjoying the hustle and bustle of someone else in this house.''

''Is China opening up to you any?''

''Not about personal things, no. But we get along fine. There's just one thing that bothers me about her.''

''What's that?''

Mattie hesitated, then blurted it out. ''Did you know that girl thinks she's ugly?''

Ben frowned, remembering the day she admitted that her stepfather, Clyde, always said she was homely.

''Yes. It's hard to believe, isn't it?''

''She's absolutely stunning. All that black hair and those big blue eyes. I can't imagine what has happened in her past to make her think something like that.''

''Just be patient with her, Mom.''

Mattie chuckled. ''You're the one who tries my patience. I hardly know she's here.''

Ben smiled. ''Hey, I do what I can,'' he said.

Mattie laughed. ''Come home safely.''

''Yes, ma'am. I'll be there around six-thirty or seven.''

Fifteen

Mattie was behaving like a teenager, tossing one out-fit after another aside while trying to find something to wear for her date with Dave. She'd dragged China into her room on the pretext of asking her for advice, but truthfully, she felt guilty about going out, and she wanted someone to talk to—to keep her mind off what she was about to do. All these years, the guilt of making love with Dave when her husband had been dead only a week had weighed heavily on her conscience. Rationally, she knew it had happened because of a need for emotional release, an affirmation that she was still alive although her husband was not. And instead of accepting the weakness for what it was, she'd blamed herself and Dave for something that was no more than an act of desperation.

"So, what do you think about this one?" Mattie asked, holding up a dark-navy sheath.

China frowned. "Too somber. I like the dark-pink one better."

Mattie groaned. "I can't make up my mind."

China smiled. "Yes, that much has been obvious

for the past fifteen minutes. May I make a suggestion?''

Mattie threw up her hands. ''Anything!''

''You go shower and fix your hair, and let me pick out what you'll wear. When you're finished, you come out and put on the outfit I've laid on your bed. You put it on without fussing and go out and have a wonderful time.''

''Oh, no,'' Mattie moaned. ''My hair! I'd completely forgotten. How am I going to wear my hair?''

China got up from the chair and pushed Mattie toward the bathroom.

''Go away,'' China said. ''You're making me nervous. Do your hair like you always do. Pretend you're going to church or something. It's not going to matter to Dave what you look like, and you know it. He'd be happy if you went in what you're wearing.''

Mattie looked down at her rumpled jeans and sweater and then sighed.

''You're right. Oh lordy, you're right.''

She started toward the bathroom, then stopped.

''China…dear?''

''Yes?''

''Thank you.''

China grinned. ''It was my pleasure.''

Still Mattie hesitated. ''You know, when I was younger, I'd always planned on having a large family, at least three children, maybe more. When I lost my baby, I lost my dream. Adopting Ben was the best thing we ever did, but as I look back on the years, I wish we had adopted a dozen. I always wanted a daughter. Someone like you would have been perfect.''

She gave China a quick hug and then escaped to the bathroom, leaving China speechless.

Someone like me? China walked to the mirror. The woman looking back at her was all eyes and too thin. And when she thought about what she looked like beneath her clothes, her stomach knotted. *No one would want someone like me.*

But as she moved about the bedroom picking up the clothes Mattie had tossed aside, the sweet words of praise kept echoing in her heart. Even though she didn't really believe them, they'd been nice to hear.

When Mattie came out a half hour later, her hair in hot rollers, her robe flapping about her ankles, China was gone and her room had been picked up. One complete outfit was lying on her bed, with matching shoes on the floor beneath it.

Mattie sighed. It was the most daring outfit she owned. A black velvet pantsuit with a rather audacious neckline. The shoes were gold, but with nearly flat heels, which would be perfect for dancing. Even the little black shoulder bag lying next to it was just large enough for a compact and lipstick and a few dollars for emergencies.

With an anxious heart, she began to dress. But by the time she had finished her clothes and her hair, her anxiety had turned to excitement. She looked at herself in the mirror and then did a quick pirouette. For a woman pushing sixty, she decided, she looked pretty darn good. Then she heard the sound of a car driving up and glanced at the clock. That would be Ben. The plan was to leave now with Dave, go to his place so he could change, and then the evening would start from there. She grabbed her bag, gave herself one last look, then opened the door.

As she passed China's room, she noticed her door was ajar. Wanting to thank China again, she peeked in. China was sitting in a chair by the window, her hands folded in her lap in quiet repose. Mattie started to speak when China turned. The tears on her face said it all.

"Oh, sweetheart," Mattie said. Moments later, she was at her side. "Is there anything I can do?"

"No. You look beautiful."

"Somehow this seems wrong," Mattie said. "I'm going out to a party, and you—"

"This isn't about me," China said. "This is about you and Dave and a lot of wasted years, okay?"

"Okay," Mattie said, then held out her arms. "How do I look?"

China smiled. "Like a woman in love."

Mattie looked a little stunned. "I don't want to look that good," she said. "At least, not just yet."

"Time is precious. Let yourself be happy."

"I'll be late coming home, but I promise to be quiet," Mattie said. "Tomorrow is Ben's day off, so we can all sleep in. Take care of yourself, dear, for me, as well as for you."

"Yes, I will," China said, touched by the woman's concern.

Mattie kissed her goodbye and then waved again as she left.

The room seemed empty after she'd gone. China turned back to her post at the window, although it was already dark outside and there was nothing to see but an occasional set of headlights from a passing car on the road beyond the ranch. The sudden yip of a coyote on a nearby ridge sent a shiver up her spine, and she had to make herself stay still, although she was haunted by an image she couldn't forget. Her child— a child who had never known the sweetness of a single breath of air—lay alone in the dark, in a box, very deep in the ground. In her heart, she knew the baby was with God, but she hadn't been able to turn loose of that pain. Maybe if she'd had a chance to say goodbye…

As she sat, she heard laughter from the front of the house and then, a few minutes later, the sound of a car leaving the yard. That would be Mattie and Dave, off for the night. She struggled with herself, trying to unload the depression. Ben would be looking for her any minute, and she didn't want him to see her cry.

She got up from the chair and washed her face, then contemplated brushing her hair. But the effort was still too painful, so she gave up the thought. As she was leaving the bathroom, it dawned on her that she and Ben would be alone. She shivered. There was no denying the fact that she was attracted to him, and as good as he'd been to her, she was afraid to trust her own judgment. Then she heard him calling.

"China? Where are you?"

She lifted her chin and walked out of her room.

"I'm here," she called.

He met her just outside the kitchen. "Wait," he said. "Close your eyes."

"Why?"

"I have a surprise."

She smiled in spite of herself. "Really?"

"Yes, really. Now close your eyes and hold out your hand."

She did as he asked, letting him lead her into the kitchen.

"Okay," he said. "You can open them now."

She smelled the surprise before she saw it, and still her delight was real.

"Oh, Ben, Chinese? I love Chinese food."

"Great. I wasn't sure what you liked, so I got a little bit of everything."

She smiled as she saw all the boxes. "That's for sure. How many boxes are there, anyway?"

"I'm not sure. Maybe thirteen or fourteen, counting the one with the fortune cookies."

"Oh, I love those. Let me see."

"No fair," he said. "They come last. Now sit your sweet self down. I'm the chef tonight."

China sat, and as she watched him digging through the boxes with such pleasure, her mood began to change. Dejection shifted, giving way to brief moments of peace. For tonight, it was enough.

"Here," he said. "You have to eat with chopsticks."

"I don't know how."

He grinned. "Neither do I. But tomorrow is a whole new year, and we should have at least one new skill to go with it, don't you think?"

"It's a grand idea, but chopsticks? Don't you think something enlightening would have been more in order?"

"After the day I've had, this is just about all the challenge I care to handle."

China tried to pick up a bite with her chopsticks. When it fell back on her plate, she frowned.

"Yes, I see what you mean."

"Want a fork?"

"No," China said. "I can do this." She bent to the task.

Ben watched for a minute, admiring her concentration. When she suddenly crowed with delight and got a bite of stir-fried shrimp in her mouth, he fell a little bit further in love. The meal continued in the same vein, with more laughter and jeers and the occasional flight of a bite of stir-fried rice. It wasn't until China opened her fortune cookie that the evening changed.

She was smiling as she broke the cookie in two. When she pulled out the fortune, she waved it beneath his nose in a teasing fashion.

"Mine will be better than yours," she said.

He grinned. "We'll see about that." He broke his open as well and began to read.

"'You are having dinner with the woman of your dreams.'"

"It doesn't say that," she muttered.

"It does. Here, read it for yourself."

She looked, then sat back in disbelief. "You made that happen."

"No, I didn't. I swear," Ben said. "Read yours. If I'd fixed it, it would say, 'You are having dinner with the man of your dreams,' right?"

"I guess," she muttered, and turned hers over to read.

She scanned the bit of paper and then went suddenly pale. It fell from her hands as she got up from the table and quietly left the room. Ben picked it up and read it.

There is a thing you have left undone.

He read it again, still uncertain as to what had upset her, then went to find her. She was back in her room, sitting in the dark. He went to her. Her face was in shadows, but he could tell she was crying. Tears were thick in her voice.

"China, I don't understand."

"I know."

"Then talk to me. I can't help unless I know what's wrong."

"My life is out of control."

"I know, but it won't always be."

"I've always taken care of myself, and I feel so helpless, even worthless."

"No, honey. Never worthless."

"You don't know. You can't understand. I don't belong anywhere. I don't have an address. I don't have a job. There is no one alive who remembers anything about me. I let myself fall for some pretty words. I let myself get pregnant, and then I let that baby die. I wasn't even there when she was put in the ground." China stood suddenly, her voice rising as she continued to talk. "Do you know how that makes me feel?

Ben hurt for her in so many ways. "No, but you can tell me. You can tell me anything and I will understand."

She grabbed him by the arms, her fingers digging into his flesh.

"I play at being all right. I pretend that things are getting better. But I need to see my baby. I need to see the place where she's at. I don't know anything about the...about how you..." She took a slow, shuddering breath. "Tell me what you know, and trust me, whatever you tell me can never be as bad as what I've imagined."

Ben was afraid—so afraid of what he was about to do. But China was right. She, above everyone else, had the right to know what had happened to her own child.

"You're sure?"

She nodded.

"She was very, very small, a little over three pounds, I think. The coroner said she died instantly."

"How?"

"One of the bullets ricocheted off a rib and into her."

China moaned.

Ben took her in his arms. "I picked out a little white casket with an angel on the lid. We wrapped her in a pink blanket."

China sighed. "To keep her warm."

It was all Ben could do not to cry. "Yes, it would have kept her warm—very warm."

She laid her face against his chest as the panic began to recede.

"I need to see," China said.

"Cemeteries are locked after dark, and taking you there in the daytime would be a risk I'm not willing to take."

"It's not your risk to take, it's mine," China said.

Ben tensed. She had asked nothing of him until now. But this? Should he dare?

"Please," she begged.

He sighed. "They will unlock the gates at sunup. I'll take you then. Most of the city will probably be sleeping off the aftereffects of ringing in a new year."

"Thank you. Thank you so much," China said.

His voice rumbled deep against her ear. "Don't thank me yet. I won't rest easy until this is over."

She looked up at him then. "Now you know how I feel."

Midnight came and went. A couple of hours afterward, Dave brought Mattie home. Ben heard the car drive up, and a few minutes later the front door opened, then closed. He heard his mother pause in the hallway, probably to take off her shoes, because afterward he could no longer hear her footsteps. A bit later, he heard the bedsprings creak as she crawled into bed.

He got up then, walking barefoot through the house, checking all the doors and windows one last time, but he knew that no amount of caution in this house was going to offset the danger of taking China back into the city, yet he could not refuse her. Until she said her goodbyes, she was never going to heal.

As he passed her room, he noticed the door was half-open. He stopped and looked in. She lay on her back with one arm outflung, the other beneath the covers. He hesitated, then walked to her bed, lifted the covers and gently put her arm beneath the warmth. She sighed, then started to turn, wincing aloud in her sleep as pain pulled her back. Without waking her up, he put a hand beneath her back and helped her turn. She settled into a comfortable position with a soft, quiet sigh.

Ben straightened, satisfied that all was well, and then paused at the foot of her bed to watch her sleep. In the dark, she looked a bit like a child, but he knew there was a strong, resilient woman beneath all that pain. He gripped the footboard with both hands until the tips of his fingers ached. There in the dark, in the quiet of the night, he made her a promise to keep.

"I will bring that woman to justice. She will pay for all you've lost if it's the last thing I ever do."

Then he closed her door and went back to his room. Sunup would come far too soon.

The gates of Restland Cemetery were already open as Ben slowed the car down to turn in. Except for a few brief comments, he and China had not spoken to each other on the way into the city. He glanced at her now. She was pale and quiet—almost too quiet. But they'd come this far. It was too late to turn back.

"I'm not sure if I remember the exact spot," Ben said. "It may take me a couple of minutes to find the place."

"I remember where Mother is buried," China said. "Take the second gate and turn right at the third road."

He did as she said, and soon memory began to return. A few minutes later he saw the new grave just up the slope and stopped.

"This is as close as we can get with the car," he said.

China looked. The pile of freshly turned dirt was like a sore upon the earth. It would take time for it to settle, just as it would take time for the pain of loss to settle within her.

Ben jumped out quickly and ran around the car to help China out. The air was cold, the sky cloudy and overcast. He pulled the hood up over her head and handed her his gloves.

"Here, honey. Put these on. They'll be too big, but they'll keep your hands warm."

She held out her hands as if she were a child, too numb to do anything more than what she was told. The softness of the fine leather and the lingering warmth inside the gloves made it seem as if Ben were actually holding her hands. She folded her arms across her chest and then took a slow breath. Ben slipped a hand beneath her elbow to steady her.

"Are you ready?"

She paused, then looked up at him, her eyes full of unshed tears.

"I have to do this alone."

He hesitated, uncertain. But when she started across the dry, brittle grass, he found himself standing and watching her go.

For China, everything seemed surreal. The sound of the grass crunching beneath her shoes. The cry of a hawk somewhere high above her in the sky. That particular scent that cold air has when it's almost too cold to breathe. The hammering of her own heartbeat, thumping in her ears. And the dark musky smell of earth that had been recently disturbed.

She stopped at the edge of the mound and stared down at the grave. The tiny marker and the name, Baby Brown, were evidence enough of her loss. The child had not even been named. Subconsciously, her hands splayed across her stomach as they had so many times before. But this time her belly was flat and the bulge was in the earth at her feet. Her gaze shifted to the small headstone just to the right of the dirt.

Clara Mae Shubert—A good mother—Rest in Peace.

She shuddered. Rest in peace. And in that moment, a knowing came upon her. That was what she'd forgotten. For her baby to rest in peace, she had to let go.

She closed her eyes then, remembering the moment of her death, and the journey they'd taken together. Her baby wasn't here in the ground. She was already gone.

With aching regret, she lifted her head. As she did, the sun broke from behind a cloud, and the unexpected warmth on her face was like a kiss. She looked up beyond the horizon to the bit of blue peeking through the clouds and let go of what was left of her guilt. It *wasn't* her fault she'd left her daughter behind. There was a reason she'd been sent back—to help find the woman who'd killed her.

She turned then, searching for the man who'd brought her. He was standing beside the car, and even from this distance, she could see the concern on his face. Despair shifted, just enough to let in the memory of their shared kiss.

The promise man.

China began to retrace her steps, and as she did, she saw him move away from the car and start toward her. Another measure of despair fell away from her heart. Whatever she had to do, Ben would be there. She wouldn't have to do it alone.

* * *

One day led into another, and then another. Ariel Simmons was touring the country, taking the Word to the masses and battling a growing sense of depression. She'd done everything she knew to protect herself from the fallout of Chaz Finelli's murder, but it didn't seem to be working. Too many people believed in the old adage of where there's smoke, there's fire, and she was suffering the consequences. Hate mail came on a daily basis. Obscene phone calls were a constant recurrence. Instead of leaving it behind, her shame traveled with her. She was losing weight and taking pills and praying as she'd never prayed before. But nothing seemed to work. No amount of prayer could rid Ariel of the guilt of what she'd done.

Connie Marx had all but gone underground. She had become a recluse in her own apartment, living off her investments and biding her time as she researched everything she could about Charles Finelli, as well as the killer's other victims. She spent her days clipping items from the newspapers regarding the ongoing case and taping every soundbite of television coverage. When the case blew open—and she knew that it would—she was going to be ready.

Mona Wakefield was missing from the compound of Dallas society, preparing herself for a comeback. She had convinced herself that a new hairstyle and new clothes would remove the old problems in her life.

Bobby Lee was back in D.C., circling among the movers and shakers of the nation's government and basking in the glory of his growing popularity. In his mind, the past was past. He'd tied up all the loose ends of his problems and was concentrating on the task at hand—that of becoming the next president.

But they weren't the only ones who were trying to put the past behind them. From the day they'd come back from the cemetery, China had been a changed woman. Her body was healed, her heart in the process of repair. Her bouts of depression were all but gone, and she grew stronger with every passing day.

A month passed, and then another, and while no one was watching, spring appeared.

"I'm going to the barn," China announced, and sailed out the back door before anyone offered to accompany her.

Dave started to follow when Mattie caught him by the arm.

"Let her be," she said. "There's no way anyone can sneak up on this house. You'll see them coming long before they arrive. Besides, something tells me that the danger has passed. There haven't been any killings in months. The woman is probably long gone to another state."

"I'll keep my distance," Dave said. "But I don't know about everything being over. In my experience, a serial killer can't stop. It's part of the pattern that drives them to kill in the first place."

Mattie frowned as she watched China stride off the porch.

"I've come to love that girl," she said. "I couldn't bear it if anything ever happened to her."

Dave put an arm around her shoulder and gave her a quick hug.

"You aren't the only one who loves China. Your son is so far gone he doesn't even know it."

Mattie sighed and then looked up at Dave and patted his cheek.

"Thank you for being here," she said.

He grinned. "Never thought I'd hear you say those words."

"Go find something to do," Mattie said. "I'm too busy to fight with you."

His chuckle followed her as she left the room.

Meanwhile, China was in a world of her own. The day was mild, although there was a fairly brisk breeze. She'd braided her hair to keep the wind from yanking it in tangles and had a pocketful of Cowboy's favorite treats. Today she'd seen buds all over the lilac bush in Mattie's backyard, and she stopped again, testing the fat round buds with the tip of her finger. As she did, she saw a small brown worm inching its way up a stem.

Time stopped. In her mind, she was a little girl of six, hiding from Clyde beneath the porch and watching a brown caterpillar wend its way through the grass. Then she'd felt like that worm. Brown and ugly, of no consequence to anything in the world. She'd tried to make herself small, hoping to hide from Clyde. It hadn't happened.

She still felt small and of no consequence, a homely little thing that mattered not at all in the world, but something was changing inside her. She no longer wanted to hide. It was a day for new beginnings, and it made her heart beat fast, as if something wonderful awaited her just out of sight. She moved on, anxious for her playtime to begin.

As she entered the barn, she blinked several times in succession, allowing her eyes to adjust to the dimmer light. Down the aisle and then out in the corral beyond, she could see Cowboy. She whistled and then started to run. He came to meet her at a trot.

"Hey, baby," she crooned, and began to climb, straddling the fence panels as she dug in her pocket for his treats. He nuzzled at her hands, and she laughed. "Give me a minute," she said. "I've got them here somewhere."

Eagerly, he took the first one out of her hand and was begging for the second before he'd swallowed the first. She laughed as he ate, and when they were all gone, she slipped off the fence and onto his back without benefit of bridle or saddle. Then she stretched out, aligning her upper body along the length of his neck, held on with her legs and threw her arms around his neck. He stood in the sunshine, accepting her affection as easily as he'd taken the sugar.

"You big, old, pretty baby," China whispered.

A horsefly buzzed around Cowboy's head. But other than a twitch of his tail, he didn't move.

Ben found her there, half asleep on the back of his horse with the sun hot against her back. Breath caught in the back of his throat as he watched them. From the first, their bond had been magic. It was as if the old horse had sensed all her wounds, both physical and mental, and given her his complete devotion. China had returned it a thousandfold. Even if she was shy about returning affection to people, she gave her love without question to the old, gentle horse.

Quietly, Ben walked up to the corral and climbed the fence. Cowboy nickered softly. Ben smiled.

"Yeah, I see you, boy, and don't start making excuses. She has you as buffaloed as she has me."

China roused at the sound of his voice and sat up sleepily, her hair loose and wild about her shoulders, her lips tilted in a half smile.

"I almost went to sleep," she said.

"I saw you," Ben said. "There wasn't any almost to it. Now come here to me, sweetheart. I don't know how long you've been out here, but you're getting too much sun."

China felt the back of her neck. It was hot.

"Oooh, you're right," she said, and held out her arms.

He lifted her off the horse and held her until she was steady on the fence rail. Then she climbed down herself, brushing off the bits of horse hair and hay from the front of her shirt.

"You're home early."

Ben nodded. "Took a half day of personal leave."

China really looked at him then. He had already changed from the clothes he wore to work and was in an old pair of boots and jeans and a soft denim shirt.

"Are you sick?"

"No, just tired and missing you."

The words wrapped around her heart. She gave him a bashful smile.

"Really?"

"Yes, really," Ben said, and then took her in his arms. "How are you feeling?"

"Good," she said.

"Not sore anymore—anywhere?"

"No. I'm completely healed."

"Good," Ben said. "Then come with me. I have a surprise."

"Where are we going?" China asked.

"Not far."

Her eyes were dancing with excitement, and she was trying to imagine the surprise, when he came to a sudden stop no more than thirty feet from where they'd started.

"Is this it?" she asked, looking around at all the open doors and empty bins.

"Nope," he said. "We're going up," he said, pointing to the ladder built against the wall.

"To the loft?"

He nodded. "You first. I'll go behind, so I can catch you if you fall."

If I fall. China sighed. Safe. She always felt safe with this man.

"What's up there?" she asked.

"You'll see when you get there."

Stifling a nervous giggle, she began to climb.

Sixteen

As China reached the opening, a pigeon took flight from the rafters and disappeared out the window. She paused, peering cautiously around the vast open space to make sure there were no more surprises.

"You okay?" Ben asked.

"Yes, just making sure," she said, and climbed the rest of the way through, leaving him to follow.

It was even warmer up here than it was down on the ground. There was an old mattress leaning against the wall, with a tarp draped across it. A pile of burlap sacks lay in one corner, a pair of hay hooks hanging on the wall above them. An incubator had been pushed against the wall, a dinosaur from the days when Ben's parents had actually hatched their own baby chicks. Other odds and ends of ranch history lay about the area. It was like walking into someone's attic and looking at bits and pieces of their lives.

"What's this?" China asked, as Ben came up behind her and picked up the item she was looking at.

"It's a sad iron. That's what my grandmother used to iron their clothes before electricity came to the country. She heated it on the woodstove and then ironed until it cooled and then heated it again. I think there used to be a couple of extra bottoms to the thing. You know, two could be heating while she was using one and then she would unfasten the cool one and clip another one on.''

"Makes you think the good old days maybe weren't so good after all," she said, and then turned, her eyes dancing with excitement. "You said you had a surprise?"

He smiled. "Yes, over here." He took her by the hand and led her toward the far corner of the barn. "You have to be quiet, though. Old Katie doesn't much like strangers."

China's eyes widened apprehensively. "Old Katie?"

"Shhh," Ben whispered, and then pointed at a wooden crate.

China leaned over and at first saw only a jumble of magazines and papers. Then a crumpled pile of papers suddenly moved and a cat peeked out from beneath. Ben lifted the paper off the cat and laid it aside, revealing the secret beneath.

"Oh, Ben."

The reverence in her voice said it all. There in the middle of the crate lay a calico cat nursing a litter of babies. When the cat saw them, she hissed.

"Easy, old girl," Ben said, and then grabbed China's hand before she could reach out and touch her. "Don't try it, honey, not when she's feeding the babies."

"Oh, right," China said, and took a quiet step back, but she couldn't take her eyes off the box and the four tiny squirming babies the old cat was nursing. She stood there for a while, staring intently at the scene, then announced, "We have to name them, you know."

Ben grinned. "Yeah, I guess we do. Why don't you pick the names? Old Katie won't mind."

China kept staring, looking for differences in their markings, but without holding them, it seemed impossible.

"They all look like her," she said.

Ben laughed. "Yeah, Old Katie has a tendency to mark her babies all the same."

She studied them some more and then suddenly smiled. "I know. We'll call them Eeny, Meeny, Miney and Moe."

Ben chuckled. "But which is which?"

"With those names, it won't matter."

Ben laughed. "Come on, honey, we'd better let Old Katie alone for now."

"Can I come back?" China asked.

"Sure, but not too often, or she'll just get nervous and move them and then you won't know where they're at."

Her eyes grew round. "Really? She would do that?"

"Yeah, it's part of her mothering instinct—a way she protects her young."

China flinched as if she'd been struck and had to

take a deep breath to continue. "I can understand that. Keeping them safe is all that matters."

Ben saw the look on her face and silently cursed himself for all kinds of a fool. He touched her arm, then her face, wanting to wipe away the sorrow.

"China, sweetheart, I'm sorry. I didn't think when I—"

She put her fingers on his lips. "Don't. There's no need."

He took her hand and lifted it to his lips. The sensation of his mouth against her palm did funny things to her heart, and an ache began to grow in the pit of her stomach that had nothing to do with grief. She tried to say his name, but all that came out was a groan.

Ben lifted his head and then froze. He'd prayed for this day—for that look on her face—and now that it was here, he was afraid he would do something that would make it disappear.

He laid her hand on his chest, letting her feel the rapid beat of his heart, and watched her eyes widen in disbelief. He touched her face, trailing his thumbs across her lower lip and then tunneling them through her hair.

He pulled her close, and when she didn't resist, he went a step further and cupped the back of her head. When she wrapped her arms around his neck, he slanted a slow, tender kiss across the middle of her mouth.

She sighed and took another step toward him, until

they were completely aligned and she could feel the imprint of his body.

"You make me crazy," Ben whispered. "Crazy in love."

She looked at him, at the hunger on his face. For her. It was for her. The knowledge was exhilarating and powerful.

"I want to make love to you, China. I need to see joy on your face and know that I put it there."

He kissed her again, and China melted against him. Suddenly she was in his arms and he was carrying her across the floor toward the mattress leaning against the wall. With a kick, he sent it tumbling. It landed on the floor of the loft with a muffled thud, sending up a cloud of dust that neither one of them seemed to mind. He laid her there, then stretched out beside her.

Like a magnet, she turned toward him, pulling him close. It had been so long—an eternity—since she'd felt so alive. She was out of control, and it just didn't matter.

Ben traced every inch of her face with his kisses, memorizing the shape of her lips, the texture of her skin and the silent plea in her eyes as his hand slid beneath the waistband of her jeans.

Then suddenly she was rolling off the mattress and scrambling to her feet. Her hands were shaking as she clutched at her shirt, holding it close around her neck.

"I'm sorry, I'm sorry. I can't let you see the... It's too awful to—"

Ben stood. The pain in his voice was too obvious for her to ignore.

"All you had to do was say no. I would never hurt you," he said, and started to walk away.

"No, wait!" China cried. "Not like this. I don't want you to think I didn't...that you—"

Ben turned, confused and more than a little bit hurt.

"Then what? Tell me, China. What the hell went wrong?"

She turned loose of her shirt, then dropped her head, unable to see the disgust on his face.

"It wasn't you, it's me," she whispered, touching her breasts, then her stomach. "The scars...they're terrible...so ugly. I can't even look at myself. How can I—"

Ben cursed. His anger startled her, and she gasped and took a sudden step back.

"You think I'm so shallow? You think I don't know the consequences of what happened to you?"

"Not shallow, not you. It's me. I—"

"Stop it," Ben muttered, and took her by the shoulders, making her look at him. "I've seen your wounds. I saw them the night they picked you up off the street. I saw them in the hospital when your belly was nothing but a long line of staples. I sat by your bed and prayed for you to open your eyes and talk to me, and not one Goddamned time did I think to myself that what had happened to you made you less of a woman."

Horrified by what he was saying, China wanted to

run. She couldn't look him in the face and know that he'd seen a part of her that even she couldn't face.

"Don't you turn away from me," Ben said, his voice rising in anger. "Don't you do that to me. You can hide from yourself, China Brown, but you don't hide from me. I'm not afraid of what's beneath your clothes. You're the one with the problem."

She watched in horror as he suddenly ripped off his shirt and threw it on the floor.

"If you're so turned off by scars, then you'd better see mine." He lifted his arm and then turned. The light caught and held on the thick, jagged pucker of flesh across his ribs.

"Car bomb, my rookie year on the force. Every time I look at that scar, I remind myself how blessed I am to be alive."

China jerked as if she'd been slapped, knowing how deep the wound must have been to leave such a horrible mark.

"Oh...my...God."

He took one look at the horror on her face and knew it was over. Tired of fighting a losing battle, and tired of being the only one in love, he reached down to pick up his shirt when she caught his hand.

"You shame me," she whispered, and laid the palm of his hand against her breast. "Please. Help me. Teach me to love myself as much as I love you."

Joy spread within him in quiet increments. "Teach you? I can't teach you anything, China. All I can do is love you. The rest is up to you."

"Then bear with me, Bennett." She lowered her head and began unbuttoning her shirt.

He stopped her with a touch, then a kiss. "Let me," he begged. She dropped her hands to her sides and looked down at her feet.

"No fair," he said softly, tipping her chin up to meet his gaze. "If you have the courage to confess your love, then you have to follow it through. Test me, China. See the look on my face and know the truth in my heart."

So she did—watching him with a steadfast gaze as he undressed her, one piece of clothing at a time. When he was through, he took off the rest of his clothes and then stood before her, unashamed of his obvious need.

"Beauty is in the eye of the beholder, China Brown, and to me, you are the most beautiful woman in the world. I've loved you far longer than it made sense to care. You took me into your heart. Will you let me the rest of the way in?"

She held out her hand, and he took it, letting her lead him back to the mattress. Then she pulled him down beside her and took him into her arms.

"Make love to me, Ben."

He rolled, covering her body as he captured her mouth with his own. Time ceased.

The old cat in the corner was through nursing her kittens and now slept with them curled all around her. The pigeon China had frightened away circled high above the barn, looking for a safe place to land.

Cowboy stood beneath the shade tree at the far corner of the corral, asleep on his feet, while high in the loft, Ben made love to the woman of his heart.

Their bodies rocked in perfect rhythm, carrying them from one sexual plateau to another—from the moment of first joining, to the beginning of the end. They could no more have stopped than they could have quit breathing. Somewhere within the act, a knowing came upon them that this pleasure couldn't last.

It started first with China, building low and hard and fast. She arched, meeting the power of his thrust with a strong need of her own, and as she did, she lost herself. It burst within her in a blinding flash of pleasure so vast she thought she would die.

The scream in her throat came out as a groan, and she locked her legs around Ben's waist in a subconscious act of holding on to the feeling.

Ben's endurance was just about gone, and when she pulled him the rest of the way in and then couldn't let go, he gave up to the feeling and spilled himself into her in shuddering thrusts.

The silence that came afterward was as powerful as the act had been. They clung, one to the other, stunned by their joining until their skin began to chill. He needed to get his weight off her body, but he couldn't find the strength to move. Finally he rose up on one elbow to look down.

Her hair fanned the mattress beneath her head like a puddle of dark silk. Her eyes still reflected the shock of climax. But her body was limp, satiated by the power of their lovemaking.

"You take my breath away."

She looked up at him and saw the reflection of her own face in his eyes; then she sighed. "It was good?"

He groaned. "No. *Good* is not a word for what you did to me. I may never walk again."

"Good," she said, and then wrapped her arms around his neck. "At least then I'll know where to find you."

He groaned and then laughed. "I love you, China Brown. Do you doubt me now?"

"No."

He nuzzled his face against the curve of her neck. "Then I'll give you something else to think about between now and the rest of our lives."

"What's that?" she asked, then moaned as he rolled the tip of her breast between his fingers.

"One of these days, when all this mess is over, we're going shopping. I'm going to buy you the biggest diamond I can find, and then you and Mom are going to plan our wedding. You once told me that you didn't know where you belonged. Well, I'm telling you now, my love. You belong with me."

They made love again in the loft before climbing back down. And while China held his promise close to her heart, there was a part of her that didn't know if it would ever come true.

The woman stormed into the cabin, her frustration level at an all-time high. She needed an outlet for the anger that burned deep in her gut, but she couldn't play the game. It had been months since that sketch had come out in the *Dallas Morning News,* but there was too much at stake to take a chance, which left her with only one option. There had to be a witness some-where—someone she'd known nothing about—but time was on her side. All she had to do was wait and one day she would know who it was.

A new lead in the Finelli murder came in the form of a telephone call to a journalist at the *Dallas Morning News,* offering information for money—a lot of money. The journalist was busy, trying to meet a dead-line.

"This is not a tabloid, buddy. We don't pay for news."

"Your loss," the caller said, and hung up.

The journalist hung up, but there was a niggle of curiosity, wondering what the man had been trying to sell. It wasn't until that night, as he sat in his apartment with a box of pizza in his lap and a long-neck beer on the table by his feet, that he realized what he'd prob-ably turned down.

Randy Boyle, the anchor for the ten o'clock news, was smirking like the proverbial Cheshire cat. Even though the journalist doubted that Channel 7 was in the business of paying off snitches, he wouldn't put it above the likes of Boyle. He upped the volume on the remote and took another drink of beer as Boyle began to speak.

"This evening, Channel 7 has learned that there is a surviving victim of the serial killings here in Dallas. A pregnant woman, who officials now believe was just an innocent bystander to the murder of Chaz Finelli, is in seclusion and waiting to do her part in bringing the killer to justice. The baby she was carrying died on the scene, but she survived, due to the gallant efforts of the doctors and nurses at Parkland Hospital. Her identity is not being released, for obvious reasons."

"Well, hell," the man muttered, then swallowed his last bite of pizza and turned off the TV.

Out on the English ranch, China was in the living room alone when the bulletin was announced that there was new evidence in the serial killer case. She bolted to her feet and then yelled out Ben's name.

He came running, his mother right behind him.

"What's wrong?" he asked.

"The TV. Just listen to what they're saying."

They sat, as the journalist had done, listening to Randy Boyle knock down the carefully laid blocks around their world.

Before he'd even finished the bulletin, Ben was on the phone to his captain, struggling with disbelief.

"Someone sold her out!" he yelled. "She might as well stand on a street corner with a sign on her back that says Shoot Me."

"They didn't give her name," Floyd said, although that was a weak excuse and he knew it.

"Well, hell, Captain, if someone knew there was a witness, then they're bound to know her name. As soon as enough money is offered, that will be common knowledge, too."

"Maybe so," Floyd said. "But it's done, and there's nothing we can do except what we've been doing."

But Ben wasn't buying that. "There's something I can do," he said. "I'm putting myself on round-the-clock guard duty with our only witness, and don't start telling me that detectives aren't bodyguards. You tell it to the governor. He's the one riding your ass to solve this case."

"Don't tell me what to do," Floyd snapped. "You've got yourself involved personally, and we both know it."

"Hell, yes, it's personal!" Ben yelled. "I'm going to marry China Brown, but I can't do that until the woman who shot her is behind bars, and she'll never be behind bars if we don't protect China."

China was shaking so hard she couldn't stop. She needed to run—to hide—but there was nowhere to go but to Ben.

He saw the panic on her face and grabbed her, then wrapped her in his arms.

"Either grant me the authority for what I want or fire me," he said.

Floyd cursed. English was just crazy enough to do

what he said. The last thing he needed was to lose a good man, as well as their only witness.

"Fine," he snapped. "But this is temporary, until we can come up with a better plan."

"The plan is to find that woman," Ben said. "There are no other options."

He hung up in Floyd's ear and then tossed the phone onto the sofa and held China instead.

"It's going to be all right, honey, I promise. I'm not leaving here again until this is over."

Then he looked at Mattie, who'd listened in horror to what had happened.

"Mom, call Dave. If he wasn't watching the news, tell him what happened. We're going to have to set our watches in shifts."

"Oh, my God," China moaned, and turned in Ben's arms. "Mattie, I'm sorry, so sorry. I never should have come here."

"You hush," Mattie said, as she reached for the phone. "You're part of our family, and we protect our own."

"Mom's right," Ben said, as his mother left the room to make the call. He sat down on the sofa and pulled China into his lap.

"I suppose we've been kidding ourselves that this wouldn't happen. We've been fortunate that it took them this long to get onto the fact that there had to be a witness for the composite to even be made."

China thought about what he said, and as she did, her panic began to recede. He was right. It was an inevitable part of this whole ugly mess, and maybe it was time. She was well now—stronger than she'd ever been before. If she was ever going to have a normal life, this had to be over.

"You're right," she said, surprising herself as well as Ben by how calm she felt. "It was the shock of hearing it that frightened me, but I think I'm actually glad. I want this over, and if it means being a Judas goat for a killer, then so be it."

Ben turned pale. "You're not putting yourself up as any target. Don't even hint at such a thing."

"But I am, Ben, don't you see? It won't take her long to figure out who I am. She's seen my face. All she'll have to do is ask around. It's only a matter of time before someone puts two and two together and remembers the woman under guard at Parkland Hospital, and then someone else will remember the detective who bent all the rules to be with her and... Well, you get the picture."

"Jesus," Ben whispered, and pulled her close. "You're scaring me, China."

"I'm scaring myself," she said. "But I'm more angry than scared. She took something from me that I can never have back. I want to be able to walk through a mall without wondering if I'm going to be shot in the back. I want to buy groceries and go to movies and sit in the park. I love you, but I'm tired of hiding. She took my life. I want it back."

"You're right, China, and understand...I'm with

you in this all the way, and I swear on my honor, I will keep you safe.''

China shook her head. ''I don't need your promises, Ben English, not when I already have your love.''

Ben and China weren't the only ones who'd been rocked by the bulletin. Far away, in the middle of Dallas, another viewer had sat glued to the news. When it was over, the remote was aimed and the television went dead. Images of faces from the past began flashing one by one.

Someone survived. But who? The game only involved one man at a time, and except for Chaz Finelli...

Understanding dawned.

The pregnant woman—the one who'd begged not to be shot! But the papers had said two had died that night. So how could...?''

The baby! Of course! How stupid I am. It was the baby that died, not the woman.

Son of a bitch! She saw and heard everything. My God, my God, she can bring down the whole house of cards.

Connie Marx was at her computer, her fingers flying fast and furious as she added this latest bit of information to the file she was creating.

A witness! All this time there had been a witness. Anger spiked. Then why the hell would they assume it had anything to do with her? As soon as she asked herself the question, she realized the answer. Until they'd been able to question the victim further, all they'd known was that the killer was a woman. Considering the people Connie knew had been seriously questioned, probably a tall, blond woman. It was only after the composite had been created that they'd eliminated her from the list.

Connie hit another series of keys, called up a list and hit Print. As soon as the printer spit it out, she moved to a filing cabinet and pulled out a file, then spread the contents on the table, sorting them one by one. Someone in this stack could very well be the killer, and then she stopped and rocked back on her heels.

Or not.

What if the killer was someone who had escaped Finelli's net? What if it had nothing to do with Finelli's blackmail scheme? What if Finelli had been incidental to the larger picture? Of course! After all, the other victims had been a party to strange sexual activities before their bodies were discovered. And their murders had been done execution style, while Finelli's was an act of impulse spurred on by rage. Possibly rage at being discovered. But what had Finelli known that the rest of Dallas did not?

Connie laid down the file and then strode to the window, letting her thoughts run free. If only she could talk to this witness. Ben English had almost promised her an exclusive. He would know who she was.

She started to reach for her phone, then stopped.

No. She'd already made a mess of her life, and this wasn't about her any longer. She was just an observer, waiting to report the truth.

Seventeen

China's existence had become big news. The next day, all over Dallas, people were talking, speculating as to who it could be. Rumors flew thick and fast that had nothing to do with the truth, but they were enough to stir up the story all over again. The composite of the serial killer was reprinted in the papers and flashed at every televised newscast. It became an all-out media war to see who could top whom. Beauty shops were doing a booming business. Women who had been blond for years were changing the color of their hair for fear they might be mistaken for the woman the police were looking for.

Charlotte Humbolt, society editor for the *Dallas Morning News,* was sorting through the picture files of Dallas's finest when she came across a handful of pictures of Mona Wakefield that had been taken at a charity event. She grimaced, remembering what a scene the woman had made by showing up in a sheer georgette dress. In the sunlight, the damn thing had become see-through. Toby Walters, the president of Lone Star Savings and Loan, had been gawking at her so hard that he'd misstepped, fallen into a rock garden and broken his leg.

Charlotte grinned, then laid them aside. As she reached for some others, something about the picture on top caught her attention. She looked back at the stack and then picked another one up—a close-up of Mona guzzling champagne. She stared at it for a minute, trying to figure out why it bothered her so much. Again she shrugged off the thought and started to lay it down, and then it hit her.

"I've got to be crazy," she muttered, and her heart began to thump as she shoved aside the mess on her desk, revealing the morning paper beneath.

Then she laid the picture of Mona beside the killer's composite and started to grin. The resemblance was uncanny. She kept thinking of all the times she'd been snubbed by Bobby Lee Wakefield.

She sat for a moment, contemplating the wisdom of what she was about to do, and then thought, *To hell with it* and picked up the phone. Even though she didn't believe for a minute that the Wakefields would have anything to do with murder, it would serve them right to suffer a little hassling by the Dallas police.

She started to use the phone on her desk and then realized it could be traced, so she took the elevator downstairs to the pay phone in the lobby. There were hundreds of people coming in and out of the building on a daily basis. There was no way they could trace the call to her and Senator Bobby Lee would have to do some fancy dancing for the cops, which suited her just fine.

"Hey, Red, phone call for you on two!" someone yelled.

Red Fisher picked up the phone, hoping it was going to be Ben, telling him he'd changed his mind about staying at the ranch with China and was coming in to work.

"Detective Fisher, Homicide."

"Compare your killer to a photo of Mona Wakefield."

A click, and then a dial tone buzzed in Red's ear.

"Hello? Hello? Who is this?" he asked, but it was no use. The caller was gone.

Although it was pretty far-fetched, they'd followed up on every lead that had been called in to date, and insulted some pretty important people in the process. The way he figured it, they'd already pissed off the mayor. Just because it was a senator's mother, there was no need to ignore the lead. He looked up and yelled out into the room, "Hey, anybody got a picture of Bobby Lee Wakefield's mother?"

A couple of rude remarks came flying back about what they'd like to do with her, but no one had a picture on hand. Red reached for the phone and dialed a friend at a local paper.

"Mike, it's Red. I need a favor."

"Yeah, and I need a thousand bucks to cover my ass at the bank."

"Can't help you there," Red said. "I told you to quit betting on those horses. You aren't any better at picking winners than you are at picking women."

The man chuckled in Red's ear and cursed him lightly. "So, what's the favor you need?"

"Fax me a picture of Mona Wakefield."

"Bobby Lee's mother?" Mike asked.

"Yeah, one and the same. And make it a head shot if you've got it."

"Oh, we've got it," he said. "When there's nothing new to be said about her, she makes something happen. I'm not too crazy about my last mother-in-law, but I'm damned sure glad she wasn't anything like Mona. Man, can you imagine having a mother who looks and acts like that?"

Red grinned. "Just fax me the picture ASAP."

"In the works," Mike said, and hung up the phone.

A few minutes later, Red stood at the fax, watching a photo printing out. He turned it over and then stared in disbelief. The woman was almost a ringer for the face in the sketch. The ramifications of pursuing this were staggering, but if there was even the smallest chance…

He headed for the captain's office.

Aaron Floyd was at the point of no return. His phone had been ringing nonstop ever since he'd gotten to the office with people wanting verification that a witness actually existed. When Red knocked on his door, he was actually glad for the reprieve—until Red tossed the photo onto his desk.

"That's Mona Wakefield," Floyd said.

"Lay it beside the sketch of the killer," Red said.

Floyd snorted. "Are you crazy?"

"Just do it," Red urged.

Floyd reached for the paper that he'd laid aside and opened it. Before he even laid it down, he was on his feet cursing.

"Who put you onto this?" he asked.

"An anonymous caller."

"Son of a bitch."

"No, actually, it was the bitch herself," Red said.

Floyd's thoughts were racing. "Was she ever interrogated?"

"No, sir. To our knowledge, she wasn't in any of Finelli's pictures, so her name never came up. However, now that I think about it, if even half the stories about her are true, it's a miracle she wasn't a part of his files."

"So maybe she was—once upon a time. Check it out."

"Yes, sir."

"Call Ben. Let him know what's happening. He might want in on this."

Red grinned. That was the best news he'd had all day.

Dave and Mattie were in the middle of a spirited game of Scrabble, and China was in the hayloft making friends with Old Katie with a leftover piece of ham from their lunch. Ben was in the front yard washing his car. It wasn't that the damned thing was all that dirty, but it was the only thing he could think of to do that would keep him within seeing distance of the barn. He didn't want China to feel as if she had no freedom at all, but the truth was, right now, she had little to none.

Just as he was turning off the water, his mother yelled out the door, "Ben! Phone! It's Red."

He dropped the hose and ran to answer.

"Yeah…what's up?"

"We got an anonymous call a while ago. It may amount to nothing and it may not. Captain said to give you a call, that you might want in on the interrogation."

"Is it worth anything, or is it just his way of trying to get me to come back to work?"

"It's a picture of Mona Wakefield. Damned if she isn't almost a dead ringer for the sketch."

Ben's mind was turning over everything he knew. "Was she ever one of the names from the Finelli file?"

"No."

"Now that I think about it, and knowing her reputation, it's a little amazing that she wasn't, right?"

Red grinned. "That's why we're partners. I had the very same thoughts myself. So, do you want in on the visit?"

"Oh, yeah," Ben said. "But I'll meet you there. It's on my way into the city. Give me thirty minutes."

"You got it, Ben. How's China taking all this?"

"About how you'd expect. But she's tough, Red. I've never known anyone as focused on making someone pay."

"Except maybe you?"

"Yeah, maybe. I'm on my way."

Ben was stripping off his shirt as he hung up the phone.

"What's going on?" Mattie asked, as he bolted past them on his way to his bedroom.

"Maybe a break in the case, maybe not. Tell China I'll—"

"I'm here," China said.

"Come with me to my room," he said. "I'll tell you what's happening while I change."

A skitter of anxiety threaded its way through her pulse, but she made herself relax and followed him into his room. He was already down to his underwear and reaching for a pair of slacks when she entered.

"Is it about me?" she asked.

"It's about the case," he said. "An anonymous tip has turned up a new face. Someone we never interviewed before."

"Does she look anything like the composite?"

"Ever see Mona Wakefield before?" he asked, as he tucked a clean shirt into the waistband of his pants and then sat down to put on his shoes.

"Senator Wakefield's mother? Sure, I guess."

"Think of it, honey…does she look anything like the woman who shot you?"

China's heart skipped. "I can't really picture her face, but she is tall and blond, that I remember."

"I'll bring something for you to look at when I get back. Dave is here and—"

"Just go," China said. "Do whatever you have to do to make this be over."

He grabbed his jacket from a hanger and then took her in his arms. She leaned against him, then wrapped her arms around his waist and laid her cheek against the front of his shirt. Ben held her close.

"So, did Old Katie let you feed her today?"

She looked up and smiled. "Yes. I even got to look at the babies, except I didn't touch them, like you said."

"Once she gets used to you and they get a little older, she won't mind if you play with them. Now give me some sugar, honey. I told Red I'd meet him at the Wakefield estate."

She lifted her lips, meeting his halfway, and the fire leaped between them.

"Mmmm-hmmm," Ben murmured as he reluctantly let go. "You hold on to that thought until later, will you?"

She nodded, then added, "Be careful."

"I'll be fine, and I won't be long, I promise."

With that, he was gone. China watched him leave, his long strides making short work of the distance to the front of the house. Then he got in his car and drove quickly away, leaving a cloud of dust behind him.

"He's going to have to wash that car all over again," Mattie muttered.

China turned. She hadn't known Ben's mother was standing behind her.

Mattie saw the fear on China's face and gave her a hug.

"You just never mind about what he's doing and come back in here with me. I think Dave's cheating again."

"I heard that!" Dave yelled.

China sighed and then made herself smile. But the rest of the afternoon, her heart was with Ben.

Red was waiting when Ben pulled up behind his car in front of the Wakefield estate.

"You made it in good time," Red said, as Ben got out of his car and into Red's.

"Had a good reason. Now let's go. I've got a feeling about this."

"Yeah, buddy, you're still reading my mind."

A short while later, they were standing on the portico of the three-story mansion and listening to the chimes of the doorbell as it rang throughout the house. Shortly thereafter, a maid answered the door.

"Afternoon, sirs. How may I help you?"

Both men flashed their badges. "We need to see Mona Wakefield. Is she in?"

"Yes, sir, I'll just—"

"Delia?"

The maid turned. "Oh, Senator Wakefield, these detectives want to talk to Miz Mona, and I was just going to—''

Bobby Lee hid his dismay behind a wide, open smile.

"You just run along now and tell Mother we have company," he said. "I'll see what I can do to help these fine men." Then he stepped aside and pulled back the door. "Y'all come on in now, you hear?"

They followed him into a library just off the foyer, and it was obvious that the Senator was about to give them the full benefit of his good-old-boy routine.

"Don't suppose I could offer you boys a drink?" he asked.

"No, sir," they said in unison. "On duty," Ben added, and then continued before Bobby Lee could stall them again. "Senator, we need to speak to your mother."

"Why sure, but could I inquire as to the reason while she's coming down?"

But Ben was firm in his resolve. "I'd rather wait and speak with her first, sir, if you don't mind."

Bobby Lee smiled, but he wasn't real happy. He liked things done his way, and this detective wasn't cooperating.

"If you'll just take a seat, then, I'll see if I can hurry her along," he said, and left them standing.

Red glanced at Ben. "Quite a place, isn't it?"

Before Ben could answer, they heard angry voices out in the hall, although they couldn't hear what was being said. Moments later, Mona Wakefield entered the room with her son right behind her. She was dressed in a pale-blue designer suit with a skirt that went just past her knees. Her hair was strawberry-blond and cut in a style that cupped the curve of her chin, forming a frame for her elegant face.

Ben's hopes dropped. He felt like he'd stepped into Alice's rabbit hole and was coming undone. This woman looked nothing like the picture that Mike had faxed to Red, and he had a moment of panic, wondering if he'd sent the wrong one by mistake.

"Welcome to our home," Mona said. "Please take a seat." Then she turned to the maid, who was standing at the door. "Delia, bring some coffee to the library, please."

"None for us," Ben said. He didn't want the questioning to become a social event.

"Nonsense," she said, and waved the maid away before sliding sensuously into a wing-backed chair. "Now, what can I do for you?"

Ben plowed ahead with the questions, even though he was beginning to doubt.

"As you know, the Dallas police have been working diligently for some time now trying to bring a serial killer to justice, and we follow up on every lead, no matter who is involved."

She smiled. "Yes, I've heard. In fact, several of my acquaintances have been targeted." Then her eyebrows rose, as if in pretend delight. "Surely you're not here to interrogate me?" She looked at her son and laughed. "Bobby Lee, are you playing a joke on your mama?"

He grinned, but it was Ben's opinion that the man looked as if he'd just swallowed a bug along with it.

"No, Mother, it's not a joke, although I must say, it feels like one."

Mona's face was alive with curiosity as she gave the men her full attention.

"I'm sorry. I just assumed…please continue."

"I need to ask you where you were on the night of December 11 of last year."

She rolled her eyes. "Well, mercy, son. I couldn't begin to remember."

"Check your calendar, Mother. If you had a social engagement, I'm sure your secretary had it written down."

"Yes! Of course. If you men will pardon me a moment, I'll be right back."

She rose with the grace of a model and sauntered out of the room, well aware that three pairs of eyes were watching her go.

The moment she was gone, Bobby Lee attacked. "I want to tell you now that I don't appreciate the insinuation that my mother could possibly have anything to do with murder," he snapped. "Why, she doesn't even know how to shoot a gun."

"Oh, but I do," Mona said, as she reentered the room with a book in her hand. "Your daddy taught me how to shoot rattlesnakes before you were born." Then she smiled at Ben as she took her seat. "We lived in Amarillo back then, and you know how snaky that part of Texas can be.''

''No, ma'am, but I'm assuming you do,'' Ben said. ''About December 11?''

She rifled through the pages, then ran her finger down a list before looking up.

''I was at a little Christmas party at the country club. I remember arriving a bit late on purpose.'' She smiled. ''It makes for a grand entrance, you know.''

''What time did you arrive and what time did you leave?'' Ben asked.

''Why, it was almost eight-thirty when the driver let me out, and I didn't get home until after two in the morning. I remember that because Bobby Lee was waiting up for me.'' She flashed her son a sweet, motherly smile. ''It was snowing that night, wasn't it, Bobby Lee? You fussed at me for being out so late in bad weather and were about to go looking for me when I arrived.'' She gave the detectives a similar smile. ''He was all bundled up in his coat and overshoes, ready to look for his mama. Now that's the kind of son every mother wishes she had. Why, he even gave me a wonderful get-away to Hollywood for a Christmas present. Said I needed a change, and he was right. Had a few collagen injections to get rid of some of those nasty old frown lines. I've had the same hairstyle for at least twenty years, so I had one of those make-overs. Got my hair done over. It used to be really long and platinum blond, remember? But this strawberry-blond is so much more me, don't you agree?''

''Mother! These gentlemen do not want to hear about your experience at the hairdresser,'' he said, and then flashed the detectives a smile. ''Sorry, boys, but you know how women are when they start talking about hair and makeup.''

''That's all right,'' Ben asked, suddenly curious as to when this outing had taken place. ''Exactly when were you in California, Mrs. Wakefield?''

''It was just before Christmas, because Bobby Lee flew out and spent Christmas Day with me at the spa.''

''Yes, ma'am,'' Ben said. ''Just so you'll be aware, we will be checking your alibi for the eleventh.''

Mona took offense at the word, *alibi* and stood abruptly, signaling an end to her willingness to talk.

''Call the country club and ask for Carl. He can give you a list of who attended.''

Just then Delia the maid entered carrying a tray of coffee. Mona waved her away.

''I'm sorry, Delia, but that won't be necessary after all. Take it back to the kitchen.'' She turned then, her eyes flashing as she glanced at her son before looking at Ben. ''Will there be anything else?''

''That's all for now,'' he said. ''If something comes up, we'll be in touch.''

They were in the car before they spoke to each other.

''It's a real puzzle as to why Bobby Lee should suddenly want his mother to change her appearance, isn't it?'' Red asked.

Ben nodded. ''I would also be interested in the time

line between the day that composite hit the front page of the *Dallas Morning News* and the day she left for California.''

''Partner, do you know what a stink this is going to raise?'' Red asked.

''From the looks on their faces, they're already smelling it,'' Ben said. ''You mind writing up the report? I want to get back to the ranch before dark. China isn't sleeping so well these days.''

''Nightmares?'' Red asked.

''Wouldn't you?''

Red sighed. ''Sometimes this job really sucks.''

They drove away, unaware of what a tempest their questions had unleashed in the Wakefield home.

Bobby Lee made himself stay on the other side of the desk, because he knew if he got too close to his mother, he would hit her.

''You couldn't just answer their questions, could you?'' he screamed. ''You had to keep talking and talking, like the white trash you are.'' He picked up a paperweight and pitched it across the room, knocking a picture off the wall and sending glass flying in all directions.

Mona was devastated. She'd spent her entire life living down her humble beginnings and now, to hear it from her own son's lips, was more than she could bear.

''If I'm white trash, then what does that make you?''

''Unfortunate!'' he screamed. ''I've spent my entire

life trying to live down your escapades. No matter how hard I try, you keep pulling our reputations back down to the gutter where you seem so at home.''

Mona paled. The pain of his words were more than she could bear.

''You don't know the depths of my sacrifices for you,'' she whispered.

''The only thing of depth between us is the shit you keep getting us in. Now we've got the police meddling in our business because you can't keep your pants on your ass. You've ruined everything...everything! I've just run the shortest presidential race in history. Hell's fire, it was over before it began.''

Mona lifted her chin, her eyes blind with tears. ''That's not the only thing that's over,'' she said, and strode out of the room.

Bobby Lee cursed and yelled and cursed some more, blaming his daddy for marrying a sprawling whore and then himself for not being an orphan. Long minutes passed before he began to calm down, and when he did, he realized what he'd done. He stormed out of the library and up the stairs to his mother's room. But she wasn't there. He ranted as he went, calling her name from room to room, but no Mona. It wasn't until he breached the kitchen doors and sent Delia into tears that he learned she was gone.

''What do you mean, she's gone?'' he yelled.

''Just that, sir,'' Delia sobbed. ''She picked up her keys and walked out the door without ever going upstairs.''

"Did she say where she was going?"

Delia's sobs deepened. "No, sir. She just thanked me for taking such good care of her and told me if I ever had any children to drown 'em."

Bobby Lee paled. This was worse than he'd imagined. He pivoted sharply and headed for the library on the run to call his campaign manager, Ainsley Been.

Ainsley was enjoying a blow job when his phone began to ring.

"Don't stop," he groaned, knowing the answering machine would pick up while the prostitute continued to do her thing.

But his mood went limp when he heard Bobby Lee begin to shout. He shoved the prostitute aside as he scrambled for the phone.

"Hello, hello," he muttered, cutting Bobby Lee off in midcurse.

"Ainsley, Goddamn it, where the hell have you been? We've got trouble, big trouble. Mona was interrogated by the police about the Finelli murder, and now she's gone."

Ainsley blanched. "What the hell do you mean, she's gone?"

"Just that. We had a little fuss after the police left, and she took it all wrong," he said. "I need you to get someone on it. Find her, damn it, and get her back here before the police find out. Hell's fire, do you know what the police are going to think if they know she skipped?"

''Now, Bobby Lee, I'm going to ask you something, and I don't want you to take offense.''

''What?'' Bobby Lee yelled.

''Does she have a reason to be afraid of the police?''

Bobby Lee groaned. ''Hell if I know, but I damn sure do. If this gets out, I'm ruined.''

''I'm on my way.''

Eighteen

China was waiting for Ben when he came home and went out to meet him as he pulled up in the front yard and parked.

The sight of her running out the door and then flying into his arms overwhelmed him. She laughed aloud as he swung her off her feet. The sound touched his heart in a way that made him want to cry, and he remembered the day when he'd wanted to be the one to make her laugh.

"This is one fine way to be welcomed home," he growled, and buried his face in her neck.

She smiled. "I thought it had merit," she said, and then kissed him square on the mouth, drawing out the last bit of his good sense.

He groaned. "God, how I love you," he whispered, and then held her close to his heart. No matter what else there was between them, she finished what he was meant to be.

"What happened today?" she asked.

"Let's go inside. There's something I want you to see."

"You brought a picture? Is it her? Did you find the woman who shot me?"

"I don't know," Ben said. "You'll have to tell me."

They started inside as Dave was coming out. "I'm off to go check on the stock. Want me to come back later?"

"Yes," Ben said. "Now more than ever."

Dave's eyes widened. "What's happened?"

"We may have ourselves a pretty good lead."

"You're kidding."

"Senator Wakefield is not laughing," Ben said.

"Wakefield? How in hell does he fit into this?"

Ben pulled a picture out of his pocket and handed it to China. "I think we'll let China tell us."

She took it from him upside down. As she began to turn the picture, it was as if a face from her nightmares began to come into view.

"Well, honey, what do you think?" Ben asked.

China moaned. Her legs went weak. She dropped the picture and covered her face.

Ben grabbed her as she staggered. He'd expected a reaction, but not one this intense.

"China...honey...talk to me. Is it her?"

"I'm going to be sick," she muttered, then tore loose from his grasp and headed for the bathroom down the hall.

Ben ran went after her, leaving Dave in the hall alone. He bent down and picked up the photo. "Christ almighty," he muttered. "Mona Wakefield. How in hell can this be?"

Mattie came out of the kitchen as China dashed past.

"Honey, what's wrong?" she cried, but China didn't stop. When Ben raced down the hall behind her, Mattie knew something had happened. She followed. If something bad was going on in her house, she needed to know.

China was leaning over the sink and washing her face when Ben burst into the bathroom.

"Are you all right?"

China braced herself on the sink with both hands and shook her head no. Ben grabbed a towel and began to dry her off as Mattie came in behind them.

"Somebody better start talking," she said.

China sank down on the side of the tub and put her head in her hands, leaving the talking up to Ben.

"I showed China a picture of another suspect. This is the reaction we got."

Mattie gasped, and then sat down beside her. "Honey, is it true? Did you recognize the woman who shot you?"

China shuddered. "It looked like her. Oh, God, it looked just like her."

"That's all I needed to hear," Ben said. "I'm calling Captain Floyd. We need an arrest warrant."

"Who is she?" Mattie asked.

"Mona Wakefield."

Mattie gasped. "*The* Mona Wakefield? The senator's mother?"

"One and the same," Ben said.

"But, Bennie, why on earth would a woman like her become a murderer?"

"Who the hell knows?" Ben said. "But she's not getting away with it. Stay with China, will you? I need to make a few calls."

"Are you going to arrest her tonight?" China asked.

"I've got to call my captain first, honey. I'll let you know in a bit."

"I want to be there when you go," she said.

"Hell, no," he muttered.

She stood up then, facing him squarely, without any sign of fear.

"I have to, Ben. I need to see her face. I need to see her in handcuffs and know she can't ever hurt me again."

His shoulders slumped. "We'll see," he said softly.

"I'm coming with you while you make your calls," China said. "I have to know what's going on."

He held out his hand. She grabbed it, holding on as if it meant her life.

"You still here?" Mattie asked, as Dave passed Ben and China in the hall.

"I've been in on this ever since Ben brought her out to the ranch, and since it looks like everything's about to hit the fan, I wouldn't miss it for the world."

"That's what I love about you," Mattie muttered. "Bloodthirsty to the end."

Dave took her by the shoulders and gave her a quick kiss.

"So you love me, do you?"

Mattie blushed.

"When are you going to do something about it? We're not getting any younger."

"Is this a proposal?" Mattie asked.

"Would you say yes if it was?" he countered.

"When this is all over, I might," Mattie said, and took him by the hand. "Looks like supper is going to go all to hell tonight. Let's at least make some popcorn. I'm starved."

"Lead the way," Dave said. "I'm right behind you."

They could hear Ben on the phone in the living room as they walked into the kitchen. Dave wanted to listen, but Mattie smiled at him, and he followed her instead.

"Look, Captain, I have a positive identification from our only witness. She says Mona Wakefield is the woman who shot her. How much more do you need?"

China watched, aware that Ben's captain must be arguing a point Ben didn't want to consider.

"I know," Ben said. "Yes, she said she had an alibi, but we haven't checked it out. She was at some country club Christmas party. You know how those things are. She could show up and circulate for a while, then disappear without anyone missing her, do the deed and then come back to the party without anyone being the wiser. Remember China's first description was of a woman in a beaded evening gown and a full-length fur coat? Pretty typical wear for a country club party, don't you think?''

Ben started to pace. China tried to catch his eye, hoping she could glean something from his expression, but he wouldn't look at her. And then he exploded.

''That's just great! And give her time to skip the country? I don't agree.''

But Aaron Floyd wasn't caring whether anyone agreed or not.

''I don't give a flying you know what whether you agree or not,'' he said. ''We're not arresting a senator's elderly mother until we bust her alibi.''

''Mona Wakefield is a barracuda on the hunt, not an elderly anything. And if your eyewitness's say-so isn't worth anything, then you make your damned case without her.''

He hung up the phone and then threw it on the sofa.

''Son of a bitch,'' he muttered.

China was almost afraid to ask.

''They won't arrest her?''

''Not yet,'' he said. ''Afraid to step on too many political toes, but don't give up on us yet. Red already has the country club list, and Captain Floyd has assigned two sets of detectives to contact the people who were at the party. Before morning, I'll know what Mona Wakefield was wearing, even what she had to eat. If she has a secret, I'll find it.''

''Am I still in danger?''

Ben hesitated, then nodded. There could be nothing but truth between them.

"Probably now more than ever," he said. "But Dave and I are here. We'll take turns watching the house. I don't think anyone knows your name, let alone where you are. However, we can't take any chances."

"It's almost over, isn't it, Ben?"

He crossed the floor and took her in his arms. "It's getting close, honey. Hang in there for me, okay?"

"Okay."

"Are you hungry?" he asked. "Suddenly, I'm starved."

She smiled. "That will make your mother very happy. If there's one thing I've learned about Mattie, it's that she uses food as a cure-all."

"And it works, doesn't it?" Ben said.

"Unless you eat too much of it, and then it's a whole other problem," China said, and then laughed.

Mona was driving south without aim. She'd emptied her bank account of cash with the purpose of getting as far away from Dallas as she could. But the farther she drove, the more painful her memories became.

Bobby Lee, her own son, had called her white trash. He'd said he would rather have been an orphan than be tied to her name. My God, how could this be? Hadn't she spent her life for her husband and her son? After she'd been widowed, she'd had plenty of chances to remarry, and some of the men were not only rich but good-looking. But had she? Had she given one thought to her own personal needs? Hell, no. She'd stayed for Bobby Lee.

She'd known from the start that he was special—always trying harder than all the other boys his age. He was never satisfied with second best. Always pushing, pushing, pushing for more. Even during his brief marriage, she'd been at his beck and call, and when that had fallen apart, she'd been there for him, picking up the pieces of his life and helping put a home back together again.

Granted, she didn't have a college education, but that didn't make her stupid. She knew things—lots of things.

She stifled a sob and blew her nose with one hand as she changed lanes on I-35. She needed a plan, but in the meantime, she needed a place to hide. In spite of the fact that her son had cursed her existence, she knew him well. He would want her back, but not because he would be sorry. Oh, no. It would be for the sake of his image, and that alone. He needed to have her back before word got out that his mother had run away from home. She'd already decided that motels would be too obvious. Even if she used cash to pay, he would find her.

It wasn't until she realized she was entering the outskirts of Houston that she remembered her old friend from back home. If Bitsy Chance still lived in Pasadena, she would help her. She and Bitsy went back a long way.

Happy to have a plan, she pulled over at the first

gas station she came to and headed for the phone booth just outside the door. Luckily there was a phone book inside and she began to scan the pages, looking for Bitsy's name. To her relief, she found a listing, but it wasn't until she began to dial that she realized the phone book was almost five years old.

"Oh lord, let her be there," Mona said, as the phone began to ring. On the fifth ring, a man answered.

"Hello," Mona said. "Is Bitsy there?"

"Who wants to know?" he growled.

"I'm a friend of hers from back in Amarillo. Tell her it's Baby Doll."

"Hey, Bitsy," the man yelled. "Some woman calls herself Baby Doll wants to talk to you. Says she knowed you from Amarillo."

Mona heard Bitsy squeal and started to cry, but they were tears of relief.

"Baby! Baby! Is that you?"

Mona swallowed a sob. "Yes, Bitsy, it's me."

"Ooh, girl, I've been following all the fuss about you and your boy. Aren't you just the thing, now? I'm surprised you even remember someone like me."

"Oh, Bitsy, I think I'm in trouble. I need a place to stay."

Suddenly, whatever envy Bitsy Chance might have harbored was gone in a flash. It was just like the good old days when she and Mona had sneaked out on their parents and gone honky-tonking in cowboy bars.

"Where are you, honey?"

Mona squinted through the filthy glass, trying to read the sign on the station.

"I'm in Pasadena at a place called The In and Out."

Bitsy squealed again. "Honey! This is fate! I'm twelve blocks from there."

"Will your husband mind?" Mona asked.

Bitsy laughed. "Girl, that fool's not my husband, and don't you worry. He'll be gone before you get here."

"Don't tell him who I am," she begged.

"Don't worry, and don't move," Bitsy said. "I'm comin' to get you."

Mona hung up the phone and then locked herself in her car and waited to be rescued. She would cry later, after she didn't need to see to drive.

It was six-thirty in the morning when Bobby Lee opened the door to Ainsley Been. Ainsley started talking before he got a foot in the door.

"I'm sorry, Bobby Lee, but it's as if Mona vanished from the face of the earth," Ainsley said.

Bobby Lee groaned, and grabbed the man's arm and pulled him inside.

"This is awful, just awful. Put some more men on it. She has to leave some kind of a paper trail."

"She cleaned out her checking account, Bobby Lee. Was there a lot of money in it?"

"Hell, yes. Probably a good twenty or thirty thousand," he said, and began to pace.

This was worse than he'd thought. He'd expected

her to pout and then come storming back this morning
with some young buck in tow just to prove she hadn't
lost her touch, but if she'd taken all that money, this
didn't feel good. It didn't feel good at all.

He thought of all the loose ends of his own life, but
he couldn't get past the obvious. The presidential race.

"I've thought about it all night," he told Ainsley.

"Thought about what?" Ainsley asked.

"I want you to schedule a press conference."

"What the hell for? Surely you're not going to talk
about this mess?"

"No, I'm going to get myself out of the public eye
as much as possible before it all falls down around me.
I'm still Senator Wakefield. I still have my pride and
my reputation. I can always run for president again
another time. Besides, I have to be back in Washington, D.C., by the weekend. I can't leave Dallas with
all this hanging over my head."

"What are you saying?" Ainsley asked.

"I'm going to renounce my candidacy for personal
reasons and let that be that."

Ainsley groaned. His future was now as bleak as
Bobby Lee's. No one would want to hire a campaign
manager who hadn't been able to keep scandal away
from the candidate he was representing.

"Are you sure?" he asked.

"Yes. Do it," Bobby Lee said. "Set it up at the
Wyndham Anatole for tomorrow morning before I
change my mind. That's where I made my announcement, that's where it will be rescinded."

"Yes, sir," Ainsley said. "I'll call you with the details later."

As he left, Bobby Lee was already in gear, planning his speech. Maybe if he managed to cry as he said it, the press would put a different spin on the news and make him look like the hero, broken and sad, but nevertheless a hero who was willing to put his family before his personal ambitions.

Mona woke up on her back just as a giant-size cockroach skittered across the ceiling above her bed. She stared at it in sleepy fascination, wondering how creatures like that managed to defy the laws of gravity. It wasn't the first time she'd awakened and not known where she was, but it had been a few years since the last occurrence. Then she heard Bitsy hawking and spitting in the bathroom across the hall and remembered where she was—Pasadena, Texas—and that she'd run away from home.

She rolled over and sat up on the side of the bed. Ignoring her nudity, she stood and headed for the bathroom.

"Bitsy, you 'bout through in there? I need to pee," she yelled.

"Give me a second to rinse my mouth," Bitsy hollered.

Mona waited. Moments later, Bitsy opened the door and then stopped in her tracks, her eyes bugged out in disbelief.

"Ooowee, girl, you ain't changed yourself a bit,

have you? You still parade around in your birthday suit every morning, just like you used to."

Mona shrugged. "It's just flesh and bone," she said, and shut the door behind her as she pushed Bitsy aside.

"Yeah, but it always looks different on you!" Bitsy yelled, and then ambled back into her bedroom and took off her nightgown to dress for the day.

As she passed a mirror, she paused for a look. She was almost ten years younger than Mona, but it didn't show. In fact, Mona didn't look much older now than she had in her forties. Bitsy frowned at the bulges and wrinkles on her own body and then shrugged it off. What the hell did it matter anymore? It wasn't as if she were looking for a man. She'd had plenty of them and not bothered to keep a one.

By the time Mona came out of the bathroom, Bitsy had coffee brewing and the television blaring.

Mona sauntered into the living room with a towel wrapped around her. Bitsy jumped up and pulled the shades on her windows.

"Lord, Baby Doll, you have a funny way of trying to hide, paradin' around all nekked in front of the windows and all."

Mona shrugged. "I didn't think."

Bitsy grinned. "Get yourself a cup of coffee and then set down and tell me all about it."

Mona poured the thick brew, but now that night had passed, she was loath to discuss the mess she was in with someone she hadn't seen in years. What if she said something that could ruin Bobby Lee's chances at the White House? No, she'd better just keep her troubles to herself. And she was saved from having to answer Bitsy so soon when her phone began to ring.

"That's probably my boss," Bitsy said. "I called in sick this morning, but I don't think he believed me. I'll take it in the bedroom and play it up right, okay?"

"Whatever," Mona said, and turned her attention to the morning news on the TV. It wasn't until she heard her son's name mentioned that she sat up and began to take notice. She turned up the volume and then took a sip of her coffee, and, not for the first time, thought of what she'd left behind. Fine clothes, clean sheets and Delia's hot buttered biscuits were the first to come to mind.

> *"Senator Wakefield has called a press conference for this afternoon at the Wyndham Anatole in Dallas. Sources are saying that they're expecting him to withdraw from the presidential race. If he does, this will be the shortest candidacy in presidential history. He hadn't even announced a platform and he's already falling off it."*

"No," Mona moaned, and sat up with a jerk. "No, Bobby Lee, you can't do this to me."

Bitsy came back into the room ready for a gabfest and found Mona scrambling to get up.

"What's wrong?" she said.

"I've got to get home," Mona said. "Bobby Lee's

about to make the biggest mistake of his life, and I've got to stop him before it's too late.''

''But you just got here!'' Bitsy cried.

''Yes, and I can't thank you enough for helping me out,'' Mona said. ''But I've got to get back to Dallas by noon.''

''You're crazy. You'll never make it in time.''

''I have to,'' she said. ''Everything depends on it.''

Within five minutes, she was dressed and gone, leaving Bitsy Chance with an unmade bed, four wet bath towels and a dirty coffee cup. It was Bitsy's opinion that Mona had been rich too long to be fun anymore.

However, money was the least of Mona's worries. When she finally got back on I-35 heading north, she pressed the accelerator to the floor.

China woke up to find herself wrapped in Ben's arms. The last thing she remembered was Ben seeing her to bed. She'd heard the front door open, then close, and knew he'd gone outside to relieve Dave on guard duty. There were dark shadows beneath his eyes, and his cheeks had a gaunt, almost haunted look. China felt guilty, knowing that the stress of her presence in his life was the cause of all that.

She snuggled a little closer, sighing with satisfaction as he unconsciously pulled her closer. It seemed a miracle that the man loved her, but love her he did. He told her on a daily basis and showed her in every way he knew how. All she had to do was trust that it would last and their lives would be perfect. After the killer was put behind bars, of course. For now, that was their top priority.

Just as she was thinking about going back to sleep, the phone began to ring. Ben came awake within seconds and was answering before he'd even opened his eyes.

"Hello."

"Ben, this is Red. We've got our warrant."

Ben was rolling out of bed as he spoke. "Her alibi didn't hold."

"Everyone remembered her there, but no one could vouch for the entire time, or even when she left."

"Did you get an ID on what she was wearing?"

"Yeah. A floor-length sequined gown. A couple of women said it was dové gray. The rest we asked said it was something pale blue."

Ben's heartbeat skidded. A blue beaded gown. "What about a fur? Was she wearing a fur?"

"Hell, yes. In fact, that caused the biggest fuss. About half the women we talked to were animal lovers and berated Miz Mona real fiercely for wearing dead critters on her back."

"Hot damn," Ben muttered, and rolled out of bed. He winked at China, who was now on her knees, following his every word.

"Is the warrant arrest and search?"

"Yeah. The clothes were the clincher for the captain. After he heard that, he said screw the senator, or something to that effect, and told us to go for it. He made a couple of calls, found a judge who doesn't much like Bobby Lee's politics and we're in like Flynn. When can you be ready?''

''What time is it?'' Ben asked.

''Almost seven.''

''I'll meet you at eight outside the Wakefield mansion.''

''We'll be waiting,'' Red said.

Ben hung up the phone. ''We've got a warrant,'' he said.

''I'm going with you,'' China cried, and jumped out of bed on the run, grabbing her clothes as she went.

Ben hesitated. ''Honey, I don't know if this is such a—''

She stopped, her jeans in her hands. ''We've already talked about this.''

He sighed. ''Then hurry up. There's no time to shower. Just get dressed and see if Mom's made any coffee. I've had about three hours' sleep, and I don't want to run into a light pole before I put the cuffs on that woman's hands.''

Nineteen

Bobby Lee was still in his pajamas when the doorbell began to ring. He grabbed a robe and headed for the stairs on the run. Please, God, let it be word about his mother. But his hopes fell when he saw the two detectives from yesterday and the uniformed officers behind them.

Delia was already there, looking wild-eyed and ready to burst into tears.

"Oh, Senator, these people are looking for Miz Mona. I didn't know what to say."

"You go on to the kitchen," he said. "Tell cook to bring my coffee to the dining room."

"Yes, sir," she said, and hurried away.

Bobby Lee smoothed back his hair with the palms of his hands and then tightened the belt of his robe.

"Gentlemen, I would appreciate it if you would step inside. You're lettin' in the flies."

"Our business is with your mother, sir. We have a warrant for her arrest."

Bobby Lee's ears began to buzz, and he felt the blood actually draining from his face. He wondered if, for the first time in his life, he was going to faint.

"You can't be serious," he muttered.

"Oh, but we are," Ben said. "She has been positively identified as the woman who shot Charles Finelli. And, as you know, the gun that was used to kill Finelli has also been linked to a number of other crimes in the city. Now, either you call her down, or we'll go up and get her."

"No, no, you don't understand," Bobby Lee said, as Ben motioned for the officers to proceed upstairs. "She's not here. I swear."

Everyone stopped. For a moment there was total silence. And then Ben took a step forward and grabbed the senator by the lapels of his robe.

"What do you mean, she's not here?"

"We had an argument yesterday after you left. She stormed out, and I haven't seen her since. I've had my men out looking for her all night, but we can't find a trace."

Ben pushed him up against the wall. "If you're lying to us, you'll find yourself arrested for aiding and abetting, for harboring a fugitive and for anything else I can think of."

"I'm not, I'm not, I swear," Bobby Lee mumbled. "As for this other, you've got to be mistaken. My mother wouldn't hurt anyone. She's not capable of something like that."

Ben turned him loose in disgust. "Officers, commence the search," he said, and then turned to Red. "I'm calling in an APB on Mona Wakefield while the senator here shows you her room."

"Yes, of course," Bobby Lee muttered, and started up the stairs just as China walked through the door.

Ben turned. "I told you to wait outside," he said.

"Where is she?" China said. "I need to see her face-to-face, just like before."

"She's not here."

China moaned. "She got away?"

"I don't know what happened," he said, and took her by the arm. "Please, honey, wait outside in the car with the other officer, okay?"

She nodded and had started to leave when she saw someone standing on the stairs. It was the first time she'd seen the senator in person, and he didn't look as good as she'd expected. In fact, he looked as if he'd seen a ghost.

"You're the witness...aren't you? The woman my mother is supposed to have shot."

China took a step forward, moving beyond Ben's reach.

"My baby is dead because of her."

Bobby Lee moaned and then sat down on the stairs, his legs too weak to stand.

"This is all a horrible mistake."

But no one seemed inclined to believe him. "Senator, you were going to show my partner to your mother's room?"

"At the head of the landing, first door on the left. Help yourselves. I don't feel so good."

The officers moved forward, led by Red Fisher, leaving the senator on the stairs.

Ben took China by the arm and pulled her to the doorway.

"In the car. Now."

"I'm going," she said.

"The captain wouldn't be too happy with me if he knew you were here, so let's don't push the issue, okay?"

"Is she going to get away?" China asked.

"Hell, no. Mona Wakefield's face is as familiar in Texas as McDonald's Golden Arches. She'll turn up, and when she does, we'll arrest her. Wait for me outside. I'll have to go by the station, but we should be home before noon."

It wasn't what she wanted to hear, but it was enough. She went back to the patrol car, while Ben joined the officers in their search of the estate.

Bobby Lee had retreated to the library and was frantically searching for his lawyer's home phone number. Cursing every woman on the face of the earth, he decided to call Ainsley instead. Ainsley answered on the first ring.

"It's me," Bobby Lee said. "The police have a warrant for my mother's arrest, and my house is being searched as we speak. What time did you schedule that press conference?"

"Christ almighty, Bobby Lee, is that all you can worry about?"

"You just answer me, damn it. I know what I'm doing."

Ainsley sighed. "It's set for noon."

"That's too late," Bobby Lee said. "Make it ten."

"This morning? That's only two hours away. I'll never be able to change all of the—"

"Just do it," Bobby Lee snapped. "I'm going to break the news myself, not the other way around. I refuse to look like I'm part of this mess."

"You do this, and you'll be selling your mother down the proverbial river."

"She sold herself years ago," Bobby Lee said. "They're just finally coming to collect."

"All right. I hope you know what you're doing."

"I always know what I'm doing," Bobby Lee said, and hung up in Ainsley's ear.

Then he went to his room to dress, bypassing the destruction of his mother's quarters. He didn't want to know what they found. The way he figured it, the less he knew, the more innocent he would appear. By the time he was ready to come back downstairs, he had everything all figured out. By God, he was going to come out looking like a hero again or know the reason why. It wasn't going to be easy, but he was about to announce to the citizens of his fair city that when he'd discovered her duplicity, he'd turned in his own mother for her horrible crimes.

After that, he had one last chore to attend to, and then everything was going to fall back into place. So he wasn't going to run for president. So what. The more he thought about it, the more he began to convince himself that it had been his mother's dream, not his, all along.

* * *

As fate would have it, Mona had a flat tire just outside of Austin. She pulled off the highway into a rest stop and popped the trunk, although she didn't have the faintest idea of how to remove the spare, let alone take off the flat tire. But she reminded herself that she'd come from hardy pioneer stock. Her great-great-granny had walked across the country from Boston to Texas, following her family wagon to a new land. If that woman could walk several thousand miles and live through Indian and Mexican wars, then by God, Mona could figure out how to change a flat tire.

She rolled up the sleeves of her designer suit and leaned into the trunk to study the setup. The tire seemed far too small, therefore it must be flat. But just to be sure, she got the manufacturer's book out of the glove box and began to read. Before she'd gotten past the directions on how to change the digital clock to daylight savings, a trucker was pulling off the highway and coming to a stop behind her.

"Thank you Lord," she said, and stood up, pasted a smile on her face and sauntered toward the man.

He got out of his rig, thinking this was his lucky day. Before he knew it, he was showing her how to take the spare out of the trunk and where to place the jack to make sure the car didn't tip.

"I don't know what I would have done without your help," Mona said, playing helpless to the hilt.

"It's my pleasure," the trucker said, as he tugged on the doughnut, but it wouldn't come out. "Dang thing's stuck on something,'' he said, and leaned a little farther into the trunk.

He gave it another couple of tugs, and as he did, the layer of carpeting inside the trunk came up in his hands.

"Something had spilled on it," he said. "Looky here. It plumb glued the carpet to the spare. Don't look like it's ever been used, or you would have found this before."

Mona nodded, pretending great interest, but she didn't really care. All she wanted was to be on her way.

"I'll straighten the carpet," she said. "You just take that little old tire and do your thing, okay?"

The trucker grinned. He was going to do his thing, and he hoped that she'd be willing to do another little thing or two when he was through.

Mona knew what he was thinking, and she'd play hell before she bumped bellies with some stranger. She hadn't ever been that hard up. She leaned into the trunk and began pulling the carpeting back down. As she did, a flash of something shiny caught her eye. She lifted up the carpet again and peered under, and as she did, her heart skipped a beat.

A gun. Jesus Christ, it was a gun.

But where had it come from? This car was hers. She'd bought it off the showroom floor less than a year ago. No one drove it but her. There was no way this could have…

A strange look crossed her face. She glanced toward

the trucker to make sure he hadn't seen, then calmly smoothed the carpet back down. A few minutes later, he was finished.

"Just put that dirty old flat right in here," Mona said. "And tell me, what do I owe you for your help?"

The trucker tossed the flat and the jack inside the trunk and slammed the lid.

"You can't drive over forty or fifty miles an hour on one of these things," he said. "As for what you owe me, well, I'll just let you decide." Then he rubbed his hand down the front of his fly and grinned.

Mona smiled. "Why don't you just crawl up in that big old truck of yours and stretch out in your cute little bed and I'll see what I can do."

When he grabbed her by the hand and headed for the truck on the run, she thought she would break a heel. But her chance was coming. She needed to put some time between her and this moose, to get lost in the traffic without having to worry about him following her and she knew what she was going to do.

The trucker climbed in, then pulled her up. He was tearing off his pants and climbing into the sleep cab as she slid into the seat. Mona took one look at the limp flesh hanging between his legs, yanked the keys from the ignition, and jumped out of the truck.

She hit the ground with a thump, felt the heel of one pump give as she landed, but was too full of adrenaline to care. She hauled back her arm and flung the ring full of keys as far out into the grassy pasture as they would go. She had one glimpse of the sunlight on metal as they spiraled out of sight, and then she began to run.

The trucker was pulling up his pants and cursing as he practically fell out of the truck, uncertain what to follow, the bitch or the path of his keys. But she was already in the car and driving away before he had his pants zipped, which left his keys. He headed for the pasture, cursing with every step.

Mona vaguely remembered his warning about not driving too fast, but she didn't have the time to waste. She stomped the accelerator to the floor once again and held on for a very rough ride, unaware of the fate that awaited her in Dallas.

Hours later, as she hit the city limits, she realized she had come back too late. The radio stations were full of the news. Dallas's favorite son had withdrawn from the presidential race. Her despair was cut short by the horror of the news that followed.

There was a warrant out for her arrest. According to the news, her own son had been the one to turn her in. Hurt beyond belief, an instinct for self-preservation led her to the cabin on Lake Texoma. She hadn't been there in years, but it would be a good place to hide while she figured out what to do next. She wasn't going into hiding as much as she was retreating to lick her wounds.

All the way through the city, she kept imagining everyone who passed her would know who she was. Fear kept her moving, even though the car was low on gas. She'd missed the turn to the cabin and had to retrace her steps. By the time she pulled up, the gauge was registering Empty.

She got out, her legs shaking, her stomach rumbling from hunger. But it couldn't matter. She would think about that later on. All she wanted was a bed and a shower, and if the utilities weren't on, she'd bathe in the lake.

It didn't occur to her until she turned the knob that the door would be locked. She started to cry, pounding on the door in frustration. It was the last straw. As she pounded, something fell from the ledge above her head, landing at her feet with a clink. A key. Of course! The spare key.

She opened the door and slipped inside, expecting almost anything except what she found. Instead of furniture covered in drop cloths and a layer of dust, everything was spotless, and if her eyes didn't deceive her, it was new, certainly newer than when she'd been there last.

She turned on a light and then walked through the rooms, looking in closets and poking through drawers. They were full, as if someone were living here. At the thought, she spun and raced toward the door, locking it firmly and then sliding the dead bolt, just in case. It seemed obvious that Bobby Lee had rented the thing out and hadn't told her. This was a fine mess. Someone could come back at any time, and then she would be found out. This wouldn't do.

But she was so tired and so filthy. The least she could do was shower and maybe find a change of clothes. She could eat, leave some money behind for the food that she took, and then get to the lake bait shop for gas before it closed. She was too tired to drive, but it didn't look as if she would have a choice.

Frantic, she raced into the bath and stripped off her clothes. Minutes later, she came out of the shower, dripping water and heading for the bedroom in search of something clean

The first bedroom had furniture, but the closets were empty. But when she went into the other, she knew she'd hit the jackpot. Makeup was on the dresser, as if the woman who lived here had just laid it down and walked out of the house. The closet was full of dresses. Mona shuffled through them in haste, searching for something comfortable, but to her surprise, she couldn't find anything but lingerie and evening gowns. It didn't make sense. These weren't the types of clothes she would have expected a lake dweller to wear. She closed the door and headed for the armoire, hoping she might find some jeans or slacks inside.

She flung back the doors and then screamed before she realized what she was seeing. At first glance it appeared she'd uncovered a stash of decapitated heads, and then she cursed herself for panicking when she looked again and saw it was nothing more than some long blond wigs on hair stylist's dummies.

"Heavens," she muttered, as she fingered several strands. "Talk about trashy. All these wigs, and not one of them of good quality."

She continued to search and was about to go back

to the closet for another look when she found a pair of jeans and a shirt in the last drawer down.

"Thank goodness," she muttered, and yanked them out, then began to put them on. To her surprise, they actually fit. The waist of the jeans was a little large, but the leg length was almost perfect. The shirtsleeves came all the way to her wrists, which was uncommon, considering her height.

It wasn't until she crammed her hands in the pockets and pulled out a handful of receipts that she realized her surprises weren't quite over. Curious, she sat on the edge of the bed and began to unfold them. One after the other, she read in silence. But the longer she sat there, the greater her understanding grew.

She looked up, her gaze centering on the clothes hanging in the closet, the wigs sitting in the armoire on faceless plastic heads, then back down at the receipts in her hand. She thought of the gun in the trunk of her car. The police were looking for her for murder because her son had turned her in. She thought back to the vacation he'd sent her on and the makeover he'd insisted she have. Her stomach turned. She needed to throw up, but there was nothing in her stomach to regurgitate. She dropped her head between her knees and remembered the day he was born. All that blood. All that pain. All those sleepless days and nights of his childhood—and it had come to this.

"Oh, God…oh, dear God, what have I done?"

After a while, she crawled on top of the covers and rolled herself up in a ball. Whatever happened to her was going to have to wait until tomorrow. She was too tired to do anything but sleep.

It was all over the national news. A warrant had been issued for the arrest of Mona Wakefield, Senator Bobby Lee Wakefield's mother.

Ariel Simmons was sitting in a Motel 6 when she heard the news and started to laugh. Thank God it was over. But the longer she laughed, the worse she felt. Before long, she was crying. It wasn't over. It would never be over. Her reputation was ruined, despite no longer being a murder suspect. The people who came to hear her preach were few and far between, old people with little to no money to donate to her ministry. It didn't pay to preach when the only people who came just wanted to hear the Word of God. It was the ones who thought they could buy their way into heaven who had been paying her bills.

With their absence, she was reduced to places like this, rather than the opulence to which she'd been accustomed. Finally, she wiped her eyes and went to the bathroom to wash her face. This was the last stop on her tour, not that it mattered. When tonight was over, she'd been giving some thought to moving south— maybe Florida—someplace where she could get lost in the crowds and create a new world, even a new identity for herself. If she sold her home in Dallas and the rest of her holdings, she would have enough to live on comfortably for the rest of her life.

The more she considered it, the better it sounded.

After all, as long as there was life, anything was possible.

It was dark when the shot came through the window near the chair where China was sitting. One second she was screaming and the next thing she knew she was on the floor and Ben was on top of her, telling her to stop. She sucked in a breath and clung to him in horror as he ran his hands across her body in frantic sweeps.

"Tell me you're all right. Tell me it missed you."

"I'm fine," China said, and stifled the need to shriek.

"God," Ben groaned, and then pushed her up between the sofa and the wall. "No matter what you hear, don't move, do you hear me?"

"Ben! Bennie! Are you all right?"

Ben could hear his mother's footsteps as she started down the hall.

"Mother! Get back! Get down on the floor and stay there until I tell you it's okay."

He could hear her starting to cry, but she did what she was told, although her need to know her loved ones were all right outweighed the prudence of keeping silent.

"Bennie, are you and China all right? What about Dave? He's outside, isn't he? Oh, dear God, what if he's—"

"Don't either of you move. I've got to go."

Seconds later, China watched him crawling belly-fashion across the floor and then into the kitchen, where the lights were out. She knew he was going out to danger. All she could do was pray.

It was impossible for the shooter to know if the shot had connected. One second the girl had been right in the sights and the next she was gone. One thing was certain, he needed to finish the job.

He started running in a crouch, circling the ranch house, searching for a way to enter, when all the lights in the house went out. A silent curse slid through his mind. This raid was a bust. He'd taken a shot at the woman. Maybe he'd gotten lucky.

Something rustled in the grass off to his left. He pictured the cop inside the house and thought of the one he'd left unconscious out near the barn. What if there were more? He couldn't afford to take a chance.

Within minutes, he was gone.

Ben found Dave's limp body just as he heard the sound of a motorcycle starting somewhere toward the highway. The shooter was getting away.

Dave moaned, and it was the prettiest sound Ben could have heard.

"Dave, buddy, where do you hurt?"

"My head. I think I hurt my head. What happened?"

"I'll explain later, but I need to get you in the house."

Within the hour, the ranch was crawling with the police, from Christopher Scott, the Navarro County

Sheriff and every deputy he could raise, to part of the homicide division of the Dallas P.D. Everyone knew why it had happened, but the shooter was gone. The good news was that China Brown was still alive.

Sheriff Scott was waiting for Ben as he came up from the barn.

''Your shooter is gone, Ben. We found tracks, also where he stashed his bike, but we need daylight for anything else.''

''I know, Chris, and thanks for coming out,'' Ben said.

''Just doing my job,'' he said. ''Although I don't relish something this ugly happening on my watch, if you know what I mean.''

''Yes, I do.''

''I'll leave a man on guard up around the highway, although I don't expect another attempt tonight.''

''Thanks. And thanks for getting an ambulance out here so quick for Dave.''

''He's probably got a concussion, but he'll be all right,'' Scott said. ''Did Mattie go with him?''

Ben nodded, thinking of China alone in the house. ''I'd better go check on China. The last few months have been pretty hard on her. This didn't help.''

''Anything I can do, don't hesitate to call,'' Scott repeated, and then he was gone.

A few minutes later, there was nothing left to indicate the turmoil they'd just been through but a few drops of Dave's blood on the front porch and a yard full of tracks. A couple of the deputies had tacked a piece of plywood over the broken window. Something that would be dealt with tomorrow. For now, Ben needed to hold China in his arms and reassure himself she was still in one piece. He couldn't get past the image of her smiling at him as she sat down in her chair, and then the glass shattering all around her as she started to scream.

He entered the house calling her name.

She came out of the kitchen, carrying a knife. Shock still lingered in the nervousness of her expression. Ben locked the door behind him and then took away the knife.

"Here, honey, let me have that, okay?"

She handed it over without a word.

Ben smoothed the hair away from her face, wishing he could make that look in her eyes disappear as easily.

"The sheriff left a deputy on guard, but the shooter is long gone."

"It's not over. It will never be over until I'm dead."

"Don't say that," he said, and then picked her up and held her close. "Don't ever say that again."

She sighed. It seemed inevitable. No matter how hard the good guys tried, the bad boys would win in the end.

"I don't want to die," she said. "Not anymore. I haven't wanted to for a long, long time."

"And I don't want you to, either, honey. I won't let that happen. I promised. Remember?"

She cried herself to sleep in his arms, and then Ben

held her while she slept, with her head stretched across his lap and one hand clutching the fabric of his jeans. He sat propped against the headboard with one hand on the middle of her back and the other beside his gun. Tears ran freely down the middle of his cheeks as he waited for dawn. He was scared. As scared as he'd ever been in his life. If something didn't happen soon in their favor, it was going to be damned hard keeping that promise he'd made.

It was midmorning by the time Ben and China got to Commerce Street. Ben's stomach was in knots as he pulled into the parking lot of the Dallas P.D. He needed to check in with his captain, apprise him of everything that had happened last night and try to figure out where to go from there.

"Come on, honey. Maybe this won't take too long, and then we'll go check on Dave. Mother said he was okay, but I want to see for myself."

China hated herself for the gut-wrenching fear of getting out of Ben's car, but she was so tired of hiding that she could almost wish it was over, regardless of the outcome. She clung to Ben's hand as he hurried her inside. Once there, she began to relax. Everywhere she looked she saw uniforms and badges and officers with guns. Safe. In here, she was safe.

He introduced her to Captain Floyd, who promptly decided she was too thin and needed to eat. He set her in his own office with a Coke and a box of doughnut holes.

"The chocolate-covered ones are the best," he said, and handed her the remote to his TV. "Why don't you kick back, watch a little TV, have yourself a snack? If you get tired, stretch out on my couch. We'll take our meeting to the room across the hall."

"Thank you for being so kind," she said, and then smiled.

At that point Floyd was lost. He cleared his throat gruffly and then frowned.

"Yes…well, come on, English. Let's get this show on the road. I want to know everything that happened last night, and I want a full report from the Navarro Sheriff's office ASAP."

Ben winked at China and then followed his boss across the hall, where the task force had assembled for an update. The main focus was on Mona Wakefield. She was still missing, and China had been shot at last night. The nails were getting tighter in Mona's coffin.

China set the pastry aside, but she kept her drink, occasionally sipping as she flipped through the channels for something to watch.

Time passed and she dozed. The program changed, and a replay of Senator Wakefield's press conference began to air. In the back of her mind, she heard what was happening but couldn't bring herself to care until she heard a reporter shout over the background noise, trying to be heard.

"Bobby Lee…Bobby Lee…are you going to—"

She came up on her feet, her eyes wide and filled with fear, her heart pounding so hard she could scarcely breathe. Instinctively, she took a step backward and splayed her hands over her belly, just as she had that night on the South Side of Dallas.

"No!" she screamed. "Don't shoot! Don't shoot!"

She might as well have screamed "Fire," because every cop on the floor, including Ben, was in the office with their guns drawn before she woke all the way up.

It was obvious to them all that no one was in sight, and they were ready to attribute it to a bad dream when she started to cry.

"Oh, my God, oh, my God." She covered her face with her hands. "I didn't remember until now. Oh Lord, all this time and I didn't remember."

"What?" Ben said, and took her hands away from her face. "What didn't you remember?"

"The photographer. He yelled out at that woman. When she heard him, she turned. The flash started going off on his camera. She was in such a rage. She pulled a gun and started shooting. Then she shot me. But I didn't remember until just now that Finelli called her by name."

"What, honey? You mean you actually heard him call her Mona?"

"No," she moaned. "He yelled, 'Bobby Lee.' Three times and real loud. That's when the woman got mad. That's when she pulled the gun."

A moment of stunned silence passed over them, and then everyone started talking at once. China dropped back onto the sofa, and Ben followed her. He took her by the shoulders and looked her straight in the eye.

"Are you telling·us that Finelli called that woman Bobby Lee?"

"Yes."

He looked up at his captain. "Well?"

Floyd stared, struggling with the implications of what she'd just said, and then he yelled, "Avery! Somebody get Matt Avery."

When a young officer appeared, China recognized him as the one who'd helped her compile the composite of the killer's face.

"Avery, if you have a picture of someone, can you scan it into your program and then make the changes you normally do?"

"Yes, sir."

Floyd yelled again. "Somebody get him a head shot of our beloved senator. I want to see what comes out of this pot."

Twenty

It was magic. One minute Bobby Lee Wakefield's face was on the screen, and then, with a few keystrokes from Officer Avery, he'd become a she, right down to the long blond hair and come-hither eyes.

"China?"

"Yes."

"Jesus," Floyd whispered, and sat down with a thump.

"This could explain why Bobby Lee decided to take the credit for turning his own mother in. It certainly shifts the blame, doesn't it?" Red said.

Floyd shook his head in disbelief. "But he's a football star and a war hero and a Goddamned United States senator. This doesn't make sense." He looked at China again. "Are you sure about this? I mean…you picked out his mother before."

"And no wonder," Ben said. "Look at the resemblance. They could be twins. As for making any sense, killers never do. However, if I remember anything about Psych 101, killing men who are into perversion could be a symbolic way of trying to kill himself."

''But Finelli wasn't into that, was he?'' China asked.

''No, honey. He may not have known about the other victims. But catching Bobby Lee in drag would have been the picture of the century. No telling how much money he would have made off that one single shot.''

''Instead, Finelli made the headlines,'' Floyd said, and then wiped a shaky hand across his face as he stared at the image on the screen. ''Go get the son of a bitch. I'll have the warrant by the time you arrive.''

China stood.

''You wait here, little lady,'' the captain said.

''Let her go,'' Ben said. ''She's earned it.'' Then he took his cell phone out of his pocket.

''Who are you calling?'' Floyd asked.

''Just keeping a promise to someone I know.''

Connie Marx was coming out of the shower with a towel around her head when her phone began to ring. She crawled across her bed and grabbed it, letting the wet towel fall to the floor as she did.

''Hello.''

''Connie?''

''Yes?''

''This is Ben English.''

She froze. ''Yes?''

''You know where Senator Wakefield lives?''

Now her heart was skipping beats. ''Yes, of course. Is it Mona Wakefield? Are you going to arrest her?''

"No, not her."

There was a moment of silence, and suddenly she knew.

"You're kidding," she muttered.

"We're on our way there now," Ben said.

"Oh, my God, this is great."

She hung up in Ben's ear and was scrambling for her clothes before she remembered she needed a cameraman to make this all work. She grabbed the phone again and dialed the station where she used to work, disguising her voice so no one would suspect.

"I need to speak to Arnie White, please." Then she hit the speaker button and continued to dress.

"This is Arnie."

"Arnie, this is Connie. You still hungry?"

He knew exactly what she meant. They'd shared one passion, and that was moving up to bigger and better things.

"Oh, yeah. What's happening, doll-face?"

"This is big, Arnie. Real big. Get a camera and meet me at Senator Wakefield's estate as fast as you can. We're about to get the hottest piece of news in Texas history on tape."

"I'm already gone," he said, and hung up in her ear.

She smiled. Justice. She'd waited a long time for justice, and now it was about to come.

Bobby Lee was on the phone, checking in with his office in Washington, as he heard the sounds of a number of arriving vehicles.

"I think I've got company," he said. "Just follow through on that EPA lobbyist and I'll talk to you when I get in. Yes, tomorrow around noon. We'll have lunch."

Although he wasn't expecting guests, after the bombshell he'd dropped yesterday, it was to be expected. And he wasn't about to turn the media away. Not when he was riding the airwaves on a sympathetic high.

But it wasn't the media who Delia admitted, and when he saw China Brown at the head of the group, his stomach started to roll. She knew. He didn't know how, but she knew!

Ben took the senator by his hand and twisted it around behind his back. One handcuff went on with a snap.

"Bobby Lee Wakefield, you are under arrest for the murders of Charles Finelli and Baby Girl Brown. You are also under arrest for the murders of Tashi Yamamoto, LaShon Fontana and—"

When the other handcuff snapped around his wrist, Bobby Lee's mind went blank. He could see the detective's mouth still moving, but he could no longer hear the words. His world had narrowed to the woman who was pointing her finger, saying things he didn't want to admit.

"You shot me," China said. "I did nothing to you, and you still shot me as if I were a stray dog."

"No," he mumbled. "Not me. It wasn't me. You've got it all wrong. It was my mother, remember? You identified her already, and you were right. She's crazy white trash. Who knows why she did it, but she was always into sex. Every kind of sex with all kinds of men."

"You lie!"

Everyone turned.

Mona Wakefield stood in the doorway like an avenging angel, her hair a mess and still wearing her son's clothes. She tried to push her way past the officers, and they immediately stopped her.

"Let her pass," Ben said, and then from the corner of his eye, he saw another car arriving out in front. It was Connie Marx. She hadn't wasted any time. The way he figured it, she'd earned at least this much redress.

Mona's legs were shaking almost as hard as her voice. Seeing all these officers in her own home and knowing why they'd come was almost more than she could bear. She couldn't look at Bobby Lee. Not yet. Not until she'd said what she had to say.

She stopped in front of Ben and then handed him a fistful of receipts.

"I found these in my son's clothes at our cabin at Lake Texoma," she said. "I believe there's a receipt, in his name, for a particular gun that the serial killer is known to have used—the very gun I found beneath the spare tire in my car. The car I so graciously loaned to my son whenever he wanted to be on his own.

There's also a closet full of dresses at the cabin, some that I dare say will bear traces of blood, and an armoire full of interesting, though cheap, blond wigs. Not at all my style.''

''Mother! What are you saying?'' he gasped. ''You can't blame me. I'm your son.''

Mona flinched, and then she slowly turned to stare her son in the face. The death penalty. He would get the death penalty. Texas was not a forgiving state in matters of justice. Man or woman, young or old, if the courts sentenced you to die, then die you did. Her lips began to quiver as her eyes filled with tears.

''Not anymore. As far as I'm concerned, you are now the orphan you always wanted to be.''

''No,'' Bobby Lee wailed. ''I didn't mean it. I never mean what I say, you know that. Tell them I'm sorry. Tell them and make it okay.''

She stared at him as if she'd never seen him before, and, truth be told, she wondered if that was true. In her mind, had she made him the son she'd always dreamed of, rather than the bastard he'd always been? It didn't matter now. Nothing mattered. She turned away, and as she did, she saw a woman standing near the wall. Immediately, she knew who she must be.

''You…are you the woman he shot?''

China didn't answer—couldn't answer.

''You are, aren't you?'' Mona sighed, and the tears began to roll. ''I don't know what to say to you. Because of my family, you lost your child. I understand your pain, because I just lost mine, too. I'm sorry. So sorry.'' Then her shoulders slumped, and for the first time, Mona Wakefield looked every one of her sixty-eight years. ''Detectives, do your thing. I will be making a statement to the press in the morning. I assume the charges against me will have been dropped by that time.''

''Yes, ma'am, and thank you for coming forward,'' Ben said.

''Had I known what I harbored, I would have done it sooner.''

The room became a turmoil of shuffling feet, along with the sounds of Bobby Lee Wakefield's shrieks and promises to repent. China stood for a moment, pinned against the wall by the crowd of people and a woman with a camera.

''China?''

She turned. Ben was calling her name, a worried expression on his face.

''I'm okay,'' she said, and pushed her way through the crowd and walked out of the house.

Lifting her face to the sunshine, she closed her eyes and drew a deep breath of air. A light, sweet scent filled her nostrils, telling her that somewhere nearby there were lilacs in bloom. The warmth on her face, the sound of a bird chirping in a nearby tree…the peacefulness of it all filled her heart.

She could walk a street when she wanted to.

Shop in a mall if she chose.

Walk in the sunshine and never have to fear she'd be shot in the back.

It was over.

Epilogue

Spring was moving on toward summer. Bluebonnets were in bloom and everything had turned a vivid shade of green—from the pastures on the English ranch to the trees along the highways. Everywhere the eye might see, the earth was alive and flourishing.

China sat on the back porch, watching Ben cut hay in the pasture beyond the house. Behind her, the house was quiet, the rooms echoing only with the sounds of her own footsteps now that Mattie and Dave had married and she'd moved up the road to be with him.

There had never been a question of China leaving. She belonged here now, just like she and Ben belonged together. There were days when she saw the hunger on his face, the times when she knew he held his tongue for fear of pushing her too fast. She loved him with a passion she hadn't believed existed. But he wanted his ring on her finger. He wanted to call her more than China, more than the woman of his heart. He wanted to call her wife.

It was strange that she'd resisted. She couldn't imagine being anywhere else or with any other man. Something in her was changing, though. She could feel it day by day. She glanced at the sun, judging the time against when she would need to prepare a meal. It would be hours yet before Ben would come in from the field.

Restless, she stood abruptly, dusted off the seat of her shorts and started toward the barn to see Cowboy. As she walked, she stopped at the gate as she always did, burying her nose in the burgeoning bank of the honeysuckle and inhaling the rich, sweet scent. As she did, a flutter of motion caught her eye, and she lifted her head to look.

There, hanging from what appeared to be a tiny gray thread, was a splitting cocoon, and emerging from the hanging sarcophagus was a small butterfly, its wings still wet and folded against its body.

It was a miracle, this witnessing of rebirth, and she held her breath as she watched the butterfly crawl to a nearby branch and hang, like a piece of silk in the wind, while it waited for its wings to dry. Little by little, the wings began to flutter, then open, revealing shades of vivid yellow framed by whorls of shining jet. It was like staring into the pattern of a stained-glass window and seeing light through all the pieces.

China held out her finger and, as if sensing the warmth of her skin, the butterfly crawled on and then stayed there, postponing its moment of flight.

Somewhere in the back of her mind she was a child again, hiding from Clyde beneath her mother's front porch. She could see that small brown worm inching its way through the grass, could remember feeling as ugly and insignificant. She'd lived her life in that frame of mind, never seeing herself as a vibrant woman but through the eyes of a bitter man. He'd called her ugly and tried to drown her the way people drown animals they no longer want.

Even though she'd grown and flourished, there was a part of herself she'd kept hidden away. And it had hung in the back of her mind just like the cocoon was hanging on the bush, unaware that all the while, her thoughts were changing—changing.

As she watched, the butterfly suddenly lifted from the end of her finger, fluttering upward like a helicopter lifting off from a pad. Then, caught by a passing breeze, the bright yellow butterfly disappeared beyond the house.

She stood there in shock, looking around at all there was before her, and then slowly lifted her hands to her face. They began to tremble as she felt her features, sculpting them anew in her mind. Then, suddenly, she had to see for herself if what she felt was really true.

She bolted into the house, running through the rooms until she came to the mirror in her room. She stood, staring at the woman who looked back.

Her hair was thick and long and tied at the back of her neck with a piece of ribbon that was as blue as her eyes. Her face was flushed beneath a light tan, and there was a smile on her lips that came from within. She reached out toward the mirror and laid trembling hands on the glass, but the woman she saw wasn't there. She moved her hands to her own face and felt the heat of her skin, and then closed her eyes in quiet joy.

Somewhere between the loss of a child and the arms of her man, she'd turned into something grand—a woman who was beautiful because she was loved.

She moved back, loath to tear herself away from the joy on that woman's face, and then she smiled. The woman smiled back, as if to say, *It's okay. I'll always be here.*

China laughed and walked out the door, her stride lengthening with each step she took. By the time she cleared the yard and headed toward the pasture where Ben was cutting hay, she was running.

Ben saw her coming. Fear leaped within his heart when she began to run. And then he saw her face and realized she was laughing. He didn't know what had happened, but he wanted to share her joy. He stopped the tractor in the middle of the field and crawled out of the cab in haste. As he started toward her, it seemed as if she were flying as she leaped one windrow of hay after another, bounding from place to place, like a butterfly darts from flower to flower.

He caught her, laughing, although he didn't know why. And when she dug her hands through the sweat-dampened ends of his hair and told him that she loved him, he knew something had changed.

"What happened?" he asked.

But there was no way she could explain the way she felt inside. So she did the only thing she could. In so many words, she handed him her heart.

"Bennie, if I asked you something serious, would you tell me the truth?"

"Always."

"Promise?"

He grinned. "I promise."

"I'm beautiful to you, aren't I?"

Breath caught in the back of his throat, and his eyes filled with tears.

"Yes, baby, more than words can say."

She laughed, and then threw her hands up over her head as if she'd scored a major victory.

He didn't know what was happening, but he was beginning to like it.

"Then don't you think you should marry me quick before men start lining up at the door?"

His lips tilted upward as joy began to fill his heart.

"China Brown, are you proposing to me?"

She grinned. "Yes."

He picked her up and then turned in a slow, silent circle, savoring the sound of her laughter and the soft, sexy curves against his chest.

"So, is this a yes?" China asked.

He started to smile.

"It's yes!" she crowed. "The man says yes!"

"I don't know what happened to you, but whatever it is, I am eternally glad."

China kissed him soundly, savoring the truth in her heart.

"It was nothing," she said. "I just saw a butterfly."

SUSAN WIGGS

THE MISTRESS

*A penniless maid
and a society gentleman
act on impluse when
Chicago is burning...*

SNOW IN SEPTEMBER

A daughter who's run away from home. A mother who's run away from herself.

Rachel Lee

Published 20th July
Available from all good paperback stockists

M226